W9-DCV-702

FIRST YEAR

THE BLACK MAGE BOOK 1

Rachel E. Carter

First Year (The Black Mage Book 1)

Copyright © 2016 Rachel E. Carter
ISBN: 1-946155-00-4
ISBN-13: 978-1-946155-00-9

All rights reserved. No part of this publication may be reproduced, distributed or transmitted in any form or by any means, without prior written permission.

Publisher's Note: This is a work of fiction. Names, characters, places, and incidents are a product of the author's imagination. Locales and public names are sometimes used for atmospheric purposes. Any resemblance to actual people, living or dead, or to businesses, companies, events, institutions, or locales is completely coincidental.

Cover Design by Deranged Doctor Designs
Edited by Hot Tree Editing

To Kitty & Shells,

Before everything, there was our fan fiction over the novels that shaped our lives. Thank you for cheerleading me all these years and putting up with some really, really terrible stories about J & D and our girls Cat & Trenity.

To Christina,

Because even though life gave us more than our fair share of lemons, we just threw 'em right back.

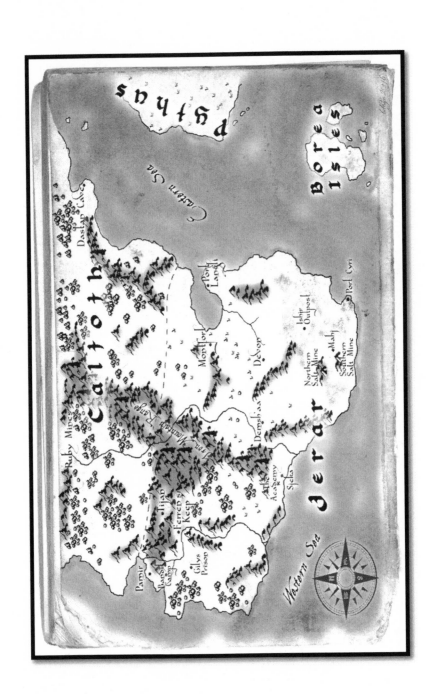

ONE

"DON'T LOOK NOW," I said softly. *Do I sound calm?* I hoped so. It was hard to tell with the frantic beating in my chest. "But I think we're being followed."

My brother paled, hands freezing on the reins. Almost unconsciously, his head began to turn in the direction of my warning.

"Alex!"

He jerked his head back guiltily. I hoped the movement would go unnoticed by the four riders trailing a quarter of a mile behind us. They hadn't appeared too concerned with our procession thus far, but the fact that the men were still following us after the last main road had ended left an unsettling taste in the back of my mouth.

It was getting dark fast. At the elevation we were traveling, there wouldn't be much light left for long. Already the sun had wedged itself behind one of the larger outcroppings of rock, and the rest of its rays were fading much too quickly for my liking.

I'd hoped the party would stop to make camp at one of the few sites we'd passed—after all, what weary traveler wouldn't prefer the comfort of an easy alcove and a nearby stream? I, for one, would have insisted as much if it hadn't been for the uncanny appearance of those behind us.

Our horses continued their steady climb into the dark hillside above.

"How do you know they are following us?"

A pit settled in the base of my stomach. "Their saddlebags are far too light for a trek through the mountains."

"So?"

I clenched my jaw and then released a long breath. It wasn't Alex's fault he didn't understand my concern. He cared about healing people, not studying the monsters that harmed them.

"Only fools—or bandits—would travel so empty-handed. We passed the last main road to an inn hours ago." I tried to keep the trickle of fear out of my throat as I added, "Only a bandit wouldn't bother with supplies. They'd be taking ours instead."

My twin slowly mulled over my words. I wondered if he thought I was overreacting. I wasn't exactly known for my easygoing temperament. I hoped he didn't think this was just another one of my "rash judgments," as our parents were wont to assume.

While I waited for Alex's response, I pretended to check the footholds, giving myself an opportunity to spy on the others. Though the men were much harder to study in the dark, there was still no mistaking the glint of steel bulging from one of the men's hips. Only a soldier or a knight was allowed to bear weapons.

A chill ran through me. I doubted he was either.

"What should we do, Ry?" Alex looked so much younger

than his fifteen years with fear in his eyes.

My twin, the rational, levelheaded, sane half of me, was afraid. What did that mean for the two of us? I refused to contemplate the answer. Instead, I scanned the trail ahead, trying to make out our route amid the lumbering pines.

Unfortunately, it was much easier to point out the problem than come up with a solution.

We should've taken the main road, I acknowledged belatedly. If I hadn't been so set on the fastest route to the Academy, we'd be on a nice, well-traveled path instead of a desolate mountain range, about to be robbed.

But it was too late now.

"Ryiah?"

I bit my lip. Alex was looking to me for an answer. This was, after all, my forte. What had I told my parents before we left home? I would join Combat or die trying.

A fine choice of words. What had been meant as a melodramatic proclamation was now to be my ironic demise. I couldn't fight our way out of this. Not against four grown, arms-holding men, and certainly not without magic.

For the millionth time, I silently questioned the gods' motive in my inability to cast. But this wasn't the time to bemoan my lack of magic. I needed a solution fast.

I peered into the trees, straining to see any sort of upcoming detour. Could we find a way to circle back, lose the men in a chase, and return to the main road... Or would we do better by taking cover under darkness and moving out again at first light?

Perhaps Alex was right, and the men would just carry on. We could just set up camp here and now and be none the worse.

Yes, and pigs might fly, I scolded myself. *You want to be a warrior mage, and yet you shirk at the first sign of danger.*

I did *not* shirk.

I sidled as close to Alex as my mount could manage. "When I say go, I want you to flee off west. I'll take the east—"

Alex opened his mouth to protest, and I clapped a hand over his mouth.

"We have to split up. Staying together would only increase their odds of catching us."

My brother stared me down defiantly. When I removed my palm, he made a face. "I'm not leaving you, Ry."

I ignored him. "We can meet up at that tavern we passed earlier just before the fork… If one of us isn't there within a couple hours of daylight, then we appeal to the local guard." I swallowed. "Bandits don't usually kill unless someone puts up a fight." At least that's what I'd heard.

"But what if they—"

"They won't."

He shook his head stubbornly. "If they find out you're a *girl*—"

I looked my brother in the eye. "It's our best bet, Alex."

Alex swore. "Ryiah, I don't like this plan one bit."

I motioned for him to get ready. Then I leaned forward to stand in the stirrups with both hands gripped firmly to the reins. Alex copied my movements, and as soon as he was in a similar stance, I nodded.

"Now."

A cloud of dirt and debris swelled up as my mare took off

at a charge. The thundering clash of hooves and the cries of surprise from the party behind us left me with an elated sense of victory. We'd caught them off guard.

I kept my eyes glued to the forest in front of me. Dark, twisting branches struck out at my face and ripped across my skin. Harsh wind tore at my already-chapped lips. I willed myself to ignore the numbing cold and sudden, jarring cuts from above.

I hoped Alex was having better luck in his bit of the woods. I could barely see five feet in front of me and had to rely on the mare for navigation. Now that she knew our general direction, it was up to her to avoid what I could not.

The sharp whistle of steel alerted me a second too late as one of the men's knives nicked the side of my arm.

I cried out and then immediately regretted the noise.

The wound was shallow, but it'd caught me by surprise. I fell back against the saddle, and the mare startled at the sudden shift in weight, slowing her gallop to a canter. I sprung to correct the error, but the mare stumbled over some loose stones and sent me pitching forward instead.

My hands, slick with sweat, lost hold of the reins.

I shot face first toward the ground and hit the dirt with a thud. Pain ignited in my limbs like a spark. I had only a second to roll before panicked hooves slammed the earth beside my head.

The mare took off before I could stand.

Mother is going to kill me. The coin to lease a horse for the trip was already a hardship as it was. Losing said horse and indebting my parents to an angry stable master would only make things worse.

I attempted to stand with wobbly knees. My muscles screamed. I had new cuts on my hands from trying to brace the fall. I couldn't tell if the thunder in my ears was from the pulsing of blood or the bandits' approach.

Maybe they hadn't seen my fall. Maybe they still thought I was astride the horse. It was dark enough, and it was quite possible they'd taken the shot in the dark.

I took a couple of hobbling steps until the hammering gave way to shouts.

Gods, no.

The bandits were giving orders to search the area.

I ducked under the nearest brush, ignoring the thorns that raked across my face and arms. I could only pray that the loud snapping of branches was just a quiet rustle outside my head.

Burrowing as deep as I dared, I waited, trying not to imagine all the horrible possibilities that awaited me if I were found.

One deep breath, and then another.

I could hear their voices. They were getting louder. A frosty breeze brought the rancid smell of days' old sweat and ale, and I cringed.

How many followed me? I bit down on my cheek as the voices drew closer.

"Saw the boy limping," one was saying.

Another man cleared his throat. "He couldn't have gone far."

I could distinguish only two men. If there were a third, he was silent.

The crunching of pine needles locked the air in my lungs.

One of the men was right beside my bush. I could hear the shuffling of feet against some of the outlying roots. I made a silent prayer to the gods that he continued on.

"I reckon he went the other way, Jared," the man said. "There's nothing this way but brush."

"Naw, he's got to be nearby."

The voices were too close. My pulse hammered so loudly, I was certain they could hear it.

"Smells good out here."

"It's the blackberries, you dolt."

There was a rustle as a hand reached into the brush and withdrew with a curse. "Bloody thorns!"

"Let me try."

A second hand shot in, grappling for a handful of berries and catching on my hair in the withdrawal. I didn't realize until the man yanked his fist back and the hair ripped from my scalp.

"Agh!"

I clamped a hand over my mouth, but it was too late.

Two pairs of burly arms jerked me out of the bush with a shout.

"Well, well," the one whose voice I recognized as Jared drawled. "Seems your appetite has it uses, Erwan." He elbowed the second man, a tall fellow with a big gut and muddy boots. "Don't it?"

It was hard to see either of their faces as I struggled in their grip. The bandits allowed me to try, making crude remarks and laughing as I squirmed in vain.

No one could save me now.

"Now, boy," Erwan said, "tell us where you and your little

friend were headed."

I sucked in a sharp breath. With all the blood and grime covering my brother's riding clothes I'd borrowed for the trip, they'd mistaken me for a redheaded young man. The tunic was baggy, and though ripped at the arms, it still hid most of my form.

I remained silent, afraid my voice would give me away.

"We asked you a question."

There was a loud, resounding slap as Jared's palm struck my cheek.

Don't cry. My face stung and bled in places the thorns had already opened, but I wasn't about to cower. Showing fear would only encourage them.

"Now," the man continued, "you get one more chance to answer before I start removing limbs." A sword dug into my ribs.

I wondered how the weapon had fallen into the outlaw's hands. Had his band cornered a lonely soldier on some deserted trail and robbed him blind, like they were planning to do to me? Or had Jared killed him to prevent the soldier from telling his tale?

From the pale light of the moon, I could see a rusty stain on the hilt. Bile rose in my throat, and I forced myself to swallow it back down. In the gruffest voice I could manage, I coughed, "The Academy."

The large man, Erwan, laughed. "Some mage! Where's his magic?"

My face burned and I looked away.

"He's not a mage. He's too young." Jared's interest turned to disgust. "The boy's no use. Just another village kid on his way to that blasted school. Bloody fools, always thinking they've a gift when they should be doing a man's work instead."

I kept quiet, hoping the men would dismiss me as worthless and leave.

"Did you travel with a purse?"

Not much. Though the Crown provided a trial year of free room and board to all of its students in the kingdom's three war schools, it wasn't enough to offset the labor Alex and I had provided in our parents' apothecary.

"The purse w-was in the saddlebags." And the mare was long gone, somewhere galloping away rider-less and free.

"Erwan, go find the boy's horse."

The pudgy outlaw groaned and started back to his mount. There was a tug on my arm as Jared dragged me toward his horse. "You come with me. Cause any trouble, and I won't hesitate to gut you where you stand."

* * *

Hours later, Erwan returned with my mare and an armful of lumber. In the meantime, Jared and I had seen to the camp.

I staggered to my feet as an order rang out to gather the wood.

How long are they going to keep me? A mountain of branches was shoved at my chest, and I swayed. Would the bandits let me go at all? Or were Alex and a patrol of soldiers going to find me gutted on the side of the trail the next morning?

I'll have to make a run for it when they fall asleep.

The men's conversation rose as I placed more wood on

the fire.

"Halseth and Karl haven't made it back?"

"Hard to see anything in this blasted forest. They probably made camp somewhere else."

"Do you think they caught the other one?"

"I don't see why not." Jared spat at the ground, and his gaze fell to me. "You, boy, is your friend a worthless brat like you, or does he have magic?" His eyes gleamed over that last word.

"N-no." My lip trembled. If they suspected my brother had magic, would they try harder to find him? To use him for his abilities?

"Shouldn't have lied."

Before I could duck, the man snatched my wrist and thrust my hand into the fire. I screamed out as the flames ate at my skin.

The man dropped my arm with a start.

Blinking back tears, I cradled my hand, careful not to touch the patch that'd turned a nasty, glistening red.

"Well, well…"

I glanced up to find Jared smirking.

"Why don't you go get us some more wood, Erwan." The man's eyes never left my face, and the corner of his lip rose higher. "I would go myself, but someone's got to watch the boy."

He knows.

Erwan shot Jared a confused look. "I just brought a whole lot of it—"

"Just fetch us more wood, you dolt!"

As soon as his comrade disappeared, the bandit turned to

me, hunger playing across his malevolent gaze. The shadows from the fire swept across his face, making every inch of him more menacing than before.

"Who would have thought?" the man sneered. "A girl."

I glanced around the site as panic took hold of my lungs. If I ran now, would I make it far? I couldn't fight in the condition I was in. Perhaps a boy my brother's size, but not someone a head taller and twice my weight.

Jared took a step closer, fingering the scabbard at his hip. "If you behave, I won't tell the others."

It was time to run.

My heels dug into the ground as the man leapt.

I wasn't fast enough. He caught me in the air, knocking me to the ground.

Two hands pinned my wrists as his knees dug into my legs.

I writhed and screamed as the man bent. A foul, sour stench assaulted my senses as his lips drew closer to my own.

My head jerked forward. I'd learned some moves from fighting with boys my own age. There was a jolting pain and a satisfying crunch. Blood sprayed across my face as the man roared, clutching his nose.

"You insolent wench!" The man's right fist struck my face just as I kneed him in the groin, earning another curse.

My face stung, but it was nothing compared to the pain in my hand. Grimy nails dug into the burn, and I shrieked. Why oh *why* didn't I have a way to access my magic like Alex?

I twisted and clawed, fighting back with my free arm.

Jared reached for the top of my tunic, and I swung my fist

as hard as I could.

The man caught my wrist.

I threw my weight into his hold for all I was worth.

But the man was too strong. He slapped me again, so hard I saw stars.

My face snapped to the side as the camp exploded in light.

Then, I started to scream.... At least, I thought it was me. But it wasn't. I was too busy choking on dirt.

The screams were getting louder.

Was my hearing damaged? *Did he hit me that hard?*

I attempted to pull myself from the ground, trying to make sense of what had just taken place.

An immense pounding filled my head as I drew up to my knees. The screams were like the screech of a rusty wagon's wheel. They kept going and going, ringing in my ears.

The cries were coming from the shimmering thing in front of me.

I blinked twice and my vision cleared.

Jared was enshrouded in flame. Fire ate away at flesh and cloth in a frantic inferno as he staggered across the camp shrieking at the top of his lungs. Somehow, someway, he'd been set entirely ablaze.

Without bothering to wait, I shoved up from the dirt. I sprinted as every muscle inside of me screamed. My trembling hands undid my mare's lead while she stared out at me with wide, unblinking eyes.

I gave swift thanks to the gods she was saddled with my bag still attached.

Then, I swung up into the saddle, wincing as my bad hand brushed the horn. Every part of me ached, but the burn on my palm the worst of all.

I gave the mare what I hoped was a reassuring pat, nudging her forward with my knees.

"What is— Get back here, boy!"

Erwan had returned, and he was racing toward camp. Pulse jumping, I leaned down, undoing the two other horses' leads.

Our eyes met across the way. He might be able to reach me in time, but his friend would burn alive.

The man swore and rushed to Jared's side.

Ha.

The last rope fell away, and I let out a loud whoop. The other horses startled and scattered as I took off into the night.

Try to catch me now.

* * *

I'd been on the run for an hour when a loud crash of hooves pierced the silence from somewhere behind the trees.

Pulling at the reins sharply, I steered my horse into a hard turn.

"Ryiah, is that you?"

Thank the gods. I'd thought I'd be searching for him all night. "Alex!"

"Lost my tail a couple miles back." He sidled closer. "Where's your two?"

"Occupied." That was certainly one way of putting it. "They won't be searching for us tonight."

It was too dark to see Alex's face, but I knew he was grinning. "What did you *do*?"

I swallowed, unwilling to tell my brother the story while we were still in the middle of the woods. "Let's get out of here first, and I'll tell you everything in the morning."

We wouldn't be safe until we were through the pass. There was still my brother's tail searching the hills. Sooner or later, they would turn back.

"Fine, but let's take the rest at a walk. My horse needs a break, and I can barely see in this awful darkness..." Alex snorted. "I don't know about you, but I've almost fallen off twice tonight."

I knew better than to comment. My overprotective brother would emerge as soon as he saw me in the light. I was in no mood for one of his rants, and I didn't want to give him a reason to go charging back after the men.

I wanted to get to the Academy as quickly as possible and leave this nightmare behind.

My brother let me lead—I had a better head for directions than he—and the two of us quietly found our way back to the main road after another hour of silent climbing.

We finally left the canopy of trees and continued the remainder of our trek across open plains. The moon's soft glow and the occasional glitter of starlight lit the way.

Fortunately for me, Alex was too exhausted to take in any abnormality of my appearance. Instead, the two of us remained silently alert, using the remainder of our energy to listen for others' approach.

Several hours later, just as the sun peeked through the towering crags off in the distance, we came across a welcome sight. A large, homely inn stood out from the road with the scent of hot, buttery eggs and sausage wafting through a wide pair of windows at its base.

Alex took off with a yelp, and I chased after my brother,

eyes glued to the vision ahead.

TWO

ALL I WANTED to do was sleep, but that was clearly the last thing my brother had in mind.

"How?" Alex's face colored with each mounting word. "How could you not tell me the moment you found me?"

As soon as we'd turned over our mounts, Alex had finally noticed my appearance. All enthusiasm had faded in the light of the many scratches, bruises, and blood mottling my skin.

And then he noticed my hand. *"Ry!"*

I hid my arm behind my back. Angry blisters marred my fingers and palm in unsightly patches of glistening red, and the pain was worse.

"It was more important to get to safety first." My apology was weak at best.

"Safety?" Alex snapped. "Don't use that *Combat* nonsense with me, Ryiah. And what happened? I thought you said—"

"I didn't say anything because I didn't want to make you upset!"

Alex made a face. "I believe I have a right to know what happened to my own sister."

The last thing I needed was his rage after he heard the

tale. "Not now. Tomorrow, please, when we are both feeling better."

Alex glowered. "One day of rest. And then you *will* tell me what happened."

I raised a brow. "Keep acting like that, and people will start to say *you're* the hotheaded one."

The two of us entered the inn, and while I inspected the grounds, Alex went ahead and ordered a room and a bath. Then, eyeing a loitering maidservant with a wink, he added on a list of common salves to be brought.

The girl scurried off, blushing at my brother and glaring at me. I knew what she was thinking. Women all took to my brother the same.

Alex and I might've been the same age, but that was where the similarities began and ended. I was a bit stubborn, a little too quick to settle my fights with a fist. My brother was assured and quick to smile. He never got into fights. He was too busy flirting with girls and charming our parents.

It wasn't that I was a brat, I just didn't have the patience that came with my twin's confidence. People liked him and tolerated me; I suspected it was also because I had what my parents joked was a "big mouth."

Alex was also a good three inches taller than me, with shoulders I envied. He barely even tried and muscle sprouted on his arms and legs like a plant. Meanwhile, my build wouldn't change. I was slim and gangly, and months of hard training back home had never changed it.

I wanted to hate my brother, but apparently I was also under his spell.

Alex had everything. Our parents' soft brown locks and

warm blue eyes that made most girls forget how easy he flirted around town. Well, that and his humor.

My eyes were blue too, but they were so light it was more common to think of them as gray than anything else. *Gray.* Take into account my quick temper, and it was no wonder people did not take to me the same.

In a lot of ways, I was more like my younger brother Derrick. Alex took after our parents.

Alex motioned for me to wash my cuts and then gave me a warning smile after I'd finished. "You are not going to like this next part."

I nodded absentmindedly. I was more than used to him tending to my wounds.

My brother pressed two fingers to my palm. There was a moment of awareness, like needles prickling against skin, and then my pain flared, like hot embers working inside my flesh. It seemed to go on for ages, and I bit my cheek.

A mage of Combat wouldn't show weakness, so neither would I.

The ache built to an unbearable point, and then it suddenly ebbed, a chill sweeping out and covering my flesh.

Alex kept the pressure steady for another minute, and then he got up to grab the tray the maid had delivered.

My brother filled a warm glass with water and mixed it with salt. He poured the mixture over my skin. It wasn't a pleasant sensation, but more tolerable than the last. He dabbed the inflamed flesh with a cold poultice a few seconds longer, and then spread a bit of honey over the top, wrapping my hand in a thin cloth when he was satisfied.

"Thank you."

Alex shook his head. "It's a shame this couldn't have happened *after* we started the Academy. If it had, I'd be able to do a lot more than this. You are still going to have to let the rest of those cuts heal naturally."

In brother speak, don't do anything else to hurt yourself before we reach the school.

I waved his apology away. "Just feel lucky you *have* magic. In two days' time, I am going to be the biggest fraud in the history of that school."

Alex sighed at the familiar argument. "You *have* something, Ry. You just haven't found it. Everyone knows twins always share the gift."

The scrolls also said magic was rare, not hereditary, and emerged in adolescence. Who's to say our shared birth played a part since blood didn't? Perhaps other twins had been the exception, and we were the norm.

I wasn't even sure when the last pair of twins had attended the Academy of Magic. It wasn't like we were a common occurrence.

"But who is to say the Council's scrolls were talking about us? For all we know, they could have been referring to *identical* twins." I fingered my red locks, a sharp contrast to the muted brown of my brother.

We couldn't be more different there.

Alex gave my knee a reassuring pat. "Gods help us, Ry. Even if you *do* have magic, it isn't as if we have a real shot."

I sighed. That much was true at least. Most applicants failed their trial year. We were just two lowborn kids without any formal training.

"Mark my words," he added, "this time next year, we'll be

applying to the Cavalry."

I knew my brother was right, but I hoped more than anything he was wrong.

* * *

The next day came too soon. I'd barely shut my eyes before Alex was shaking me awake with the reminder that we still had sixty miles of riding left, and two days to do it.

"And if we fall behind now, we'll miss the admission period."

I glared at my brother. "Not funny." I'd said the very same thing two mornings before, which had led us to that gods' forsaken overpass and the bandits in the first place.

Alex grinned in reply.

Grumbling, I dressed and walked the length of the room, gathering the rest of the supplies until we were ready to leave. Alex handed me our breakfast as we exited the inn, the same stale bread as every meal before. I eyed it unhappily. If I never saw a piece of rye again, it would be too soon.

After we'd tipped the stable boy for our horses' return, the two of us set to checking the fit of our straps and loading the saddlebags. Alex finished much sooner than me. He volunteered to assist, but I refused. Warriors dealt with pain every day, and now that the worst of mine was gone, I was determined to do the same.

Exhaling loudly, my brother mounted his charge, muttering about mule-headed sisters who were too stubborn for their own good.

I finished a couple minutes later and then swung myself into the saddle, wincing. My body was still sore, but for the most part, a full night's rest had done me good. My ribs were only a little bit tender, and most of my wounds had closed. Even the burn on my hand, while still a terrible shade of pink, didn't sting.

It did itch, unfortunately. But I had enough sense not to scratch it. I'd learned that lesson plenty of times before.

Alex moaned as we started out onto the main road. "What I wouldn't give for some creamed porridge."

My tongue salivated. "Or a honey bun."

Alex's stomach roared loudly in accord. The bread hadn't done very much to slake our hunger. After the room, we hadn't had much coin left for the inn's meals.

"The first thing I'm going to ask the masters to teach me," my brother declared, "is how to conjure food—*good* food."

I raised a brow. We both knew the Academy only taught war casting. The masters would never waste any of the faction's lessons on something so silly. Magic was too precious. If they taught us food-anything, it'd be the easiest fare for an army, hardly the tastiest.

"I look forward to hearing their responses."

Alex chucked the last bit of his roll at me. It was rock hard.

Laughing, I managed to catch it and toss it into the forest beyond.

"So," Alex said, "are you ready to tell me what happened?"

I wasn't, but I was going to anyway.

I, at least, knew the truth. Alex had only my injuries and his wild imagination to explain them. If our roles had been reversed, I would have insisted as much.

I proceeded to tell him everything.

When I was finished, Alex snarled, "That cowardly whelp! He deserved much worse than what he got!"

I cringed; that memory was anything but pleasant. There was also a nagging in the back of my mind. Something about the turn of events didn't make sense, even now retelling them. How exactly *had* Jared caught fire? We'd been scuffling close to the fire, but had he really been so senseless to roll his entire body into the pit?

He'd been on top of me, and then he'd disappeared.

In the heat of the moment, I hadn't bothered to question it.

But now I wondered. Was there another explanation for what I'd seen? I still felt like something was missing.

My hands stilled on the reins.

Was it magic?

"Ryiah?"

I glanced at my brother. We'd been riding in silence for the last couple of minutes, and now he was watching me with a curious expression.

I stared at the grassy plains ahead of us, wondering if I should say my last thought aloud. It seemed too much to hope. There'd been a couple times since Alex discovered his powers where I'd thought... But each time I'd been wrong, and the disappointment had been crippling.

No. It was better left unsaid.

But Alex knew me too well. "You think you lit the man on fire with magic, don't you?"

Was I really so obvious? I flushed. "I know how it sounds."

"But it makes more sense than anything else."

"Tell me I'm wrong." I didn't want him to. I wanted magic to be the answer, but I'd been wrong so many times.

He was quiet. I knew Alex was caught between believing in his sister and facing our pattern in the past.

I played with the reins in my lap. "The man didn't roll into the fire. And he wasn't close enough to the pit for the flames to reach him."

"Perhaps you misjudged the distance." My brother's reply was gentle. "The man could've fallen in while you were dazed."

"But he was too far away." My words were desperate, and I could hear the plea in the back of my throat. *Believe me.*

"Did anything feel different?" he pressed. "Were you unusually hot or lightheaded? Did you think of fire?" All the traditional symptoms of magic.

"My hand burned, and just about everything hurt... I wasn't lightheaded exactly, but my head did really ache afterward." I paused. "And no, I was too angry and afraid to be thinking of anything except what was happening."

Alex frowned. "That doesn't sound like a casting, or at least what it's like for me."

An idea hit me. "Do you think my pain released the magic?"

Alex appeared thoughtful. "Maybe... but then how is it that it only worked once? He hurt you several times before it occurred. And how many times have you injured yourself sparring in Demsh'aa with your friends?"

That was true, but then nothing about magic made sense. Maybe there was an answer, and I would find it at the Academy. Groping around in my bags, I eagerly pulled out my father's hunting knife.

"Ryiah," my brother yelped, "what are you—"

Ignoring Alex's cry of alarm, I dug the blade into the center of my palm, reopening freshly sealed wounds as blood dripped down past my wrist.

At the same time, I observed a yellowish-green mass that clung to a nearby tree. The moss looked like a perfect target, a furry patch of flammable tufts.

I increased the pressure of the blade.

Almost immediately, the moss began to shrivel and smoke.

"Alex!"

My brother's jaw dropped as he followed my gaze.

I continued to add pressure, hardly conscious of the pain as flames sprouted on the moss. *"Look, I have magic!"*

My voice was raspy and hoarse. I wanted to scream, but I was too afraid it would break the concentration of power on the tree.

Breaking free from his initial shock, my twin rode over and snatched the knife away with a huff.

"Alex!"

The moss crumbled to the ground in a withered heap, the flames gone.

My brother gave me a dark look, brandishing the knife. "You shouldn't have to maim yourself to cast, Ryiah." Clearly, any brotherly elation was lost in the wake of my blood.

He was right, of course.

"I wasn't even sure I could." My mind was racing. Now that I knew what it felt like, could I do it again? Without cutting myself?

Staring determinedly at a second tree, I willed my magic to take flight naturally, without inflicting pain.

Nothing.

I squinted harder, ignoring the throbbing of my hand and the pounding in my head as I ogled a yellow-green mound on the trunk. Every thought, every part of me strained as I attempted to project my magic onto the nearby moss.

Still, it remained unchanged...

I tried, again and again. And *again.*

Eventually we passed a whole forest of moss-lined trees without so much as the slightest hint of fire, not even smoke.

By the time we made camp for the evening, I was frustrated and coarse.

"What is wrong with me?" I tore into my dried jerky with vengeance. "Why can't things ever come easy like they do for you?"

Alex wasn't rising to my bait. "You'd make a great soldier or knight, but you want to be a mage. You picked an uphill road from the start."

I made a frustrated sound. "Everyone knows that mages are the best." They had the power, the status, rooms in the king's palace, and all the coin they'd ever need. A knight was a lofty goal, but how could I explain that it wasn't enough?

There was this driving pull, and it'd been a part of me for years—ever since that day six years ago when a patrol from the Crown's Army regiment stopped by our village on their way to the palace in Devon.

There'd been a swarm of soldiers and knights to captivate

my brothers and the village boys, but the person who caught my eye was the sole Combat mage avoiding attention in the back of their squad. I'd seen the way the others deferred to her. She'd had their respect, and she didn't have to lift the heaviest sword or flex her muscles to do it. She just *was*.

It was like that with all magical factions, but there was something special about Combat.

That was the day I'd started to dream of carrying that kind of power and respect. It was intoxicating, and I couldn't let it go.

"You chose the hardest path *because* it was hard. I chose Restoration because I wanted to heal people."

"I want to help them too!"

"You want to be a war mage to save people, and be the hero they remember. Healers and alchemists do the same without the fancy title."

Who didn't want to be the hero? Everyone knew the ones who chose Combat were a little power-hungry and mad, but we were also the ones who shaped a war. I wasn't going to apologize for wanting more.

Vain? Perhaps. Ambitious? Definitely. But that's the kind of mage Jerar needed. You didn't become the most powerful country from shaking hands.

"None of that will matter if I have to bloody myself every time I need to cast." Imagine that, a mage who had to slit her wrists just to fight a duel. I'd be dead in a matter of weeks.

My brother reached out to take my hand. "I'm sure the masters will be able to show you how to use your power without hurting yourself."

I hoped so. If not, I was in for a *very* troubling year.

Alex grinned. "And once you've mastered it, you can make some normal friends. Not the power-hungry ones like yourself."

Ha. "You think you're so hilarious."

"You're laughing because it's true."

* * *

We were riding along a steep switchback the next morning when the ground started to shake.

"By the gods, what is that commotion?"

Our horses fidgeted, tossing their heads and alternating from one leg to the next.

Alex swallowed. "We need to dismount. The horses are getting nervous."

It sounded like a stampede.

I left my brother with the horses and started toward the center of the road, trying to discern where the tremors were coming from. The whole area sounded like thunder, and there wasn't a storm cloud in the sky. It was right around the corner, whatever it was. In seconds, I would be able to see—

"Ry, get off the path!" My brother jerked me back just as nine tall, slick black horses emerged, taking up the entire trail with their riders. The men were riding in a two-column formation with livery that gleamed in the afternoon light.

Eight of the riders bore heavy chainmail with metal plates lining their arms and chests. *Knights*. The expression underneath their helmets was dark and unrelenting.

My mouth went dry as I took a deep breath. If Alex hadn't pulled me out of the way, I would've been trampled to death.

At the center of the procession rode a young man. He didn't appear much older than us. He wasn't wearing livery like the others, but there was something formidable enough about his posture. I had the overwhelming impression that he was anything but helpless.

Everything about the rider's dress unnerved me—his hair, cloak, his pants, the boots, even his fastenings were black. What was even more unsettling, the stranger had the most unusual eyes I'd ever seen. They were garnet, somewhere between black and a deep crimson, a juxtaposition of two colors that should never exist.

The stranger locked eyes with me as he spotted my brother and me in passing. He scowled, and I felt as if I'd been kicked in the gut. I was used to the bizarre behavior of our nobles back home, but this rider's condescension was much deeper. *What sort of person carries that much hostility toward strangers?*

Still, I couldn't look away.

It was only after the group of riders had completely passed that I recalled what the young man had been wearing. Hanging by a thick chain around his neck, there'd been a hematite stone pendant.

There was only one family in the entire kingdom who was allowed to wear a black gem of that description.

Apparently, I had just watched one of the realm's two princes pass me on horseback.

It took a moment for the shock to register.

"Do you know who that was?"

Alex nodded speechlessly.

"Do you think he's going to the Academy?" I paused. What was I saying? Of course, he wasn't.

No member of the royal family was allowed to participate.

It'd been that way since the school's founding, and in the ninety years the school existed, no one had ever questioned the Council of Magic's ruling.

Alex seemed to be of the same mind. "There hasn't ever been an issue between our king and the mages. I doubt one would arise now."

I hesitated. "Well, the prince certainly looked unhappy about something."

My brother didn't look concerned. "Maybe someone almost trampled his sister." The two princes didn't have a sister, but my brother was making a point. "He certainly didn't care about any other riders on the trail. Just like the nobility, thinking the roads were only made for them. He probably expected us to bow."

"He almost rode us off the cliff."

"Highborns." My brother gave a groan. "They are all the same."

And we were about to meet a bunch at the Academy. I couldn't wait.

* * *

When we finally reached our destination, the sun had set, and in its place was a rosy-golden hue. A soft glow chased what remained of our journey, and I followed its vague outline across the hillside below.

Tiny boxes dotted the landscape, little shops and houses at the center of the western seaside. Sjeka was the only western port for miles, but it was more famous for the war school it housed. *The Academy.*

A well-trodden dirt path wove between the huts, slithering until it finally came to rest at the base of an enormous structure.

Thick, dark slabs of grayish stone upheld a striking fortress with twin towers peaking out into the sky. Three colored cloth banners hung from poles attached to each side of the edifice. One for each faction: forest green, ember red, and raven black.

I swallowed. The castle was at least four levels high at its lowest point. It was as tall as a hill.

"If this is the Academy, what do you think the king's palace looks like?" Alex wheezed.

I had no answer.

Nudging the mare a step forward and then another, I began to make my descent. Alex followed softly behind, and in what seemed like ages but was probably only minutes, we arrived at the Academy doors.

At their center, two heavy wrought steel handles awaited.

The two of us dismounted and handed off our reins to a waiting hostler.

Taking a deep breath, I reached for a handle and gingerly pulled.

It didn't budge.

Frowning, Alex joined me, and the two of us heaved until it finally creaked open.

As soon as we were inside, I lost what little of my breath remained.

Everything I had heard... it didn't do justice to what my eyes were seeing now. Of course, I'd known the Academy would be beautiful.

But I hadn't known it would be... so much.

The floor was paved in black marble so every step we

took echoed along the hall.

In a contrast that should have been jarring but wasn't, the walls were a rough, uncut sandstone. On them, metal sconces held ever-burning torches in place, but instead of the natural, golden radiance of fire, they emitted a flickering, crystalline blue. An alchemist's work.

At the end of the passage was a large room containing an enormous, spiraling staircase.

When I approached the atrium, the sheer size of it seemed to grow. The stairs stood out at its center, steadily rising, secured by thick iron railings on either side. As it touched the second floor, the rail separated into two twisting cases with a giant, many-paned window at their base. Facing due west, the window revealed the jagged rocks and sea.

Moonlight bathed the entire room, and when I looked up, I found the most riveting feature yet. The ceiling had been constructed entirely of stained glass. Thousands of twinkling red and gold glass fragments greeted my open-mouthed gaze. *Wow*.

"Ugh. Two more lowborns."

Startled out of my trance, I took in the rest of the room. I'd failed to notice the large gathering of people at my left. A hundred or so young men and women were clustered around a figure I couldn't quite make out. Most were distracted by the speaker in the center, but a couple of stragglers were eyeing my brother and me warily.

Instantly, I became conscious of what we must look like. Five days of horsehair and exhaustion. Riding clothes stained with dirt and sweat and blood. My hair a shoulder-length tangled disaster. Even our arms bore a nice coating of dust since that morning. Not to mention the bruises spotting my arms and blisters in my fist.

So much for first impressions.

I ignored the stares and followed my brother as he pushed his way through the crowd, attempting to catch a glimpse of who was commanding everyone's attention. As I squeezed past arms and elbows, I caught my foot on something hard and tripped.

Luckily, it was so packed that I just ended up colliding with the person in front of me instead of landing face down on the floor.

I started to apologize. "I'm so—"

The tall stranger turned around.

It was *him,* the prince with the angry eyes from the mountains.

Hours later, and his expression hadn't changed.

"—sorry."

He just looked at me, irritated. I felt heat start to rise in my cheeks under his taciturn stare, but seconds later I was facing his back again.

Well, he's a delight, I thought dryly.

Having just annoyed one of the heirs to the kingdom of Jerar, I decided to move on to less provoking tactics. I safely navigated my way through the rest of the mass and joined Alex, far away from the prince.

In the front, a large man stood conversing with his audience in a layered, black silk robe. I recognized him from the insignia on his sleeve.

"Is that Master Barclae?"

Alex nodded.

Master Barclae, or as his title commanded, "Master of the Academy," was a handsome man with sharp features and a salt and pepper mustache that suited his face. He'd started leading the Academy a year or two before Alex and I'd been born. Many said it was because of him that Jerar's last Candidacy had had such strong contenders.

I strained to hear what he was saying.

"—first two months will be spent exploring the fundamentals and identifying the faction you will choose to commit your studies to. The remainder will be spent learning the foundation of its magic."

Someone mumbled a question.

The large man laughed coldly. "There is no such thing as 'rest.' If you want an easy career, you should have applied to one of the other schools our Crown sponsors. The School of Knighthood, perhaps, or maybe the Cavalry? The latter's retention is so high, I suspect they hang gum drops from its rafters."

I glanced at my brother. There was nothing easy about either of the schools the master had mentioned.

Alex returned my anxious smile with one of his own. *Too late to turn back now.*

"Why are there *only* fifteen? Because fifteen is already *too* generous. Magic is hardly common enough to justify that number—the *only* reason we have that many is because the Crown demands at least fifteen new war mages each year to enter its company. At one point it was higher, but that was a waste of resources and jeopardized the training of the few who deserved to be here. The Academy's expectations are demanding, and it would be idiocy to train incompetents. It is a privilege we allow fifteen as it is."

The students continued to pester the man with questions until he finally cleared his throat. "That is enough for tonight. It's late, and your official induction will take place tomorrow morning." He snorted. "Try to save such senseless queries for your other masters." Without bothering to wait for a response, the master of the Academy exited the podium, disappearing through a corridor on my left.

A frenzied manservant appeared before we could scatter.

"Master Barclae will return in the morning," the man squeaked. "If you haven't done so already, please check in with Constable Barrius, our master staffer, in the east wing. He will go over the expected conduct."

Almost immediately, the crowd dispersed. Most of the students set off in the same direction as Master Barclae, while my brother and I followed a handful of others to the right.

As we began to make our way down another long corridor, I groaned. Alex was already flirting with a girl in the back.

Ugh.

I caught the eye of a friendly-looking girl at the front. If I didn't make friends, it would be a long year of watching Alex's trail of broken hearts. "I guess I can see why my parents didn't want me to choose the Academy."

The girl laughed. "My older brother tried out a couple of years ago. He said it was only as hard as you make it..." Her eyes glimmered. "Then again, Jeff was one of the first to resign, so maybe I shouldn't be listening to a word my brother says."

I grinned. "I'm Ryiah."

"Ella," she told me with a dark hand outstretched.

"I'm here with my twin." I nodded to my brother. He was too busy to notice, flirting shamelessly with his infamous grin.

Poor girl doesn't stand a chance.

"You two don't look much alike."

I shrugged. People always pointed that out, even fifteen years after birth.

"So where are you from?" Ella asked.

"A couple days east. Have you heard of Demsh'aa?"

Ella nodded, ebony locks falling across her hazel eyes. "My father usually visits the apothecary there whenever he passes through. He likes the sleep sachets and swears they are better than the ones he buys from the palace alchemists."

"That's our family's store." I smiled. "Alex made those. We didn't get half as much business when it was just my parents. He's always had a gift. It was the biggest surprise when he said he wanted to be a healer."

"Oh," she paused, "are you planning on Restoration too then?"

"Combat."

Ella laughed. "Another fighter."

"You?"

"The same." She made a flippant gesture with her hand. "My family lived at court for thirteen years before they finally gave up on me as a lady-in-waiting. I spent years convincing them to let me try out for the School of Knighthood... but then my magic showed up. So here I am instead."

So Ella was highborn from court. It explained her pretty accent. But she was also stubborn, and that made me like her. It would be nice to have a friend in the same faction.

"What time did you arrive?"

"Not long before the two of you. But don't worry. We didn't miss much. I overheard someone say that Master Barclae was the only master to make an appearance."

I sighed. "Good. I would have been upset if we had. We made good time today, but it was still an eight-hour ride."

"You do look as if you've had a long day," she observed.

I fingered the frayed ends of my shirt. She was being polite. "It's been a long *week*."

Our group took a turn and found a cluttered chamber with a formidable old man and the frantic-looking servant from earlier. Each one of them was waiting with a scroll lined with names.

"Ladies first," the old man barked. "Then the boys."

Everyone called off their names, and the man checked off the applicants from the roll.

When we finished, the constable eyed us with distaste. "Well, well, young ones, welcome to our realm's own version of the Realm of the Dead. For as long as you last, this will be your new home."

No one spoke. *Is everyone here so angry?* I wondered. I'd heard some of the staff didn't like first-years, but now I was wondering if it was all of them.

"Well, not *this* place exactly, but close to it. We keep your living quarters out behind the Academy. There are two barracks to separate each of your lots."

My jaw dropped. *Barracks*? I heard a gasp to my right and

knew I wasn't the only one who was shocked.

"Frederick," the old man said, jerking his thumb at the manservant beside him, "will take you there. You will carry your own bags. We don't waste castle chambers on first-years, so the barracks are where you will spend your time when you are not eating or training here in the Academy. You clean up after yourselves. The apprentice mages are abroad most of the year, so the layout of the Academy will be at your disposal.

"We have rules you must follow in accordance with your residency," the constable added tartly. "You are not allowed to enter the residence of the opposite sex. Curfew is ten bells. Classes are mandatory. No unauthorized fighting. And you may not leave the Academy grounds. There are *no* exceptions."

I didn't want to leave it. I just wanted to survive it.

"Any infraction of these rules, and you will find yourself in my chambers." The man cleared his throat. "*Don't* let it happen. I've been known to send first-years home on a first offense."

* * *

The entire walk to the barracks was silent. Clearly, I wasn't the only one to expect a more pleasant orientation.

We reached the wooden buildings, and I bid my brother goodnight, entering the women's residence with Ella.

The inside was much bigger than I'd anticipated, even for a crowding of fifty girls. Double bunks were spread out in rows with comfortable blankets and small trunks lining each of the walls for our belongings. A large fireplace stood at the furthest corner, no fire present but probably necessary in winter. There were even a couple baths in an adjoining house, and while I'd probably have to spend half my night waiting to use one, at least I'd have the opportunity.

It could have been worse.

There were also two servants to contribute to the upkeep. As the constable had warned, the Academy staff didn't assist with personal needs, but they did build fires, clean sheets, and heat water for bathing. It was more than I'd had at home.

Almost immediately, I could identify which girls had come from a background like mine and which were used to the palace. The ones like me were far and few between, maybe ten in the crowd. We tended to be the ones smiling at our luck while the others complained loudly about the "accommodations." Ella wasn't outspoken like the others, but I could sense that even she was disappointed. Highborns were used to more.

Setting my bag on an unclaimed bunk, I pulled out a cotton nightshirt and my only pair of clean undergarments. Then I headed to the baths.

After an hour of waiting, I finally got my chance at a lukewarm wash and scrubbed until my skin was raw. There was no one else in line behind me, so I was able to take my time. My dirt and grime warded off any potential bathers.

I returned to my bunk, satisfied and clean. It was only as I wrapped the soft sheets around my chest that the weeklong journey finally hit with staggering force.

I fell asleep in a matter of minutes. But before I did, a smile crossed my lips.

The Academy. I was finally here.

THREE

"RYIAH, WAKE UP! Everyone else has already left."

Groaning, I opened my eyes. Every muscle in my body felt like it'd been hit by a thousand tiny hammers and rocks. It was not a pleasant sensation.

I forced myself out of bed and found Ella standing by impatiently.

"How much time do we have?"

"Ten more minutes before breakfast ends to report to Master Barclae."

Barclae. Immediately, all exhaustion was forgotten and I yanked my only clean dress over my head. Then I ran out after Ella, combing my fingers through my hair and wishing I had more time to put in a better impression.

Too late now.

The two of us rushed through the courtyard and into the back entrance of the Academy. We made it into the dining hall just as the platters were being taken back to the kitchens. *Just my luck.*

Ella and I took our seats at the end of a back table. I'd just spotted Alex a couple seats down when Master Barclae entered, looking stern and impressive in his silks.

"Well, it looks like you're all still here. I will try my best to discourage that."

I flinched. Master Barclae's mood was worse than the night before. Or perhaps he was happy and just hated first-years in general.

"What is *he* doing here?"

I turned in the direction of Ella's whisper and saw where she was looking. The prince was seated one row from Alex.

I'd forgotten all about him. "Maybe he doesn't know the rules?" My explanation sounded ludicrous even to my own ears.

Master Barclae coughed loudly, and my cheeks burned as his scowl fixated on Ella and me. "Have I bored you?" he drawled loudly.

We quickly shook our heads, and I lowered my own, shamefaced.

But Master Barclae wasn't done making his point. "Really, I insist, what is *so* fascinating that you needed to interrupt my lecture?"

"Nothing," I said quickly.

"Him." Ella pointed.

I quickly snuck a look at the prince and saw his garnet eyes fixated on Ella and me. The expression he wore was one of unadulterated loathing.

I swallowed uncomfortably. *Ella!*

"Ah." Master Barclae smiled sardonically. "Him. What about this *him*?"

Ella stood nervously, "The Council's Treaty states no heir of the kingdom can undertake training as a mage. T-to prevent the Crown from interfering with matters of magic."

The irritation in the young man's eyes turned to daggers. I quickly looked away.

"The doctrine was alluding to first-born children who would be inheriting the throne. Prince Darren is second."

"But we've never had a prince before—"

"*You've never had one before,*" the boy interrupted with a snarl, "*because nobody was good enough!*"

I winced. There was no mistaking the indignation and resentment in his tone.

Master Barclae laughed. "Ah, my dears, you are so young to have already made such an unpleasant impression with a member of the royal family."

Ella bit her lip and I could feel the prince's angry gaze burning us alive.

"Well, now that these two girls have finished embarrassing themselves, would anyone else like to join them?"

Silence.

"Good. Now, before I send you off to your actual lessons, I want to make a couple of things clear. Each year, students enter my school claiming to have a gift. Please understand that having magic has never been and never will be enough. The power most of you possess is nothing short of insignificant." The master grunted. "Unfortunately, it takes *months* of testing to determine this. Were it only weeks to identify potential, there would never be such a thing as a trial year."

Someone behind me snickered loudly. That person wasn't worried, a sentiment I couldn't help wishing I shared.

"The constable informed me that we have one hundred and twenty-two new faces this year. There will only be fifteen apprenticeships passed out at the end of the year. I advise you all to think long and hard on those odds. Do you really want to waste an entire year under the guise of *hope*?"

He didn't wait for an answer.

"Ten months of hard labor, course study, and endless repetition. *That* is what you have to look forward to if you choose to remain. Most of you will be gone by midwinter, if not sooner." Master Barclae eyed us coolly. "In any case, we'll have a weeklong trial for those who remain at the year's end. Which brings me to my final note before you begin your studies, and that is your faction. Each one of you walked through our doors with a preconceived notion of which magic to train for, and for most of you that faction is Combat."

An elbow nudged me in the ribs; Alex had made his way to where Ella and I sat. He gave me a crooked grin, and I shoved him back, knowing exactly what he was thinking. I already knew Combat was a long shot, but it wasn't going to stop me from trying.

"I implore you to think twice. We've two other factions with far easier odds."

* * *

Leaving the atrium behind, Alex, Ella, and I followed a winding corridor to the left. I'd just finished introducing the two when I noticed the prince watching us from the corner of my eye.

"If looks could kill," I said to Ella in a low voice, "you and I would already be dead."

The girl stiffened. "Darren can glare all he wants. Who cares if he's not first-born? All it takes is one accidental stabbing, and suddenly, he's the heir. The masters made an exception for the Crown."

"Does it really make a difference?" Alex was curious.

"It would," Ella snapped, "if you knew who he was."

"You know the prince?"

Her mouth twisted. "Oh, yes, Darren *and* his brother. Trust me when I say not knowing them is a gift."

I was instantly curious. "What did they do?"

Ella shook her head, clearly unwilling to drudge up memories of her childhood back in court.

Alex glanced at me, and I shrugged. We entered an enormous library with the rest of our class, and the three of us took our seats in a hushed silence.

Already, there was parchment and quill at our desks. Beneath my chair, I discovered three heavy leather-bound books. I couldn't imagine the coin they would've fetched back in Demsh'aa. Books were a privilege, a very expensive one that few nobles could even afford. A baron or duke might've had a small collection at home, but only the king's palace in Devon and the Academy could have so many volumes as the ones I saw now.

No matter where I turned, shelf after shelf greeted my incredulous gaze. Thousands of books and yellowing scrolls stacked high along the walls, and at the very end of each was a ladder leading up to yet another floor of, you guessed it, more books.

I hazarded a guess that the second floor was a study. There was another floor after that, but I couldn't make it out in the dark.

Back at ground level, a heavyset woman in her fifties stood at a raised platform that had two solid oak desks at its center. Her brown hair was pulled back in a wavy bun, not a strand loose, and her powder was perfectly pressed. She was dressed with strict formality in a heavy blue cloak with a high-laced collar and an emerald pendant clasped tightly around her neck. Her eyes had a severity that warned one not to fool around in her presence.

To the woman's right sat a slightly twitchy man about half her age. His vest and pants were frayed, and his hair was rather unkempt. He had an untrimmed mustache that lined his chin and upper lip, but it seemed more from neglect than the careful precision of Master Barclae's style. Though he seemed out of sorts, his eyes spoke of kindness and intelligence.

The duo introduced themselves as Masters Eloise and Isaac and wasted no time in familiarizing the class with their expectations for the year.

Magic was the very last thing on their list.

"There is no point in learning to cast if you haven't a clue what you're doing." Master Eloise sniffed. "What you need are the basics. I don't care how much tutelage you've had, one can never know too much."

"Yes," Master Isaac added quickly, "'tis far more important to know the 'why' than the 'how.' The basics will give you the foundation first."

The "basics," apparently, were the scholarly arts: history, science, mathematics, geography, and Crown and Council law. "Nothing of interest" as Ella grumbled under her breath.

I couldn't help but agree.

I wanted to cast and wield weapons with the best of them, not bury myself in books.

It would be two months before we actually commenced the individualized study of our magical factions.

I was so close to Combat, and yet so far away.

* * *

Four long hours later, I pushed my way past a slow mob of students and came close to clawing my way into the dining hall. Ella found me just as I was piling my plate high with salted pork and a wedge of cheese, and a second plate of leeks and yellow squash.

"Hungry much?"

"You have no idea." I ravaged a roll and then grimaced. I could feel other first-years' eyes on me, and I made an effort to eat a little more slowly as we sat.

"We didn't have much to eat on the road." Alex leaned down to take an apple off Ella's plate as he joined us at the table, winking. "Thanks for that, beautiful."

Ella snatched her fruit back with a huff. "I bet other girls giggle and blush when you steal their lunch. *I* want to eat it."

Alex reddened, and I snorted, drink spraying across my lap. It'd been a long time since I met a girl who was immune to my brother's charm. It was a refreshing, and amusing, change of pace.

Ella turned back to me, no longer concerned with my brother. "Ryiah, your hair is such an interesting shade. I bet you had a crowd of bumbling farm boys following your every word."

I choked into my glass. "Hardly." Scarlet red hair was a

curse, and when I blushed, it seemed to make it worse.

Alex snickered. "Ry was too tough for the lot back home. She was too busy fighting for them to notice."

I kicked his foot. "We were training, not fighting. There's a difference." I glanced at Ella. "What about you?"

She laughed loudly. "The boys at court? Hardly my type. I need a man's man, like Master Barclae."

Alex cringed. "But he's so old!"

"And mean," I added. "He was mean to us."

Ella scoffed. "He doesn't look it. Besides, most first-years are younger than us. Have you noticed that?"

"Highborns," Alex offered, "they all took advantage of the early admission at twelve and thirteen, I'd bet."

"I don't see why." Ella frowned. "*I'm* highborn, and it always seemed more of an advantage to wait until the cutoff at seventeen. A better chance to build up your powers before you apply." She laughed lightly. "But I guess it's hard to wait once you discover your magic."

"Prince Darren is older," I observed, "and so are some of the others too."

"He's one of the smart ones," Ella admitted. "But most of the students rushed admission."

Wasn't that the truth? The day Alex's magic emerged, he'd planned for the following year, and I'd been all too eager to follow. I wondered what she would think if I told her I hadn't even had my powers when we set forth for the Academy. *Rushing admission* was putting it lightly.

Still, not everyone was overwhelmed like us. "It certainly didn't seem like they rushed admission in the library." A lot of the younger highborns were the smartest in our year.

"All that extra tutoring." Ella didn't look surprised. "My parents would've done the same if they hadn't been so set on a convent."

Still, they knew so much more than me. I sighed. "In Demsh'aa, Alex and I were one of the few kids who knew how to read and write, but that was only because our parents were merchants. I didn't even realize it would be a part of our studies!"

"Well, it makes sense, doesn't it?"

I just groaned and put my head in my hands. "All the work they gave us? It's our first day, and they already expect us to read through four chapters and do fifteen sets of those horrid math equations."

"We can start on them now. We've got a half hour until our next session."

I frowned. "I would, but if I take in any more 'learning' right now, I think my head will explode."

Ella chuckled. "Your head better catch up quick."

"I'll study with you, Ella." Alex flashed my friend a winning smile.

Ella turned to me, ignoring him completely. "It's not going to get better. Remember my brother. There's a reason people leave early on."

I shook my head. That might be true, but I needed a moment of quiet to breathe. I was afraid, if I didn't take a break, the expectations would intimidate me into retreat. "I'll meet you guys at the armory before our next session."

Ella nodded. "Just don't be late."

* * *

As I started down the Academy's long corridor, I spent the

walk fantasizing about the pile of blankets that awaited me back in the barracks. I was only four hours into my year, and I was already longing for sleep. It couldn't be a good sign.

First couple weeks are always the hardest.

I sighed. *Or maybe that's just a saying, and it really is horrible all year long.*

I had just turned the corner when I suddenly collided with someone coming from the opposite direction.

"I'm so sorr—" I began, and then froze.

Seriously? *Not again.* Why was fate so determined to make me continuously cross paths with the one person who so clearly hated the world?

The prince tightened his lips and bent down to grab the papers he'd dropped. I reached down to help him, but he snatched them up before I could offer a hand.

Straightening, Darren made way as if to pass, but I stood my ground. I needed to apologize for earlier. Even if Ella was right about him—and she probably was, judging from our encounters thus far—I still owed him an apology. I didn't need to spend the year with an angry prince.

"Your grace," I fumbled, "I want to apologize for earlier—" The prince glared at me, but I continued on hastily. "It wasn't right. You deserve a chance just as much as anyone else, especially since you aren't the heir—"

"Thanks," Darren cut me off sharply, "but I don't need some backcountry peasant asserting what I can or can't do."

My whole face burned in indignation. "I didn't mean—"

"Look." The words seemed to grate across his teeth. "I didn't come here to socialize with commoners and learn about their feelings. I came here to be a mage. I've more pressing affairs than listening to you apologize for your own incompetence."

The prince pushed past me as I stood dumbfounded. Any initial guilt I'd felt was gone. I wasn't sure exactly how I'd expected the apology to go, but certainly not like *that*.

There was nothing modest about this prince, this *non-heir*. Ella was right; there was no way I would want someone like that on the throne wearing a crown *and* a mage's robes. What compelled the masters to make such a blatant exception?

"You've never had one before because nobody was good enough!" That's what Darren had yelled at us. Was that why the Council of Magic decided to make the distinction between an heir and someone who was second-in-line to the throne? Because Darren had shown exceptional talent?

If he chooses Combat, I'll wipe that arrogant sneer off his face the first chance I get, I decided. *How exceptional can a non-heir be, really? He wasn't even good enough to be first-born and get a throne.* It was a cruel thought, one that didn't even play out logically, but I welcomed it all the same. *I hope you lose out on an apprenticeship to many, many commoners.*

I forced myself to continue the trek to my barracks in stilted silence. It was useless. Ten minutes of restless pacing, and then bells were summoning students again for our next lesson. I made the walk to the Academy's field, wondering why I'd even bothered to go off on my own in the first place.

When I arrived, I found Alex and Ella at the back of a crowd facing the armory's doors. Miles of fenced-in pasture sat just beyond it.

I sidled up to my brother and friend just as a man stepped

out of the building's entry, his boots kicking up dirt.

He was easily the most intimidating man I'd ever seen, with a wall of bulging muscle straining to break free, disconcerting green eyes, and close-cropped hair. The man's dark skin was glistening, and he had several white scar lines that cut down across his arms.

The master wore the livery of a knight, not a mage.

I sucked in air as I heard several others do the same. *Is there some sort of mistake?*

"No, I am not one of your masters here." White teeth flashed in the afternoon sun. "But don't you be getting any ideas. I'll still be involved in *every* step of your development. I served on the King's Regiment for twenty years, and I've spent the last ten training young mages to fight." Aha. "I am Sir Piers, and I will be leading you in the physical conditioning needed for your factions."

"I thought we were to be sorcerers, not pages," someone muttered.

Sir Piers heard the comment and glowered.

Instantaneous silence.

"Many of you might wonder what use I am to your precious studies. Can I have a volunteer please?" No one moved. "I have my pick then." The big man almost gleefully dragged forward one of the boys who'd been whispering behind me. The boy was now shaking, and I really couldn't blame him. Sir Piers clearly enjoyed scaring his charges.

"Now, what is your name?"

"Ralph."

"Well, Ralph, it's your lucky day. Which faction do you want to end up in?"

"Combat," Ralph squeaked.

The man snorted. "Yes, *always* with you first-years."

"Now," he continued, "show me what you can do."

"It's n-not much," the boy stammered.

I watched as Ralph snatched a twig off the ground and began to stare at it with a furrowed brow.

Seconds later, tiny flames encompassed his stick. He didn't even break a sweat.

Great, I thought darkly. The boy didn't need to hurt himself to get it burning. A twelve-year-old showed more promise than me.

"Now," Piers said, "run a mile—the course of the stadium's circumference."

Ralph's face fell.

"What are you waiting for?" Piers barked.

Ralph took off like a jackrabbit, but about two minutes into the run, his pace slowed. I could sense his discomfort. None of us had dressed with a strenuous workout in mind. I was still wearing my dress.

For the next eight minutes, poor Ralph ran around the track huffing and puffing as the rest of the class watched, careful to avoid any comments that would target us as the next "volunteer" victim.

When Ralph finally returned, Piers had another order awaiting the boy.

"Light fire to another stick."

"I... need... a moment."

"Now!"

Ralph scrambled to find another branch and tried to repeat the same casting, to no avail. He was too busy taking deep gulps of air to concentrate.

"You just gave the enemy an opening, boy. You are now dead on the battlefield. Take your seat." Piers sent the boy off with disgust. "Do I have another volunteer?"

Everyone looked to the ground quickly, except for the non-heir who seemed unperturbed as he met Piers's gaze head-on.

"All right, princeling, have at it."

Darren stepped forward and picked up a twig. I breathed out a sigh of relief. He was normal like the rest of us. It would have killed me if he put on some sort of breathtaking display.

Darren clenched one end in his palm, eyeing a nearby tree.

You've got to be—

The entire trunk exploded in a blaze. Branches with crackling leaves shuddered as the tree became a writhing, red torch.

The non-heir cracked the twig in his palm.

The fire instantly abated.

Dead tree limbs scattered the grass. Darren waited for instructions.

I glanced at the knight to gauge his reaction. The commander was wearing a satisfied grin.

"Well done," he boomed. "Now, do the same to that tree—there."

We all looked to see where he was pointing. A similar oak stood half a mile off at the other end of the stadium.

I braced myself, knowing better than to hope the prince would fail.

Darren walked over to grab one of the last tree's charred branches from the ground. Part of the stick still looked red-hot beneath its ashy bark, and I wondered if it burned. Still, Darren showed no sign of pain as he rolled it back and forth between his palms, keeping his stormy gaze on the target ahead.

Moments later, the second tree caught fire. *Not as dramatic as the first, but still impressive*, I noted dryly. The fire quickly died out on the trunk but continued on in most of the higher branches until he ceased his casting.

"You may take a seat now." Piers gave the prince a much friendlier dismissal than the previous boy.

Darren nodded curtly and then made his way over to the front of the crowd.

Piers addressed the rest of us. "What did those two have in common?"

Nothing.

Not a single person spoke up.

"The dynamics of war," Piers continued breezily, "are not all about force. You think you can blast your enemy with magic, and maybe you can. But the further you are from your opponent, the less power you're able to exert. We can't waste all this time training you to be powerful mages and have you faint at the first sign of battle. Not one of you will be sitting in an ivory tower pointing your finger like a blasted fairy tale. You'll need to be close to your enemies to do damage, and you'll need to maneuver in and out of battle to safely engage.

"The Academy worked alongside the School of Knighthood to develop this training to make you more capable. None of you will be as successful as a full-fledged knight, but you'll be better prepared. Whether you're a Combat mage fighting at the head, a Restoration healer going from one wounded to the next, or an Alchemist helping with dangerous flasks, you need stamina and endurance."

No one could argue that. My brother groaned—he hadn't anticipated physical drills with Restoration.

"For the rest of our hour, I'll be gauging your physical competence. Once I understand how incompetent you are, we'll have the rest of the year to fix that."

First-years were shifting from one foot to the next, the air tense.

"*Oh*," Sir Piers added, almost gleefully, "and if any of you Combat hopefuls are wondering when we'll train with any of the fun weapons a knight handles, keep in mind you have to get through two months of my class first."

And there went my last bit of hope. Now I was groaning along with the rest.

"There is a change of clothes in the building behind me. Ladies first."

Ella and I rushed to the building with the fifty-five other girls.

A servant was smirking as we changed into the ratty, ill-fitting garb. "Those will be your attire for the rest of your time here. From here on out, you will no longer be wearing personal garments or insignia. Year one is not a cause for celebration. The Crown doesn't waste coin financing your personal fashions."

Several girls grumbled, but for the first time, I was

excited. It was just clothes, a pair of breeches and a too-long tunic and belt, but it was a chance to impress.

Masters didn't encourage status at the Academy, only power.

I might actually stand a chance.

* * *

Two hours into the torment that was Sir Piers's idea of light conditioning, I found myself dry-heaving at one of the wooden benches on the side of the field. Alex appeared at my right, similar retching noises coming from his mouth. Neither of us had prepared for *this*.

All over the stadium, first-years were dropping one by one.

Piers had decided we would run five miles. Five miles, he'd added, interspersed with twenty lunges and presses each time we completed a lap. That would've been fine—hard, but fine—if that were all.

But it wasn't.

Once we completed his first demand, the knight barked new orders for everyone to line up across from one another. When we did that, he had servants distribute weighted staffs and instruct us to "proceed."

Since most of the girls and a couple of the lowborn boys had never held a weapon in their lives, Piers had to show us how to hold the poles, where to stand, and which way to lean. He wasn't happy about it, and neither were we.

We spent just as much time rapping each other's knuckles as we did the staffs.

When one girl dared to quietly ponder the usefulness of the drill to her partner, Piers finally snapped.

"When a mage is powerful enough to send daggers cutting through the air, do you think she randomly decides their course? *No*, she studies and practices *exactly* which cuts are needed to hit those precious arteries. *Nothing* I teach you here will be pointless!"

For the remainder of our lesson, no one dared a single complaint, even when Piers decided to introduce a new routine involving the many flights of stairs raising the stadium benches around the field.

But that still didn't stop our bodies from reacting to the horrible cycle of pain.

Taking a deep breath, I told myself it couldn't get worse.

We were on a fifteen-minute break before our session with Master Cedric, but for most of us, those fifteen minutes were spent limping our way to a tower of water pitchers across the field. Refreshments were brought courtesy of Constable Barius's staff, all of whom had decided to take a late afternoon break.

I think the water was just an excuse to watch.

I scanned the field for my friend.

Ella stood a little way off, red in the face and perspiration under her arms, but somehow still charming in her disheveled state. She was talking to another girl as she attempted to stretch her calves. The two of them were laughing at something she'd said.

I winced. I couldn't even imagine laughing. My lungs were still burning from those stairs.

Shifting my gaze to the other half of the stadium, I spotted the prince. He was surrounded by a pack of first-years, all of them highborn. It was obvious, despite their lack of dress.

They oozed confidence without even trying.

I scowled. How did Darren get away with looking unaffected by our drills, while I dripped sweat like a rat drowned at sea? Weren't princes supposed to be lazy and weak?

"He's so handsome, isn't he?"

A younger boy had caught me watching the prince and was staring right along with unabashed longing. I made a face. Darren wasn't handsome; he was a plague.

Sure, those choppy, side-swept bangs and jaw-length locks could trick a girl—or boy—into thinking the prince was attractive. But not me.

All one needed was a close encounter with his charming personality.

I stifled a snort, but the boy heard it and mistook it for disdain for the girl standing at the prince's right.

"Those two are perfect for each other," he breathed. "They'll get an apprenticeship without even trying. Priscilla is the best girl."

Ah, yes. The raven-haired beauty who'd out-distanced, out-lunged, and out-pressed the rest of my gender. How someone from such high lineage was able to best those of us who'd actually foraged and hunted for our meals, I'd never know. Priscilla looked the part of an aristocrat, and I wondered why she was here at the Academy. Usually, girls like that went to convents. They didn't bother with magic or knighthood. Why did they need status when they already had it?

Priscilla was a year older than me, like Darren. I wondered if she'd followed him from the palace. They seemed friendly enough; she was constantly leaning in close to whisper something in his ear and pressing her palm on his chest.

Ugh. She was welcome to the prince.

The rest of Darren's group consisted of the two burly-looking brothers and a young girl whose skin was so pale it was almost translucent. She'd matched Priscilla in most of our drills. Still, the girl was so tiny and fragile, I wondered how she'd made it this far. She didn't talk much, and she wasn't laughing like the boys.

"All right, children, let's gather round!"

The class came together slowly, regretfully acknowledging the end of our break.

Sir Piers smirked when the last first-year arrived. "We've got more of that tomorrow. I hope you're all prepared." There was only silence, and the man chuckled, well aware of how we felt. "For now, I leave you in Master Cedric's very capable hands." He gave a respectful nod to a wiry old man in red robes waiting anxiously behind us.

Then Sir Piers left the field, whistling a triumphant tune as the older man introduced himself to our year.

For the next two hours, he was going to be leading us in some basic exercises conducive to magic.

I shared a look with Alex and Ella. *Finally.*

"Our first month will be spent in meditation. Without focus, you won't be successful in your chosen faction."

My enthusiasm died just as fast. *Meditation.* So we wouldn't be learning how to heal a dying knight or cast a lightning storm. And I had to say, I'd had enough "meditation" practice during my time on the road. Two hours of coarse physical activity might actually beat the boredom induced from focusing on a blade of grass for the same length of time.

I heard someone groan to my right. *Right about that.*

"You might have great potential," Cedric interjected loudly over his disgruntled audience, an incredible feat for such a timid-looking man, "but if you can't concentrate long enough to hold the spell you wish to enact, you'll never find yourself casting the more advanced spells that you'll need."

He went on to mirror Piers's earlier warning about the battlefield. Mages died quickly when they couldn't summon proper focus. We wouldn't be hidden away in a tower. We needed to focus in an atmosphere full of distractions waiting to tear our concentration apart. These rules applied to every faction and so on.

Nothing he said was new. I was beginning to think every one of our masters wanted to bore us to death. *We'll never reach the battlefield. We'll be too busy hauling books and taking long, deep breaths while learning foundation.*

I grudgingly joined the rest of our year, forming a giant sitting circle that spread out across the grass at Master Cedric's instruction. From this angle, we could see not only the master and his four assisting mages, but also the entire class.

At least I'll finally stand out. I might not have had practice fighting with staffs or learning the names of Jerar's eastern seaports, but meditation was easy. I'd spent years sitting by myself, trying to call on magic in my parents' bustling store, ever since I turned twelve.

Turned out, I was wrong. I wasn't terrible, but I was at

best a little better than the rest.

How many years did the others spend silently concentrating in grass? It was ludicrous, and my nails dug into my thighs. I was never going to stand out here.

For the first time, I wondered if joining the Academy was a mistake.

Master Cedric and his assistants walked around, taking note and depositing small rocks each time one of us broke free from our concentration. Their voices grew louder as time passed.

For the first half hour, we'd simply been instructed to close our eyes and keep still. To maintain an "air of calm" and to focus on a moment of peace and tranquility. That was easy enough.

But then everything changed.

The master sent pouring hail and rain one second, startling birds out of their trees so that angry screeches filled the air the next.

I tried not to flinch when an assistant trailed a blade across my shoulders through the cloth.

I couldn't suppress a tiny whimper when the serrated edge caught on my tender palm, reopening my blisters from the past.

I looked up in time to see the mages casting knives.

"Concentrate!" An assistant tossed two stones by my feet. "Pain shouldn't detract from your focus, first-year!"

I wasn't the only one who'd failed. Most of the others had a small pile forming next to them too. Most, but not all.

Darren's eyes were still shut, and he was bleeding from both wrists.

For the second part of our exercise, Master Cedric had us keep our eyes open while continuing to practice the same meditative state. Of course, sight only made it worse.

It wasn't easy to remain calm when the assistants were running around throwing daggers and casting arrows inches away from your face.

All of us were afraid one of the mages would slip up and we'd end up skewered or worse.

I wanted to do well, I really did, but meditation was turning out to be the most difficult test.

My head pounded, my muscles ached, and sweat stung the corners of my eyes. I was trying hard not to give in to the distractions Master Cedric and his assistants were casting, but pain was not an easy distraction to ignore. I knew the masters had healers and alchemy salves on hand to see to our wounds, but it didn't take away from the moment.

Eventually the session ended, and we all looked to one another, greedily eying the others' failures. No one was stoneless, not even the prince. The pale blonde girl only had two—turns out she was the best—and Darren and his cohorts had no more than five a piece.

I had twelve. Alex had even more. Ella, ten.

Not the best, and not the worst. It was maddening.

Everyone waited to be dismissed.

"How many of you have changed your minds about the uselessness of meditation now?" the master rasped.

Several of us cast our eyes down, shamefaced.

"Too often we allow sight and pain to dictate our actions. That's fine in day-to-day living, but it will not get you very far in casting. Magic commands your absolute focus.

Anything less and you risk a spell going awry. Pain will come and go, and you need to learn to push past it. If you are overwhelmed, you won't be able to do what needs to be done."

I saw myself on a battlefield, unable to cast to save a soldier because of a stray arrow crushing my lungs. Master Cedric was right. I needed to be better, but I didn't know how. Everything about this catered to the ones who already knew what to do, the masters didn't wait for the rest of us to catch up.

"Master your focus early on because pain doesn't go away." The master folded his arms. "The Academy is not meant for everyone. Best accept that now than a wasted year in denial."

* * *

I trailed off to the dining hall with the others, bitterly acknowledging the reason so many resigned early on.

Most highborns hadn't been below the top quarter of our class for any of the lessons. I shouldn't have expected anything less, but that didn't take away from my grief. Alex and I had an uphill battle, which was only growing worse. Only a third of the first-years in attendance were lowborn as it was.

The prince and his friends were the best. They all wanted Combat; we'd all heard them say it in our sessions. That was five apprenticeships right there.

If I knew what was good for me, I'd just pack my bags and leave the Academy right away. But I couldn't. I hadn't backed down from the village boys in fights back home, and I wasn't about to start now.

The prince's contemptuous comments earlier on had made it clear that he would only associate with the best. I studied the front to see who that was.

There were seven more at his table than before. Four of the newcomers were *not* of noble standing from their dress before our drills. But all of those newcomers had done well, *extremely well*, in comparison to the rest of our year.

Apparently, the non-heir would make exceptions to be around "commoners." But I, like most of the lowborn first-years present, was not promising enough to be worthy of his time.

Glancing around the commons, I saw more evidence of the changes in place. During the morning meal, students had sat next to friends or others of similar rank. Now more emphasis was spent on sitting with those who performed at one's own level during training.

At the far end of the hall, where I'd previously sat, were the rejects of our year.

I ground my teeth as I fixated back on Darren's table at the front. My frustration wasn't so much the prince—he was hardly the first highborn to look down at a lowborn—it was everything he represented that I wasn't.

I sat down at the first available seat, which just so happened to be the far end of the table of failures. I wasn't going to waste half my meal negotiating a spot based on skill.

Alex and Ella plopped down beside me without another word. Something warmed my chest, and I gave them a timid smile. It would have been difficult if they'd decided to move onto someone better.

I spent the entire course of dinner listening to a lively exchange between the two, while I pushed gravy-soaked peas across my plate. Alex and Ella seemed to be the only ones who found our entire situation humorous. They weren't exactly friends, but they'd grown closer in our sessions.

I was beyond grateful, even if I knew it was just for me. And while many of their jokes were at the expense of our own mishaps, it was nice to laugh them off.

Alex dunked a roll into his stew. "Did you see me during our drills with Sir Piers?"

"Some of us had more pressing concerns than your face."

"Well, while you girls were trying to keep up with us men—"

Ella and I both interrupted my brother at the same time. "Hey!" We'd both done better than Alex. My brother might have brawn, but he was a healer through and through. He didn't like to exert himself unless it was for a spell.

"As I was saying, *I* was trying to romance a lady while you two were too busy huffing and puffing around the track."

"And how did that go?" I interjected. "Being the slowest boy in the class?"

"I wasn't the slowest." His grin got wider. "The second, perhaps."

Only my brother would laugh over failing our drills. Just another testament to our different approaches to life.

"And which damsel in distress would she be?" Ella taunted. "I saw you entertain several before class even started."

My brother chuckled. "That was harmless conversation,

sweet. When I'm flirting, you'll know."

Ella rolled her eyes.

"It was that girl over there." My brother pointed his crust at Priscilla, and I stifled a laugh as the girl caught the three of us staring. Her frown turned to disgust in the blink of an eye.

"Seems like a fan."

"Sure it went well, lover boy?" Ella was smirking. "That looks more like disdain."

Alex just gave a maddening smile. "She's a tough nut to crack."

"That's Priscilla of Langli." Ella's brow rose in challenge. "You never stood a chance."

"What about you?" He leaned in to tuck a curl behind her ear. "Do I stand a chance with you, Ella?"

I choked on my roast as my friend guffawed. I was *not* having my brother spoil the one friendship I had. I turned the conversation back to the earlier girl fast.

"What's Priscilla's relation to the prince? Are they betrothed?"

My brother sighed. "Probably. The prince was glaring the entire time I engaged her on the field."

"They're not betrothed." Ella followed our gaze. "But it's only a matter of time."

"Did she come here for him?"

"Most definitely." Ella twisted the water glass in her palm. "Her parents are *very* well-known courtiers. Social climbers like the Langlis dedicate their lives to building close relations with the king. Priscilla is a very pretty girl, and her family is the wealthiest save the Crown."

"So why not his older brother?" I was truly curious. Why would her family pick the second-born prince when their daughter could be crown princess?

"Prince Blayne needs to marry a Borean princess to strengthen our allies. Darren doesn't have his hands tied. Every power-hungry family with a daughter has been after that prince since the day he was born."

I cringed. *Those poor girls.*

As I listened to Ella, I found myself watching Priscilla interact with the prince's group. Ella could say the girl was after the prince, but Priscilla had still performed very strongly in all of our drills.

"I don't think she's just here for the prince," I remarked, causing both Alex and Ella to start. "She's too prepared. She might want the prince, but I think she came here for a robe."

Ella just shook her head. "If Priscilla wasn't good, she wouldn't have a chance at the throne."

"Why?"

"Because power is all that prince cares about." Ella's words were curt. Again, I wondered what had happened in her past. "Priscilla and her parents were smart enough to figure that out. I'm sure, as soon as they realized how serious he was, they got her the best tutor gold could buy."

I looked back to the girl and her prince. Rumors were already flying around that they were first in line for an apprenticeship. I'd even shared the same thought.

Really, on day one, to already have that kind of reputation...

It isn't fair.

Alex noted my stare. "I heard some people have already

decided to change their faction."

"W-why?" I jerked back around.

"Some of the others were saying the odds were too stacked against them in Combat."

Master Barclae's predictions were already coming true. It wasn't even the end of our first day.

"They might say that now and change their minds later," Ella countered. "Jeff changed his mind three times before the end of his first month."

"I can see why." And I could. The prince was a prodigy, whether I liked it or not. "The masters have seen hundreds of first-years. To impress them at this point means you really stand out."

Ella folded her arms. "Well, future apprentice or not, no one is going to sway me but *me*."

I knew it was mad and foolish and possibly hopeless, but I agreed.

* * *

After dinner, the three of us headed to the library's upper study to begin the day's assignments. Most of our class had gone off to the barracks to wash. A part of me wanted to as well, but all three of us had agreed we would fare better studying in silence than a crowded library when the rest returned. And then we'd have the baths to ourselves.

There were a couple other small groups already in the study, but they were few in number. When we entered, they seemed friendly enough. I recognized one girl, Winifred, as someone from a neighboring village. Another, Clayton, was Alex's friend from Demsh'aa—we'd missed him in the crowds earlier.

Before long, we amassed a small group of our own: Alex, Ella, me, Winifred, Clayton, another lowborn boy named Jordan, a highborn girl named Ruth, and a timid first-year named James.

It was nice to study in the company of others. We all had something to offer. While Winifred spent most of her time lecturing us on the mathematical equations we were trying to break down, Alex and I helped with the sections on herb lore and science. Having parents who owned an apothecary was an advantage after all.

Jordan and Clayton assisted with geography. They'd grown up on family farms. Ruth was excellent at Crown law from her time in court, and Ella spent most of her energy on history and battles. As she explained, her father was a knight.

Apparently, Ella used to follow her father around the village as he drilled soldiers.

No wonder the girl wanted Combat. She was a warrior through and through. It also explained why she had fared better than most of us in Piers's conditioning. She'd only been second to Priscilla, Eve, and a couple of the boys.

By the time the rest of our year arrived, most of our assignments were finished. Alex and I were a bit slower than the rest, so we still had a couple problems left, but I figured we'd tackle those in the barracks before bed.

Bed.... It was a looming fantasy, almost as tempting as a hot bath to sooth my aching limbs.

I packed up my work, feeling a lot more confident than before. The only thing that detracted from my mood was the prince's arrival as we left.

I tried not to grimace as his group took over the most comfortable lounge, forcing the others to the smaller aisles on the second floor. People didn't even try to stand up to him; they just gave up their seats with a smile.

My friend's expression mirrored my own. "Just like the palace. No one's entitled like a prince."

Alex glanced between the two of us and settled on my friend. "You really don't like him, do you, Ella?"

She set her mouth in a hard line. "No."

"Care to tell us what happened?" he pressed. "Or are you just going to leave us to guess?"

I had to admit, I was curious too.

"There's nothing to tell." Her eyes flashed, but she didn't expand. That was the only answer we got.

Alex laughed nervously. "Just wanted to know what he did, so I don't repeat his same mistake."

Ella smiled, and the tension in the hall left the air. "How about this?" She leaned in, standing on the tips of her toes to whisper in his ear. "I'll punch you in the gut if you ask me again."

She blew my brother a kiss and then sauntered off, leaving Alex flushed and speechless.

My twin had finally met his match.

Alex watched the girl walk away, his mouth agape.

"Don't even think about it," I warned.

"I don't... she..." His face burned red, and he ducked his head, suddenly out of sorts. "I have t-to..."

Alex took off, thought unfinished, in the direction of the men's barracks.

Clayton snickered. "I think Ella is going to give your

brother a run for his reputation."

"She doesn't like boys her own age." I was thinking of Master Barclae and Sir Piers. Ella had the right idea. Most of our year was incompetent. *Or arrogant jerks.*

"People say a lot of things. That doesn't mean they're always true," James piped up, a bit too eagerly. Alex wasn't the only one who admired my new friend. I'd caught James openly staring more than once.

We all laughed at the truth of James's statement and parted ways.

I didn't stop to think the rule might also apply to me.

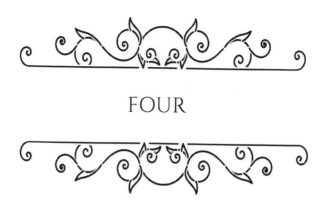

FOUR

APPARENTLY, I WAS the *only one* to not complete the first day's assignments... I'd collapsed into bed the second I'd finished my bath, and now I was paying the price.

Master Eloise glowered at me over my incomplete scroll. "This is unacceptable, first-year."

My mouth was a gaping hole. *How in the name of the gods did everyone finish?* I'd caught several girls sleeping when I arrived back in the barracks the night before, which meant they hadn't even entered the library to study. Had they copied someone else's answers in the morning?

I suspected the answer was yes.

"You will spend two hours after dinner assisting Constable Barrius's staff with the mucking of the stables."

What?

"But I didn't have enough time to finish last night's work!" I was ashamed to admit there was a bit of pleading in my tone, but how was I supposed to finish today's assignment *and* clean the stables?

"If you can't meet the Academy's demands, then you are wasting our time."

Behind me, several students snickered.

My face burned. "Just because I didn't cheat—"

Alex kicked my shin, and I paused to glare at my brother. His eyes narrowed and his expression was clear. I would only make it harder on myself if I called out the others. *Do I really want to make enemies on my second day?*

"My apologies," I mumbled to Master Eloise. "It will not happen again."

"See that it doesn't."

I lowered myself into my seat, avoiding the gaze of the rest of the class. I tried not to panic over how I would complete the day's work *and* my new chore.

After four hours sulking in the library and the shortest lunch imaginable, Alex, Ella, and I headed for what was sure to be the worst part of our day: two hours with Sir Piers.

Expectations did not disappoint.

After another five-mile run, Sir Piers had us practice again with the staffs. Somehow he expected us to have significantly improved over the course of a day.

Instead, our exhaustion just led to more mistakes than before.

When I got down the line to Alex, he and I spent our five-minute drill barely moving in order to catch a quick break. When it was Ella's turn, she spent the entire time trying to helpfully contribute tips I neither wanted to hear nor heed.

I can't do this.

Sir Piers spent the whole exercise shouting. I was convinced someone had told him the louder he yelled, the harder we'd try. It didn't work.

Half the class was at the point of collapse by the time our second hour finished. It was all I could do to walk my staff back to the armory.

"Just where do you lot think you are going?" Piers barked.

The crowd of students froze, and I turned back to see Sir Piers and Master Cedric scowling at us.

"Gods, *no*," Alex said in a hushed voice.

"We are not finished," Sir Piers bellowed. "I need all of you to return with your staffs. Master Cedric has granted us extra time."

My stomach fell. My knees were shaking, and my arms felt like lead weights.

The assisting mages from yesterday returned, passing out small strips of cloth to each student they passed. Alex, Ella, and I each accepted the offering, exchanging dubious expressions as we lined back up in the two-columned formation.

"Blindfolds everyone. Today's exercise is going to expose the problem with yesterday's performance."

I tied the rag across my eyes, clutching the staff to my chest. I felt silly standing there, unable to see anything, and I was wary of what the masters had in store.

"You are going to spar. Second column defends as the first leads the assault."

Really? Staff fighting *while* blindfolded? This was only going to make me perform a million times worse.

Grudgingly, I engaged with the gangly girl who'd been standing across from me. Attacking was impossible. My sense of balance was completely thrown off without sight. The echo of a hundred wooden staffs clashing was deafening. I couldn't find my partner even if I tried.

I spent most of my time swiping the wind or accidentally

knocking my staff into the person on my right's shoulder.

"Change positions!"

If blindly hitting someone was hard, it was worse on the defense. I had to guess where my offender was coming from. My shoulders ached from being continuously whacked.

I tried to listen for rushing air when the staff came in for a hit, but I couldn't hear anything above the clamor of our group or the barking of Sir Piers. My best bet was to try and focus on the stink of sweat when my partner raised her arm.

A couple more drills produced better results, but only slightly. If anything, I now had a nose attuned to perspiration. I wasn't sure that was a good thing. The scent wasn't exactly pleasant.

"Take a seat and remove your blindfolds."

Our lesson was over.

Relieved, I tossed the sweat-stained rag to the ground.

"Forgot about the other senses before today, didn't you?" Piers grinned wickedly. "You've been relying too much on sight."

And why wouldn't I? *It's only our second day at the Academy*, I wanted to shout.

"Every action requires more than one sense for a performance to be seamless. Just now, all of you were forced to recognize other ways of predicting an opponent's attack. Heightened listening, body heat, smell, and an increased understanding to the different points of pressure in a blow are all observations the best warriors make."

The crowd was grumbling. I'd bet I wasn't the only one who had forgotten a few of those senses.

Master Cedric cleared his throat, coming beside Piers for

the first time in our drill as he addressed our year. "If you were to engage in a casting, these types of observations would increase the potency of your magic. Your spells are derivatives of the information, experience, and desire you put forth. I'm sure all of you have desire—it's why you are here—but the amount of information and experience you put into your castings will be important indicators as well. You can want something more than anything, but if you can't build up the proper projection in your mind, it won't be very effective. You need to consider all aspects, not just the image or obvious sense of the action or thing you are trying to create."

I strained to listen, but the pounding in my head was making his words an endless drone.

"The irony of your training here at the Academy is that, while we require you to ignore your physical senses in meditation and acute focus, we ask you to embrace them in your mental casting. You are not allowed to feel what is physically going on around you during the moment of your spell, but you are expected to cast an image evocative of all those physical senses in your mind. I admit that the practice of these two things is not easy. It is not something you can master in a day or even years. All I can advise is that the more you practice, the more you dedicate yourself to exploring these two states, the better your chances at succeeding within your own magical faction."

The end of Master Cedric's lecture was spent in silence. Most of us were still trying to take in everything as we followed him out to the field to continue yesterday's meditative exercise. I hoped it would make sense after a long night's rest.

At the end of our session, we were informed that this would be the pattern for the rest of the month—half of the session practicing a heightened awareness of the senses, the second half learning to block them out. Supposedly, with enough practice, we would be able to transfer easily between the two states.

Of course, to be "competent" we'd have to continue the practice on our own during any "free time" we were lucky enough to acquire. Knowing how much free time I actually had at my disposal, it was obvious that the highborn students had a huge advantage.

Those who had grown up with a parade of tutors didn't have to be worried about the lack of free time they had now. The non-heir's group wouldn't falter under our intense workload; they were already proficient in foundation. Meanwhile, I'd be struggling for any free moment I could find to try and catch up.

It was unfair that I would be working doubly hard, but if I didn't try, I'd only be widening that gap in the months to come.

By the time dinner ended, I was in an irritable state. I forked piles of manure out of the straw and ground my teeth the entire walk back to the castle, unable to let go of my growing resentment toward the privileged class. Highborns—even Ella and Ruth—had no problem finishing each night's assignments, which meant it would always be people like me mucking out the stables.

I refused to cheat. What was the point of pretending to know the foundation if I didn't? To be the best, I *had* to complete those blasted papers in time. Copying answers would only hurt me in the end.

I'd known all along I'd have a disadvantage, but I had hoped the masters would help. Shouldn't they help the underprivileged instead of capitalizing on our weakness? Why take away free time from the ones who needed it most? Why punish me for incomplete assignments using mundane tasks that had nothing to do with the practice of magic?

No matter how tired you feel, you're going to finish today's assignments. I heaved back a sigh.

By the time I reached the barracks to grab my books, I had only an hour left till curfew. I looked for my study group as I entered the crowded library, but they were nowhere to be seen. They'd probably already left.

Grumbling, I shoved my way past a horde of students and headed to the back of the room. I could see why Ella had been so irritated the day before. With Darren's group hogging the largest, most comfortable lounge, there was little space left for the rest of us. There was crowding down every aisle on either floor, and the chatter was loud enough to set my teeth on edge. There was no way I'd be able to concentrate.

Spotting a ladder at the end of the room, I decided to leave the masses and see what the third floor could offer instead. When I reached it, I could see why no one had bothered. There was no torchlight, no books, and no seating.

The third "floor" was nothing more than a cramped alcove with spiderwebs hanging from empty shelves. At a corner on the left was a makeshift bench composed of wooden crates. The place had probably been used as a study at some point, but it had been long since abandoned.

Unwelcoming and lacking, just like me. The irony was impossible to miss.

Avoiding the darkest part of the room, which I suspected was crowded with unfriendly critters, I made my way to the only source of light. I dragged one of the crates over to sit beneath a dirty paned window that streamed moonlight and quickly commenced my study. The alcove wasn't comfortable, but it was quiet and remote.

My time passed quickly. It'd been productive, but I was nowhere near done when I heard Constable Barrius ordering the first-years to return to their quarters. I was in the midst of grabbing my belongings when I began to contemplate my situation. If I left now, I would never finish the day's work.

But, I thought as I listened to the pounding of busy feet, *I could stay up here, and no one would know*. It was risky, I knew, to stay out past curfew. If the constable spotted me, I could be expelled on the spot... but if it worked, I could actually complete the day's assignments.

Lights out in the barracks were mandatory in an hour; I could never continue my assignments there. This was the best chance I had, and the only one that made sense.

I was careful not to make a sound as everyone exited the room. I ducked down behind the crates as Barrius and his assistant made their final inspection of the floors.

They never checked the third.

Finally, after much pausing and condescending chatter, the two servants left, leaving me alone in a situation I hoped very much not to regret. I had no idea how I would make it to the girls' barracks, but I saved that worry for later. I contemplated going down to the lounge where there was more light and comfortable seating, but I knew it was too risky. Who knew how often Barrius would check the library? I'd best stay where I was and make the most of it.

I'd only been studying for twenty minutes when one of the doors creaked open below.

Carefully setting down my belongings, I tiptoed to the railing's edge and peered down into the dark study beneath. Sure enough, it wasn't my imagination. In the shadows, I could see a hooded figure quietly slinking to the couches, clutching an armful of books.

Seconds later, the servants were back.

I watched as the figure ducked behind a bookcase to the right not a moment too soon. Torchlight illuminated the library, and I watched as the constable chastised Frederick for his imagination.

"But I thought I heard someone—"

"You think you hear a lot of things, but once again, you've managed to waste my time."

"But shouldn't we still search?"

"Really, Frederick, who would sneak off to the library of all places?"

"I don't—"

"Out!" Barrius snarled.

"Yes, sir."

The two servants retreated.

After their footsteps faded, the figure below chuckled. I watched as the student settled comfortably upon the couch below and set to work organizing papers, a bright glow in hand. I squinted at the casting. It wasn't very bright, just enough to give out light to read, and see the face of my fellow rule-breaker.

The hood had fallen away to reveal black bangs and the dark eyes I'd since grown accustomed to loathing.

Darren.

The non-heir sat below, poring over the same books as me.

My jaw dropped. The very thought that he and I had shared the same idea was distressing in more ways than one. *I* had come here to make up for lost time, but Darren, who already had such an advantage in his training, he had come here to study anyway. Someone who didn't even *need* to, someone who was *already* at the top of our class...

And I bet he had come here the night before too.

I refused to consider what it meant.

Turning back to my studies, I tried to focus my thoughts and block out anything other than the problems on the page in front of me. I bit my lip resolutely. *Don't let this opportunity go to waste, especially with him down there.*

Minutes slowly trickled by as I read the questions once, twice, three times before attempting to solve them. *You can do this.* I stifled a yawn and kept at my work.

Two and a half hours later, I finally finished the assignments.

I could have left at that point, but seeing as how Darren was still working below, I decided to stay. My conscience could not allow a condescending prince to work harder than me. Especially one who had insinuated I was here to "socialize."

So I stayed. Math and Crown law were beyond

comprehension at that point, as was geography with all of its confusing maps, so I chose a history scroll instead. It was the right choice. Almost like a storybook in narration, the long and detailed accounts of Jerar's fighting mages helped retain my focus into the late hours of the night.

Our last war had been ninety years ago, but the book's breakdown of battle strategy made me feel as though I were a part of it now. I'd had no idea how intricate the planning was behind our army's attacks. Silly me, I had always assumed victory just came down to how much power a nation's mages had... That was part of it, but hardly the whole.

I'd just started reading about a particularly bloody battle when Darren stifled a yawn downstairs. Taking that as my cue, I packed up my work and stood by the rail to watch for his departure. As soon as he left, I would follow.

I barely shifted the books in my arms when my quill dropped. It echoed unsettlingly down the stairs.

Darren jerked his head upward in my direction. He didn't ask who was there, but he did get up to investigate. Rather than waiting for him to find me, I gave up my hiding place and started down the ladder instead.

Settling onto the first floor, I turned to find Darren standing with a palm full of light.

"You?" he rasped.

He sounded so surprised, and for some reason, that made it worse.

"You're not the only one who wants to get ahead," I snapped. Then, because I couldn't help it, I added, "You know, us *commoners*, not all of us are just here to 'socialize and talk about feelings.'"

Darren's eyes flashed with an emotion too quick to place. For a moment, I imagined it was shame, but I wasn't that vain. A righteous prince would never stoop so low.

The two of us stared in the ever-mounting silence: me, aware of every flaw in my appearance and the hint of manure tingeing the air, and Darren, looking as inscrutable as ever.

Sighing, I broke his gaze and squeezed my way past.

I was almost to the door when he cleared his throat.

"Wait—"

I paused.

"Don't take the right hall. Barrius had Frederick patrolling there last night."

"A-all right." Was he *helping* me?

My confusion must have shown because his next words were cold. "The last thing I need is for you to get caught and make it harder for me to come here at night."

There was the prince I expected; I was tempted to laugh. "My furthest intention," I assured him dryly.

Darren just stared, eyes dark and unreadable, and I didn't bother to wait. *I* had more pressing concerns than a royal's approval. I hurried out the door in the direction of the women's barracks.

The prince didn't cross my mind again. Not as I was quietly sloshing around in a dark tub, washing the stench of the stables out of my hair, and certainly not as I slept.

FIVE

THE NEXT TWO weeks flew past in a blur. I would crawl out of bed and rush to the dining hall with Ella in hopes of catching the last couple of minutes of the morning meal. Even then, I was too tired to do much else besides stare lifelessly ahead. The extra hours I was losing to the library had started to take their toll, and it was all I could do to stay awake.

The only comfort—besides my assignments—that made the experience worthwhile was catching sight of Darren across the hall. A part of me smirked at seeing the prince grip a steaming mug with the same bloodshot eyes as me. He might have been better at carrying an inscrutable air, but there was no denying his misery.

At first, Alex and Ella had wondered why I stayed behind studying each night, but it hadn't been hard to convince them I needed the extra time to myself. They knew how slow I was at finishing some of the assignments. No one in the women's barracks ever mentioned my absence. Ella was the only one who had noticed, and she kept it to herself.

Each day was filled with the same tedious coursework as

the last. The bright side, of course, was that I was no longer behind. My assignments were always turned in complete, and I could tell from Master Eloise and Isaac's approving remarks that I was no longer a disappointment. Mathematics was still a time-consuming ordeal, but with the extra two to three hours each night, I was easily gaining traction in the basics and moving on to more complex issues that dealt with warfare and Crown law instead.

It was a strange schedule, and a tiring one, but it seemed to be working. Still, I was beginning to wonder how much longer I'd be able to hold out. I was doing well in the first half of my day, but three weeks of sleep deprivation had weakened my performance in the remainder. I was lagging through Sir Piers's drills and Master Cedric's lessons, and while everyone else had started to improve, I was still as clumsy as the day I had started. To make matters worse, *everyone* had noticed.

The worst embarrassment came that afternoon.

"I said *stop* sparring, first-year!"

I froze, cheeks burning as I tore off my blindfold. The entire class was staring. Priscilla of Langli stood in front of me, one large, red welt plastering the left side of her face. She was furious.

"Didn't you hear me give the command to halt?" Sir Piers barked. "Or are you really that thick-headed?"

I winced. The knight hadn't hid his disdain at my progress, and today was no exception.

"I m-must have missed it." I'd been so exhausted, I hadn't heard anything other than the pounding in my head.

Priscilla dropped her staff and stormed off in the direction of the armory—but not before shooting me a look that promised repercussion later.

Sir Piers showed no remorse. "If you can't stay awake long enough to hear your commander give you an order, you shouldn't be at this Academy—or anywhere near a weapon—in the first place."

I nodded, eyes watering, and went to return my staff, avoiding Ella's sympathetic gaze.

It seemed that no matter what I tried, it would never be enough. I didn't have enough time to do everything the masters asked of me, and when I tried to make time, my work only suffered somewhere else.

* * *

My evening became progressively worse when I ran into Darren as he was leaving the dining commons. As soon as he spotted me, a smirk spread across his face. The non-heir had become less aloof since the start of our late-night studies, but it didn't mean he'd become any kinder.

"What?" I snarled. "Come to gloat?" To say I was defensive in his presence was an understatement.

Darren's expression didn't falter. "Do you always attack the blind, Ryiah?"

Several students nearby snickered, and my cheeks flushed.

"There's a first time for everything," I challenged. "Maybe I'll try a royal next."

"Ryiah!" Alex snatched my wrist just before I could throw my tray at the smirking prince.

Darren laughed and sauntered off to join his table of admirers while I was left brimming with rage.

"What has gotten into you?" my brother hissed.

"It's not fair!" I growled. "I am going to fail this place—"

"Then let's have you try something new, not challenge the school prodigy to a duel." My brother dragged me back to the table with Ella and the rest of our study group.

Ruth gaped at me. "Did you just threaten a prince?"

I stabbed at a cherry tomato on my plate. "Wouldn't matter if I did. I can't keep up with Piers's drills to save my life. Darren would have disarmed me in a second."

Alex glanced at Ella. "Anything you can do to help her, beautiful?"

My friend scowled. "Am I or am I not the daughter of a knight?"

"Does that mean yes?" I asked wearily.

Ella smiled wide. "For the girl who challenges arrogant halfwits, it's most definitely a yes."

* * *

An hour later, I met up with Ella at the armory for our first lesson. She was practicing some sort of complicated footwork when I arrived, much more advanced than what we'd gone over in class.

Another highborn advantage—I stopped myself. I had no right to resent my friend who was taking time out of her day to train me. My frustration was making me petty.

"Thanks again."

Ella tossed me a weighted staff and shrugged. "I should be doing this anyway. I need it after watching Piers sing Darren and his minions praises all week long."

I laughed and matched Ella's starting stance. "It's pretty obvious, isn't it?"

"It's downright depressing," she griped. "I grew up around

weapons, and I've trained with them almost as long. At no point should people who grew up reciting their family's lineage be besting me at those drills... Hold that pose, Ryiah."

My sore muscles protested as she adjusted my form. "Don't I need a blindfold?"

The girl snorted. "Let's not test your luck just yet."

We began the drill again only to have her stop me once more.

"Stop being so tense!" Her order was terse. "If you don't loosen up those muscles, you're going to strain something. You need to be relaxed and fluid when you block, like you are dancing."

"I hate dancing."

"Well, like you are water then." We began to spar again. "Really, you hate dancing?"

"You would if you saw what the boys in Demsh'aa had to offer." I attempted a block and overcompensated, swinging wildly to my right.

Ella chuckled. "You'll be doing this dance every day now."

"At least it's with a partner I respect."

We were practicing in the shade of the armory building, but the air was still thick with humidity. Flies swarmed about. I was almost tempted to use them for my target. At least then I'd get some satisfaction out of our endless drilling. I was so exhausted from parrying blow after blow. And after so many endless deflections, it didn't matter that Ella was holding back. I could have been facing the great Sir Piers himself.

I took my turn leading the assault. "Will I really get better?"

"I know it doesn't seem that way now." Ella blocked easily, her voice a relaxed lull to my heavy gasps for air. "But all this—the soreness, even the fatigue—if you keep at it, it's worth it."

The burning in my arms challenged her claim.

I swung a more concentrated pass, and for the first time, it met its mark with a resounding smack. Ella actually faltered for a second, more from surprise than the weight of my blow.

"Pain is a sign you are working your body to its limits," Ella continued as we kept on. "My dad always said that is why lowborns usually outperform nobility in their first year at the war schools." She paused and remarked somewhat ironically, "Though you wouldn't guess it here."

No, you would never guess it here. I held onto my groan.

Ella lowered her staff and glanced up at the darkening sky. "Well, I guess that does it for today."

I followed my friend to the armory to dispose of our weapons. My entire body ached, but for once, I was happy it did.

Not time to give up yet.

* * *

"*Come on*, Ryiah, pay attention!"

"I am!" I groaned and deflected another blow, scrambling to get my defense up in time.

I barely managed.

"Again," Ella shouted.

I made another mad attempt to defend myself.

And then another.

And then I cried out as my friend's staff came into contact with my ribs, and I dropped my pole. I'd guessed wrong again.

"Once more, where am I coming from?" She held her stance, willing me to try and see what it was I had missed the first time.

I watched my friend closely, trying to figure out where her next strike would be. All signs pointed to a low upswing from the left, but I had made that mistake before, and my ribs were paying dearly for it now.

I frowned. Her shoulders were deceptively loose with her eyes drifting ever so slightly to my right, and her hands gripped the staff at a crooked angle. I had seen it all before. What was I missing? *Pay attention...* but to what?

The grass crunched beneath her boots.

Ella had spent enough time reminding me not to be too sure of myself. Any good opponent will try to trick you, she'd said. Anyone who practiced close range fighting would know the importance of deceit. Let your enemy think they've got you figured out, make it look like they can see when you're coming—not too obvious, just enough so that they get cocky. If someone thinks they know your next move, they are more likely to let their guard down for any other attack.

"Look at me, Ryiah," Ella said again. "Where is my staff going to land?"

I tried to see the impossible. Sweat stung my eyes as my gaze traveled up and down my friend's form, searching desperately for a sign.

Then I saw it.

Her knees were slightly bent, feet apart, with the right heel slightly off the ground. It was easy to miss—her dark boots were bulky and obscured sight easily—but there was a slight indent in the leathers on the right front of the foot that betrayed where she had shifted her weight on the grass.

"You're going to come from the right with a top-swing," I announced confidently.

Ella relaxed her form. "Good job!" Her reply was a little too enthusiastic for someone who constantly assured me I was doing well. I briefly wondered if she'd really believed that, and then buried the thought at once.

"It's funny." I changed stance. "Each day Piers and Cedric ask me to practice in a blindfold, and then you make me watch whenever we train out here."

"Well, four days with me is far from an eternity. And you need to know the basics first." She gave me a nudge with the staff. "Just think, one day you'll be able to knock that prince from his gilded throne without batting an eye."

That would be the day. Though I wondered why she didn't want to do it herself.

* * *

For the rest of that week and the next, Ella and I continued our extra drills. It was an endless cycle of madness, but fortunately I did not fall any further behind.

Except in meditation. But I needed those naps...

Two straight weeks with Ella correcting my form and watching my every move had paid off. I was still as sore as that first day I'd arrived, but I could tell my breathing was much less labored in our daily sessions. Even my arms felt stronger. The weighted staff no longer felt like a foreign extension of my arm.

Sir Piers had since stopped criticizing my technique and moved on to some of the other, less fortunate first-years who were still grappling with the concept of a proper guard. They didn't have a knight's daughter to train them like me.

I had to hold back a small smile when Piers informed Priscilla she could learn from my approach after she complained about the "unnecessary repetition for highborns."

The commander jerked his chin in my direction. "That one may not have your skill, but at least she's willing to learn."

"The ones who *need* to learn shouldn't be here," the girl retorted hotly. "Highborns learn to fight with staffs in their sleep. *I* was fighting with swords at twelve."

Several students gave loud hoots of agreement. It didn't take a mastermind to figure out which.

"You would think that." Sir Piers was unruffled by Priscilla and her friends. "And, most of the time, you'd be right. But each year I've been here, there's been one or two lowborns who shame all that extra coin your families put to use. It's the ones who *need* to learn you should be worried about. They work twice as hard."

Priscilla flinched.

"The worst thing wealth does is give those who have it a false sense of security." Piers chuckled as he moved on to another student to correct. "You stop trying as hard, and there's always another who will gladly take your place."

* * *

Later that evening, my glee was still in full swing when

Ella and I retired from the armory. It seemed that Piers's speech had instilled a newfound sense of urgency to some of the more confident first-years. We were now one of six small groups who practiced near the armory after our evening meal.

Most of the students, I noticed, were practicing more advanced techniques than Ella and me, but it was a compliment that they'd shown up just the same. Maybe they didn't view me as a serious contender, but at least they were willing to consider the possibility.

Ella turned to me as we entered the library. "Feels good, doesn't it?"

I just smiled brazenly.

Alex greeted us with a hand over his nose. "Ry, you smell terrible!"

Ella gave him a look.

"Ella, beautiful flower that you are, that comment was for my dear sister alone. You—"

"Save your prose, pretty boy." Ella waved her hand with a snort. "We've got enough to worry about without your attempts at romance."

Our study session came and went without much ado. We were mostly silent because the night was our last review of the fundamentals. Starting the next day, we'd begin orientation. That meant one faction a week, beginning with Restoration. And factions meant actual magic.

We wouldn't be picking our factions until the end of the month, but everyone knew the next few weeks were important.

Tension was thick in the air as we poured over our scrolls,

each silently hoping that we'd learned enough to not humiliate ourselves in the weeks to come.

The months after were when we'd lose the most students, according to Master Barclae's ominous admission that evening at dinner. *"You can't fake it for long here,"* he'd warned.

I wasn't trying to fake it; I just wanted to survive.

The entire library was quieter than usual.

When Barrius came round for his usual dismissal, it took twice the time it usually did for him to clear the first two floors. Everyone was reluctant to leave. That also made it impossible for me to escape to the third floor unnoticed.

Irritated, I retreated with the rest of the crowd to my barracks, resolving to sneak my way back at the earliest opportunity.

After the room went dark, I pushed back my blankets and reached for my bag.

Ella rolled over in her bunk. "Still at it?"

I clutched my materials and squeezed my way past the scattered belongings strewn across the floor. "I'll see you in the morning," I told her quietly.

"Don't be up too late," she whispered. "We've got our work cut out for us tomorrow."

"I know." I grimaced. "I'll try not to."

"Will the two loud mouths please keep it down!" a girl groaned. "I'm trying to sleep."

Shooting Ella an apologetic shrug, I ducked out of the barracks in seconds.

The Academy was two hundred yards away, the path to the barracks barren and treeless. I made a mad dash, hoping for the best. The prince did this every day after curfew, but it was still early enough that Barrius's staff was patrolling the halls, and I didn't know the servants' routine like he did.

Safety. *Whew.*

I'd just shut the doors behind me when something squeaked to my left.

Please, please be a mouse.

It was too dark to see anything. Holding my breath, I waited, praying whoever was there hadn't heard me.

Silence.

I waited a couple moments longer.

Up ahead of me, a chamber door slammed open and flooded the end of the hall with light.

The servants' torches were quickly eating away the shadows and illuminating the dark.

Panic filled my gut. Who knew how far Barrius would go if he found me breaking curfew? I couldn't get caught.

I felt my way along the rough sandstone wall, inching toward the light, trying to remember if I'd seen a room this close to the back entry of the Academy. Surely the staff had quarters nearby. I was in the servants' wing after all.

The voices were drawing nearer, as was the light, and I had only a minute or so left before I was spotted. I continued my blind fumbling, ignoring the pain in my hand as I shoved it against something sharp, desperately seeking a handle in the dark.

My hand caught on a smooth panel, and I felt around for the door's knob. I twisted and something caught my wrist, yanking me inside. The door slammed shut just as a hand covered my mouth to muffle my cry.

There was the slightest bit of light coming through the cracks in the door, but it was enough for me to recognize the face of my so-called captor.

The prince dropped his hand and motioned for me to be silent just as the two servants approached.

"—know I heard something in there," the first was saying. "I'm sure of it."

"Well, come on then." There was a rattle as a man withdrew a ring of keys from his belt. "I bet you there's a first-year hiding on the other side."

I swallowed and looked wildly to Darren who stood closest to the door. The two of us were crammed in some sort of storage closet. Giant sacks of flour and wheat lined the shelves, and there was nowhere to hide. We barely had enough room to stand, let alone disappear.

Darren didn't look worried. Instead, he put a finger to his lips and then shut his eyes, leaning against the nearest shelf.

Meditation isn't going to do much good when they catch us, I thought crossly.

The knob rattled, and I held my breath as I prepared for the inevitable result.

Nothing happened. The rattling continued, but the door stayed shut.

"That's strange… This key doesn't work."

"Let me have a go at it."

The metal knob continued to shake, but it was no closer to opening.

I looked to Darren in the shadows, suspicious and relieved. The door had opened easily enough for me.

"It's not letting up."

"Well, let's check the gardens. Maybe whoever we heard made it to the outside."

"Must have," the second agreed. "This door is locked."

The rattling stopped, and the servants' steps retreated. After a couple of minutes, I willed myself to breathe more easily, taking slow gulps of air.

"They're gone now. Come on." Darren seemed impatient as he stepped out of the closet. The door swung open as if it'd never been locked.

I eyed him warily. "How did you do that with the door?"

The prince ignored my question. "Are you coming or not?"

I sighed and joined him in the hall.

Darren started off, heading toward the west corridor, and I called out after him. "Where are you going?"

He turned and gave me an odd look, or what I was convinced was one. I couldn't be too sure since it was dark again without the servants' light to guide us.

"The library. Where else?"

I felt like a fool.

"That's where you're headed, right?"

"Yes."

"Try not to get us caught this time." His brow furrowed. "And don't make any noise."

I didn't reply, deciding silence was better than the retort I had half a mind to say. He *had* saved us after all, even if he was being conceited about it.

We made it the rest of the way without any trouble. It seemed the two men we'd encountered were the only servants concerned with patrolling the east wing of the

Academy, and we didn't run into anyone in the west passage leading up to the library.

Entering the giant study, I watched as Darren shut the doors behind us and conjured a bit of magic in his palm. There was just enough light to cast a dim glow on our surroundings.

I cleared my throat, uncomfortable. "Thank you for helping me back there."

The prince scoffed. "I didn't do it for you."

"Just take my thanks." I was agitated. After all, I was thanking him. Whatever Darren's motives were, he'd helped me twice now.

The prince looked amused. "Your thanks?" His expression seemed to imply that they didn't amount to much.

I balked. "Well, you've been nasty enough that I guess fate was bound to have you do one decent thing for me." Two, but I wasn't about to admit that aloud.

The prince recoiled. "And I suppose you think you've done nothing wrong?" His jaw was hard. "In case you fail to remember, you and El—that girl you always go around with tried to get me thrown out of here."

"Well, you *are* a prince. You still have a chance at the throne." Even if you are the non-heir.

"I will not apologize for my birthright." Darren narrowed his eyes and added callously, "I don't need to explain myself to people like you."

I glared right back. "I might not be a princess, but even if I were, I wouldn't use bloodlines as a means to demean everyone else."

"I wasn't referring to your trivial heritage." He looked at

me contemptuously. "I care little enough whether you grew up in the fields or a damned palace." He took a step closer and looked down at me, speaking the next few words slowly. "When I say 'people like you' I am referring to the ones who so clearly have no real magic or potential of any kind."

I clenched my fists until I could no longer feel them. Hot blood pulsed under my skin. Prince or not, I had never come this close to punching someone outside of an arena.

"You..." I couldn't even come up with the rest.

Darren continued on, unaware of how dangerously he was treading. "Really, it's unthinkable that the masters could even consider the possibility of denying *me* in favor of someone like you who plainly has no purpose attempting the robes in the first place."

My nails dug into my palm, and I was vaguely aware of the warm trickle of blood filling my fist. Heat clouded my vision, and Darren's smug face filled my mind. *"When I say people like you."* His words were like fire, singeing my skin as they piled into an inferno of red.

"What are you—*stop*! RYIAH!"

My vision cleared, and I realized Darren was shouting, madly shaking the sleeves of his cloak, flames licking across its edges. The flames were growing higher every second, perilously close to his arms.

"Don't just stand there!" he snarled. "Make it stop!"

I looked down at my hands, which had since unclasped. There was no more pressure or pain. The fire should have snuffed out on its own like it had that time with the moss.

Only it hadn't. Just like that other time with the bandit. *What's wrong with me?*

Fear pooled in my gut. "I can't!"

"Well, it's your magic!" he shot back. "I already used up my stamina—" He swore as a flame nicked his skin.

"Ryiah!"

I raced over and bit back a cry as fire caught my skin. I helped hold Darren's sleeves while he pulled his arms out one by one. As soon as he finished, I tossed the cloak to the floor, stomping out the remaining flames against the marble floor.

"You bloody fool!" The sleeves of his thin undershirt were scorched in several places, revealing painful red swells on both wrists and part of his forearm.

"I didn't mean to!"

"Of course, you didn't mean to!" Darren was livid. "You have no control over your own magic!"

I winced. "Is there anything I can do?"

Darren lifted one arm at a time, testing the extent of his injury and frowning.

"Do you want me to help you back to your quarters?" He needed to soak those burns before they started to blister. I didn't have to be my brother to understand the basics of self-preservation.

Darren laughed hoarsely. "I'm staying right where I am. I didn't come all this way to turn back."

I gaped at him. "You can't be serious!"

"I've had worse." The prince picked up his books and carried them over to his usual chair. He noticed my stare and added, "You don't become the best if you aren't willing to stick your hand in the fire."

"I always thought that was an expression."

The corner of his lip twitched, and for a moment, I thought Darren was about to smile. "I think it was... until tonight."

* * *

For the rest of the evening, I remained on the first floor of the library with the newly injured non-heir. I could have retired to my alcove, but there was a certain amount of guilt—and curiosity—that prevented me from leaving. Whatever I thought of Darren, he was never what I expected.

I wondered what "I've had worse" meant. Darren was a prince. How much suffering could a child of the Crown have? I ground my teeth. He must've been mocking me.

Still, what if he wasn't? If anything, there'd been an edge of bitterness to his reply. It was unsettling.

What does a prince have to be bitter about?

"Are you done staring?"

Dropping my quill in surprise, I flushed and mumbled, "I-I didn't realize I was."

Darren sighed. "You know, I was wrong about you earlier."

I gaped at him. *Is he apologizing to me?*

"But I hope you understand why I wasn't wrong to assume it."

I bristled. "What are you talking about?"

Darren pointed to the book in my lap. "We've been down here for thirty minutes, and you've yet to turn the page. For someone so bent on Combat, you are making a lot of mistakes."

That was only because he'd distracted me, but I wasn't going to say that.

"How did you know I was going to pick Combat?"

"Please." Darren smirked. "I've seen you in the practice yards. No one spends that much time trying to impress Sir Piers for his charm. It would be admirable, if you actually knew what you were doing."

"Please, enlighten me," I growled.

The prince cocked his head to the side. "Hard work doesn't mean anything here if you don't have the magic to back it."

I glared at the prince. "I have magic. You saw it."

"You aren't trying to develop it."

"I'm trying!" I resisted slamming my book on the table. I seemed to lose my temper around the prince awfully fast.

Darren shot me an incredulous look. "You spend all your time in those books and drilling with your friends."

"What does that even mean?" I demanded.

He gave me a lazy half-smile. "If you really want an apprenticeship, I'm sure you'll figure it out."

* * *

The next morning, I awoke with dread. My stomach was in knots, and Darren's counsel had done nothing to help me sleep through the night. The best first-year in the school had insinuated I was making a huge mistake, and instead of telling me how to fix it, he had left me to fend for myself.

"You spend all your time in those books and drilling with your friends." What was wrong with that? I devoted more time than any other student, with the exception of his arrogant highness, to my studies. Wasn't that what I was supposed to be doing?

And what did Darren mean when he said he had been

right to assume I was one of "them," the ones with no real magic or potential? We hadn't even started casting yet. How could he even discern who the ones with potential were without seeing them cast beforehand?

He *had* to be alluding to Master Cedric's lessons. His were the only ones I continued to struggle with. But it was meditation. Who hadn't fallen asleep during it at least once?

And, sure, I hadn't exactly tried to improve my standing, but I only had so much time. I couldn't do well in everything. What more could Darren expect of me? Surely learning to fight and magic's foundation were more important than focusing on a blade of grass for two hours?

And why did it matter in the first place? Darren wasn't a master. He was a first-year, a very, *very* opinionated, arrogant first-year.

I shoved my blankets off my cot and stood resolutely. Darren didn't know what he was talking about. He was just trying to unnerve me. Maybe my potential scared him. I wouldn't put it past the prince to try and intimidate me into leaving.

Determined not to give Darren's words another thought, I hurried to the dining commons to join my friends.

Ella grinned. "Ready to embrace the magical realm of blood and bandages?"

I groaned. "No."

It was bound to be a long, arduous week.

SIX

THE FIRST DAY of Restoration didn't end. If I'd ever complained of a lack of time before, I sorely regretted it now.

Four hours were spent staring at complicated diagrams of human anatomy. Thousands of strange names for the parts of the body and the various rules one was expected to understand in order to mend. We learned the most common complaints during a warrior's service, and I was surprised to see how much time was spent going over natural maladies. Battle wounds were too advanced for the week's orientation.

Instead, we were to focus on the most common afflictions for service in the Crown's Army: jungle rot, frostbite, burns, and dehydration.

Alex and I had an advantage thanks to our years in the family apothecary, but for me most of that knowledge was lost to some frazzled recess in the corners of my mind. Alex did well, but Darren's warning from the night before kept invading my thoughts, destroying any semblance of concentration I had.

The next few hours were even more disheartening. Piers kept our regular conditioning, with its various laps and lunging and stretching in between, but he traded our staffs for heavy, weighted sacks of grain.

We were instructed to carry, lift, and drag them up and down the field. Repeatedly. For an hour.

"Those are your patients," the knight barked. "Don't think you'll always be able to treat a victim in the middle of a battlefield. If there's still a fight going on, you'll need to get them to safety first. So pick up the pace, children!"

By the end of the exercise, my arms were too weak to even reach up and adjust my hair in its tie.

Master Cedric's exercise wasn't any better. If I'd thought our first week of actual casting would change things, I was wrong. It didn't. At least not in the way I'd hoped.

With the help of his assistants, Cedric had us divide into several small groups and take turns healing one another from the maladies we had studied earlier while the rest of the group watched. We were given two tasks, describe the natural treatment aloud and then cast out our magic using a projection of that method to heal our patient. If we failed, the next person in our group would start his or her own attempt.

I did well enough during the first half of the lesson. But when it came time to cast the cures for our patients, I was useless.

"What do you think you are doing, first-year?"

I whirled around to find Master Cedric frowning. I glanced at the small knife in my fist. It was my turn to cast.

"She can't cast without injury, sir," Alex volunteered. "She's tried, but for some reason—"

"Is this true?" Master Cedric stared hard at me.

I reddened and nodded wordlessly.

"Perhaps next time you will think twice before falling asleep in my class." The master walked away without a second glance while Alex and Ella gawked after him.

"Did he really just say that?"

"He's not even going to try and help you!"

I tossed the blade to the ground, furious. What good was my magic here if the masters refused to help me?

Alex elbowed me. "Don't let him get to you, Ryiah. He probably just lost his temper because you aren't the only one."

Several other students couldn't cast at all. There were rumors they'd come without magic... I had magic, I just couldn't access it.

What was wrong with me? My twin didn't have any problem with casting.

I stared at the girl across from me. Master Cedric's assistant had given her the first symptoms of frostbite. She was waiting for me to heal her and glaring. No one in pain liked waiting.

I tried to remember what Master Cedric has said at the beginning of class.

"Use all your senses. Shut out everything. Focus solely on the projection in your mind... Once you have a strong hold of what you need to do, project your will into it, and if you've done so correctly, your magic should come through." I kept repeating the instructions over and over in my head, willing my magic to take effect.

But it never did.

At one point, I caught Darren watching me from the corner of his eye. When I whirled around to catch him, he gave me a wink before casting a healing of his own.

A perfect healing.

I felt like screaming.

"Maybe next time." Ella gave my shoulder an awkward pat.

The assistant returned to heal my partner, and I looked down to avoid any more sympathetic glances from the rest of our group. No one else had failed this exercise. Others in other groups, yes, but I was the lone wolf here ready to tear off my own arm if it would help.

"I'm sure once Master Cedric sees how hard you are trying, he will change his mind," Ella offered. Like Alex, she had no idea why my magic wasn't working. None of her suggestions had worked either.

I sighed. Judging from the mild-mannered master's response, my two dozing incidents in his class were irreparable.

Alex, on the other hand, did even better than expected. He grasped Master Cedric's lesson almost immediately. Even though I'd only seen him cast the most basic of healings back home, he was adept at putting the new castings to work. When it was his turn, it took only minutes for my brother to heal his patient of a sunburn.

I tried to tell myself that it was just Restoration, that my castings didn't matter here, but it was hard to evade the truth. If I couldn't cast now, how would my week of Combat be any different?

* * *

That evening after dinner, Ella did not come with me to the field to continue our nightly conditioning. She needed to spend the extra time studying now that we had moved on from the basics. The rest of our group went with her, including Alex.

When I arrived at the armory, I wasn't alone. Granted, there were fewer students now that we had started the first faction's orientation, but there were at least twenty first-years drilling when I arrived.

Someone had brought out a pile of staffs and blunt training swords. Glancing at the two weapons, I considered trying the blade. It would be the perfect distraction to my dismal day thus far, but without Ella's instruction, I knew the best thing to do would be continue working on my practiced routine with the pole instead.

The best choice, but not the one I ended up making.

"Do you even know what you are doing with that?"

I flinched and whirled to find Priscilla sneering. She was watching me awkwardly clutch the sword handle while Darren and the rest of his following stood only a couple feet away.

She had picked the wrong day to bully me.

"Don't you tire of playing the witch?" I shot back.

One of the two husky brothers snickered, and I was almost certain I saw Darren smile.

Priscilla, however, was less than amused.

"Go on all you like, lowborn. It will not save you from your pathetic casting. The only good use for that sword is if it ends your own paltry existence."

Ouch.

"Oh no," I countered, "is someone jealous because Sir Piers told you to worry about me?"

"The only thing I worry about is being stuck in the same quarters as a common whore."

"What are you talking about?" Now I was just confused.

Priscilla looked me up and down. "Tell me where you sneak off to every night. Explain *why* Sir Piers suddenly started to take an interest in the same halfwit he was so keen on condemning a week ago? Seems to me you must have found a way to earn his praise through your skirts—"

All I saw was red. I felt that same rage from the night before crackling and sputtering its way to the surface. "I would never!"

"Then tell me where you go," she countered. There was a malicious smile on her lips, and it took all my self-control to stop from lunging.

Behind her, the rest of our audience had fallen silent.

"Unless you've got something to hide, of course."

I loosened my grip on the sword's hilt and cast a glance at Darren. The prince didn't appear the least bit interested in defending me. Apparently, he was perfectly content to let Priscilla think the worst of me, to keep from sullying *his* reputation.

We'll see about that.

"You can say what you like, Priscilla." My eyes were locked on Darren as I spoke. "But before you go around soiling my name, you might go and ask your precious prince where it is he goes each night as well."

Priscilla blanched and immediately turned on Darren. "What did she mean by that?"

Darren kept his face perfectly still. "That lowborn doesn't know what she's saying."

"Then why did she—"

"Because she has nothing better to do." Darren glanced at me, dark eyes flashing. "The girl is trying to upset you, and you are letting her."

I folded my arms. "He's lying to your face."

Darren glared, and I ignored him.

Priscilla glanced from me to Darren and back again, unsure whom to believe: the girl she hated or the prince. "Well, I should tell the constable she's sneaking out."

"No!" both Darren and I shouted at the same time.

"What I mean," Darren amended quickly, "is that you shouldn't waste your time on someone as insignificant as her." His eyes dared me to disagree.

I reluctantly kept silent, knowing better than to say anything foolish again. Topping Darren would mean nothing if it got me kicked out of the Academy.

"Come, let's practice closer to the field," Darren took the highborn by the arm, leading her away.

As soon as his following left, I took a deep breath.

"What was *that* about?"

I glanced up and found Ella walking toward me.

"How much did you see?"

"Enough." She picked up the sword I'd dropped and snatched a second sword for herself. "It seems I'm not the only one who has a bone to pick with the prince. I was just coming down to check on you when I saw your little chat. Sword?"

I shook my head at the offered hilt. "I don't know how to hold it."

"Well, it's a good thing I'm staying."

"Are you done with the assignments already?"

Ella shrugged. "No... but I figured you needed a friend." She gave me a kind smile. "This week is only Restoration. I'll manage until Combat."

* * *

An hour later, Ella and I made our way back to the library for the last leg of study.

"The prince must really dislike you," she said as we turned the steps of the corridor. "He usually goes out of his way to ignore people."

I laughed loudly. "I'm special."

"What did you do?"

"I think my very existence offends him." That, and my lack of dedication to my magic, whatever that meant. Also my presence in the library, but for some reason I couldn't admit it. She might get the wrong idea.

"You've made a nice enemy of Priscilla too." Ella cocked her head to one side. "If I were you, I'd avoid them both."

I sighed uncomfortably. "Believe me, I'm trying."

Ella had a strange look in her eyes.

"Just be careful," she mumbled. "When people like them notice you, that's when you should be worried."

I stared at my friend, trying to understand the odd intensity to her warning. "What happened when you lived at court?" There was something she wasn't telling me. "Why did your parents choose to leave?"

Ella stared at the walls in front of us. "Just don't trust them." She looked anywhere but my face. "Don't trust them, and you can't get hurt."

* * *

When Darren arrived at the library, I was waiting for him.

"Good, you're here." He set down his books. "We have some things to discuss."

I advanced on him with a huff. "You can't let Priscilla say those things about me. I don't care if it gets us both expelled, if you don't defend me next time she does that, I'll tell everyone the truth. I swear it!"

He didn't blink. "What was I supposed to do? Defending you would have only made her hate you more. And you aren't innocent in all of this. You baited her and then practically insinuated you were lying with me instead."

I blushed. "I didn't mean for her to interpret it *that* way."

"Well, everyone did, so I hope you keep in mind that you have only yourself to thank for your tarnished reputation."

"I'm sure they didn't—"

"Oh, but they did." He exhaled. "I corrected them, but if the rumor had reached the constable or Master Barclae, you'd have the both of us tossed out of here for misconduct!"

I stared at the floor. "I had no idea."

Darren's tone fell flat. "Clearly."

Neither of us spoke for a minute. Then I remembered the other reason I'd been waiting on the prince.

"What did you mean when you told me I was training the wrong way last night?"

The non-heir shot me a look. "If you paid attention to Master Cedric's lessons, we wouldn't be having this discussion."

"I tried." I hated that I'd resorted to pleading. "But nothing he says makes any sense, and he won't show me what I'm doing wrong."

"You've fallen asleep in his class. Twice." Darren's expression was unsympathetic. "What did you expect?"

"I don't know." I bit my lip. "But is that really enough to condemn me? I'm trying. You know that!"

Darren did not reply.

"No one else can help me," I begged. "Even my brother doesn't know why I can't cast like everyone else. But you do. I *know* you do. It's why you told me I was training wrong."

"Even if I did know, why would I help you?"

"Because it's the right thing to do."

He snorted. "Well, good luck with that."

"You can't just give someone advice and then not show them how to use it!" I seethed. "It's not advice if it doesn't help them!"

Darren balked. "Well, I certainly wouldn't give it to the girl who has tried to get me tossed out of this place not once but twice now—oh, and let's not forget your most inglorious moment, when you tried to light me on fire."

"I've made some mistakes." I met the prince's eyes defiantly. "But you wouldn't have given me advice if you hadn't been feeling guilty about me in the first place."

Darren regarded me grimly. In that moment, I was aware of how near we were standing. This close, I could smell some sort of wooded musk emitting from his clothes, a mixture of pine and cloves that reminded me of home.

Why did he smell so good while I smelled like days of sweat, no matter how many times I washed? It wasn't fair.

Hair fell across the prince's forehead and into his eyes, and for some reason, I kept staring like a fool. I'd never really studied the prince up close. Now, all I could see was the dark garnet and brown of Darren's irises, which oddly didn't seem quite as opaque as I'd assumed, enclosed in those dark, dark lashes.

And right now, those eyes were doing strange, flippy things to my insides. Things I didn't like. I felt as if someone had wrenched the ground right out from under me. I wanted it back.

Darren cleared his throat. "Are you done berating me, Ryiah?"

The trance broke, and I stepped back quickly, flushing.

"I..." The prince was looking at me as though I was mad. "See here," I began again, flustered at my inability to speak.

"You want my help."

"Yes." Had I been reduced to a fumbling oaf just because he'd stood a little too close? For the love of the gods, he wasn't that good-looking.

Okay, maybe he was. But certainly not enough to affect me. I had better taste than arrogant princes.

Pull yourself together. I rolled my shoulders and regarded Darren coolly. "If you show me how to call on my magic, I swear I'll never bother you again."

He arched a brow. "As tempting as your offer is, I don't have time to help every girl who bats her eyes at me."

"I was not!" My speech impairment was gone as fast as it'd come. "And if you're really so secure in your own standing here, you wouldn't think twice about helping someone you believe might constitute a threat."

"You are hardly a threat." Darren was no longer frowning, and I had the distinct impression he was enjoying the debate. "And you really think the way to charm me into helping you is by insult?"

I glared. "Would you prefer me to fawn over you like every one of your blindsided subjects?"

He didn't bother to hide his smile. "That would be a nice change."

"Fine." I put my hands on my hips and gave my most sickly sweet impression of Priscilla: "O, valiant Darren, brave ruler among men, please help this humble first-year learn. Let me be half as magnificent as yourself."

"I changed my mind. Humility doesn't suit you at all."

I glowered. "Then why ask?"

"Because I'm a prince." He raised his eyes to the ceiling and groaned. "I'll help you this once. But not again."

I nodded. Once was good enough for me.

"Clear a space in the center of the study and come find me when you're done."

Minutes later, we were standing across from one another. I kept waiting for Darren to talk, but he was too busy studying me, probably taking in my disheveled appearance and everything else, with a skeptical expression on his face.

"Do you know how to light a fire without magic?" he finally asked.

"Of course."

"Have you ever done it with flint?"

Really? I didn't bother to reply—he was the highborn not me.

"Well, we're going to use flint as part of a metaphor for how to cast. Master Cedric has been saying the same sort of thing for weeks, but as we know—" His mouth twitched. "—your naps were more important."

I cringed.

"When you cast magic, you need to be picturing what you plan to evoke in your mind. The stronger the idea, the better your casting will be. That's where the senses come in." He looked me up and down. "You can't expect to cast something you don't understand. What is something you can describe well?"

"Fire." I felt like a fool for not coming up with anything else, but I couldn't help it. Fire was the one thing I'd been able to successfully conjure time after time.

"How inspired." His eyes narrowed. "Now describe it to me with your senses."

"Um, well, it's hot. It, uh, doesn't really have a taste. At least I don't think it does. When things get burned, there's a charred flavor... It's chalky and bitter. Sour? Flames feel like wisps of air. It looks like—" I froze as a thought crossed my mind: *like the color of your eyes.*

I looked away from Darren. "It looks like the fragmented tips of a red and yellow kite billowing in the wind." Definitely not anything else.

"You are missing two senses." Darren seemed unperturbed by my haphazard ramblings. "What does it sound like? What do you smell?"

"It sounds like low... clapping? It smells repugnant. Like wood smoke and something sweet? Spun sugar and smoke."

"Now, what do you want to do with the fire?" he asked. "What type of casting do you want to perform? Keep in mind it should be simple."

"What about holding it in my hand? I've seen people—"

"Do you want to burn yourself?"

I shook my head.

"Then don't try to do what you've seen others do. Their castings are more complicated than they appear. Try lighting a candle instead."

"Do I actually need a candle?"

"You are a beginner, so yes." He tossed me a taper. "Now think about the act of lighting a candle—but don't do it yet."

"How...?" I paused, fully aware that there had been no candle in his hand a second ago.

"Yes, well, I'm not a beginner." There again, that tone. I wanted to punch him. "Now think back to how you would light a fire naturally. This image you are evoking is the flint. You need to focus on its details, using all the senses you described, in your mind. The 'steel' that you strike this 'flint' with is your will. That's the easy part because it is rare for someone to cast something they do not want. If you have desire, you have will."

Apparently, I'd only ever been doing one side of the equation. But in my defense, the senses had been more important to a fight. The idea that I hold this complicated projection in my mind to cast... Alex had probably assumed I was already doing that.

"It all comes down to those two things: steel and flint. The resulting spark is the physical manifestation of your magic. If you have potential, it should be effortless. If you are struggling, it's a safe bet you are wasting your time trying to practice magic in the first place."

I glared at him. "Maybe I struggle because I didn't have a lifetime of mage tutors like you."

He shot me a condescending look. "I was supposed to be a

knight. I never even considered becoming a mage until four years ago. I would hardly consider that a 'lifetime' of tutors. The only reason I am here is because the palace mage insisted he'd be a fool to overlook my powers. It wasn't privilege that got me the training. It was my *potential*."

"Becoming a knight isn't so different than a mage. Most of the training applies." Me and my big mouth. I wanted to swallow the words the second I spoke them aloud.

"Every village has a local regiment of soldiers." He leveled my challenge with one of his own. "That's free training right there. Tell me why you aren't better at Piers's drills? Seems like someone wasted their youth."

I took a deep breath and told myself what Darren had to teach me was more important than mauling the non-heir to death.

Darren's lips curved up in a smirk. "Well, it appears you have *some* self-control after all."

I stayed silent.

The non-heir gestured to the taper. "Now, light the candle."

This was it. I rolled the candle in my palm, letting its smooth, waxy surface calm my racing nerves. I felt self-conscious with Darren watching me, but I hastily blocked out those thoughts, letting my anxiety trickle away until all that remained was a vision of fire. I felt its searing heat in my mind. I saw the sputtering flames. It smelled adversely sweet, and my tongue recoiled at the taste of scalded flesh. I reached further into my mind and heard the sharp sound of crackling flames against wood.

I stared at the candle's wick with the image of fire locked

in my mind. I imagined the cotton string embraced by flames, all of my senses engulfing the candle's end, a tiny flame sputtering that would carry all of my fire's features.

Please.

The sting of scalding wax hit my knuckles, and I shrieked. The candle in my hand had a flame protruding from its tip.

"I did it!" I could have screamed.

"Yes," Darren agreed, stepping forward to close the distance between us. "You did."

My breath caught and I couldn't move.

The prince leaned closer, and I froze, heart beating wildly in my chest.

And then Darren blew out the flame and took a step back. "Now do it again."

"What did you do that for?" I sputtered.

"That was too easy. I want to see you do it under duress. It's much harder to concentrate when you have distractions."

"Like what?" I was instantly suspicious.

A slow smile spread across his face. "How about I repay your favor from last night?"

What favor?

Darren snapped his finger. I glanced around frantically but didn't see any changes to the room. "What did you—" The words caught in my throat as I noticed a long shadow quickly making its way across the dark marble floor. As it trailed closer, I cried out involuntarily.

The shadow was a herd of enormous, hairy brown spiders that was racing toward me.

No. My legs went numb. *Where did they come from?* I hated spiders.

"The funny thing about magic," Darren said, eyes dancing wickedly, "is that you can't control the mind. But if you know what a spider doesn't like, you can drive it out of hiding." He grinned. "I'll send them back the moment you light that candle."

I swallowed as I looked to the incoming mob. "Can't you try something else?"

"Stop making excuses."

My eyes shot to the extinguished candle in my hand. The wick was tinged black from the previous flame, and I willed it to light once again. *Please.*

I tried to visualize a fire using all of my senses, but it was much harder to actualize with the pounding in my chest. I couldn't stop thinking about those spiders getting closer and closer.

Why did he have to choose them? The anxiety had my blood racing, and I kept losing focus to peek down at the ground.

"Ignore the spiders, Ryiah!"

I bit my lip, and inadvertently my gaze slid down to the insects again. They had just reached my boots and were beginning to climb. My insides froze.

"RYIAH!"

I shut my eyes and tried to picture a fire. The image came swimming back. I took a deep breath and tried to drown out the desire to run screaming and shaking the creatures off my legs. I recalled the candle and opened my eyes, practically throwing my impression at it with a stifled huff.

Instantly the candle's wick caught fire, but it was quickly diminished as a mountain of wax spilled out over my hands.

Not only had the wick caught fire, the entire candle had melted. There was nothing left but wax. I glanced down at my tunic and saw the spiders were scurrying back to wherever they'd come from.

Thank the gods. I glared at the prince, hands on my hips. "You didn't have to use spiders."

"I could have used fire. Or a dagger cutting you up, slowly." His eyes dared me to challenge him again. "I chose something harmless."

Spiders weren't harmless if you got bitten. I told him as much.

"How will you get better," the prince countered, "if you aren't willing to face your fears? I did you a favor. Maybe now you'll stop napping during Cedric's lessons."

I peeled the wax off my hands, wincing at the swollen flesh beneath. Darren was obviously enjoying this lesson too much. "I haven't done that in days."

"Well, I've done my part." Darren waved a dismissing hand and sat down in his chair with his books.

Over so soon? I still had questions.

"Can you answer one more thing?"

"What?" The word was drawn out and clipped at the same time.

"How did you know I was training wrong?" I bit my lip. "You seemed to know something was wrong before you'd even seen me cast."

"It was a guess. And after you attacked me with that fire, it was pretty obvious you didn't know what you were doing."

"How come no one knew how to help me? Even my brother couldn't help and he's my twin."

Darren narrowed his eyes. "You really know nothing about magic, do you?" He didn't wait for a response. "You can *pain cast*, Ryiah. Most people can't. Your magic operates at a different level. You can't expect the same rules to apply to us."

"Pain cast?" My voice squeaked.

Darren studied his fingers. "For the weak, castings come easy. Projections are harder when you have two different sources of magic. Most only have one, and that's enough. Your brother is obviously one of them."

"But where does our magic come from? Why don't the masters teach us this?"

"The masters don't teach it to first-years because it's advanced. They care more about foundation." He exhaled. "And pain casting comes from instinct. It's why your natural response is to call on will instead of taking the time to build up a projection before you cast. Your second source wants to take over the first. People like you and me have to work harder to project because we are fighting our natural response."

Was that what I was doing—taming my magic when I cast the way Cedric taught? It was certainly harder than picking up a knife.

I frowned. "So why do we bother fighting it?"

"Because it's reckless." Darren gave me a hard look. "The powers you exert are unpredictable and much harder to control. Your flames didn't stop last night, did they?"

I sighed. "No."

"Exactly. It's dangerous, and you should be grateful you haven't lost a limb."

I winced.

"Of course, if that's your intention, it would be very amusing to watch."

I threw my quill at his head before I even had a chance to think. The prince caught it with a grin.

For a moment, I faltered.

He has a nice smile.

Arrrrrgh. Where in the name of the gods did *that* come from?

I ducked my head and started toward the third floor's study. I couldn't care less whether the bloody prince had a nice smile. The only thing that mattered was his help and my success at the Academy.

SEVEN

"FASTER!" PIERS'S ROAR boomed across the stadium. "All of you are pathetic excuses for war mages. I've seen horses with more spirit than you!"

He's trying to kill us.

I swallowed back a mouthful of bile and continued running along the stadium's track. I was a limping fowl chased by a pack of rabid wolves, only instead of the beasts of the forest, I had Piers's insults tearing me limb from limb. My legs burned, my arms ached, and my entire chest was on fire.

I could barely breathe.

I had fifty more minutes. Fifty minutes of sprints, *endless* sprints, and the horrible obstacle course we were required to complete at the end of each mile's lap.

Today, after all, was our third week of orientation. In other words, Combat.

Today's drill, Piers had promised, would make it clear whether we were "cut out for the hard life of Combat, or the cushy life of the other two factions." None of us wanted to disappoint him with that kind of introduction, but his new routine was proving quickly how difficult that would be.

I ran my fastest mile ever—seven minutes to the second—only to lose the momentum I'd built during the second half.

The obstacle course was Piers's worst invention yet. Somehow he, his assistants, and the constable's staff had created a breeding ground of misery.

Now we had sacks of barley to haul, a towering rope to climb, a tightrope to cross, flying arrows and throwing knives to dodge on the way to each station, and, last but not least, a quick three-minute joust with one member of the constable's staff.

All ten of the constable's men just happened to have some experience wielding a pole. They weren't very apt, but after twenty minutes of trying to complete Piers's course, it didn't seem to matter much.

"I'm not joking. Pick up the pace, first-years!"

I kept running, trying to block out everything but the goal.

My feet were in pain. Raw, excruciating pain. A couple slivers of glass had somehow made their way through the supple leather of my boots, and it was all I could do not to sit down and pull them out. I'd managed to avoid any flying arsenal, but I still had three more laps to complete. We had healing mages on duty to treat us once we completed the program, but unless we were near the point of immediate death, we were stuck fending for ourselves.

"All of you are still here." Piers marched along the field with a scowl. "I promised Master Barclae that I'd send five packing by the end of this week. It's time to sink or swim, my children, sink or swim."

I was halfway into my second lap when the weather changed.

Gone was the hot and sweltering sky, the temperature had dramatically plunged. I could hear the soft rumble of thunder. The sky was drenched in a purple haze.

"D-doesn't... look... good." Alex caught up to me on the turn. "Not... natural..."

I nodded. It cost too much to speak.

Seconds later, the class was being pelted with rain and small pellets of hail.

Lightning flashed, and I scrambled to make it to the next destination: the climbing rope. My arms were still weak from my last attempt. Lucky for me, there were three people ahead, so I had a couple minutes to recuperate.

Grimacing, I bent down and slowly, *carefully*, pulled a protruding shard from my boot.

"No more sheltered training!" Sir Piers's voice was louder than thunder. *Sheeesh.* "All of you want Combat—no, don't you dare shake your head at me, Karl! You want a black robe, prove it. I don't want to see a single one of you stopping unless every bone in your body is broken! If you are waiting in line, you had better be jogging in place, or giving me crunches!"

The class groaned, and I hastily jumped up to begin running in place. This was insanity. I had no idea how I would complete the course two more times.

When I finished climbing the rope, my hands were raw and my arms were limp noodles. Thanks to the rain, I'd slipped on the rope, and now I had a hefty burn to show for the effort.

The hail was getting bigger and the little pebbles *hurt*. The ground was turning to slush, and my clothes were soaked through.

I made my way over to the next station: the tightrope. Broken glass glittered in the mud beneath it, waiting for the victims to slip.

The tightrope wasn't particularly challenging. It was maybe three yards across, no more than a yard above the ground. But I wasn't exactly known for my balance—I'd already slipped once, and now with the rainstorm and my slippery boots, I was especially wary.

"Hurry up." Jake, one of the two stocky brothers from the prince's following, shoved me to the front.

Taking a deep breath, I forced myself to take one solid step after the next.

At first, everything was fine. I was gingerly making my way across, inching one foot in front of the other, but then the wind picked up, and I slipped.

My foot started to slide and only an awkward twist saved my balance.

Whew.

I crossed the remainder and hopped to the ground. Two down, two more times to go.

The first-year after me charged the rope. A second later, Jake was cursing and hopping on glass. *Ha.*

I grinned and started jogging to the final task in the course—

A dagger came whipping through the air mere inches from my face.

I ducked with a second to spare. *That was close.* Too close.

One of the assisting mages had probably seen me laugh; I

resolved not to do it again. I wasn't so sure the attack was by chance.

I snatched up a staff from a pile on the ground and turned to face a swallow-faced manservant. This one was thin and wispy, and he clutched his weapon awkwardly. Then again, he wasn't a fighter.

I made the first move.

Feigning a downward swoop and attacking from the left, I caught my partner off guard and placed a satisfying hit.

My partner snarled, undoubtedly angry at his new bruise, and he lunged at me with vengeance.

I deflected his oncoming blows. It was a short three minutes, but it was tiring just the same.

One of the assistants gave an approving nod, and I set onto the next lap.

By the time I reached my final sparring session, I was at the point of collapse.

The disgruntled servant was scowling at my approach. I'd barely beaten him in our last round, and he was determined to punish me for the second. I had a feeling most of the constable's team was doing the same—seizing the opportunity to take vengeance on all the first-years who had made their lives difficult, even if our only crime was inhabiting the Academy.

"What's the matter, first-year?" The servant spun the staff in his hands as he circled me, looking for an opening.

I refused to respond and focused all of my senses on the pole in his fist.

"Too good for me, are you?" The man lunged left.

My arms shook as I parried. Again and again.

Two more minutes, Ryiah, I promised, *two minutes, and then this is all over.*

Smack!

My ribcage stung from a sudden impact. I doubled over, cursing. I'd stopped paying attention for a second, and the manservant had delivered an especially hard blow to my chest.

"Don't know why you first-years bother," the man taunted. "It's the same every year, and yet you still come here thinking you're different." He positioned himself to strike left again, and I braced myself, too tired to read into the telltale signs that he was feigning the movement.

Wait...

Too late, I saw where he intended to land his staff. With all the strength I could muster, I cast out an image of the block I was too slow to carry out. It was the same technique I had been practicing all week, but I'd never tried it in class.

There was a loud clap as wood and wood collided. The casting worked!

The servant turned to Piers a couple paces away. "She cheated!"

The knight shrugged. "She used her magic. Any soldier would use what skills he possessed in a battle."

The man snarled and stomped off the field while I stood there in shock.

"Very good, first-year."

My chin shot up and I saw Master Cedric beside Piers. The old man was wearing a smile. "You paid attention to my lessons after all."

After my lesson with Darren, I'd been casting with

success—not every time, but enough. This was just the first time the master noticed. He'd probably written me off until today. I bowed my head and hurried off to join the group of first-years who'd already finished across the way.

The prince and his friends were present, but so was Ella.

When I reached the stadium benches, I grabbed a flagon of water and sat with my friend to watch the rest of the class complete our drill. Alex was still out there, huffing and puffing across the field.

"Your poor brother," she said.

"I know."

The two of us grinned. After watching Alex flourish in Restoration, it was a nice change of pace.

Ten minutes later, the ordeal was over.

Piers ordered everyone to a final hour drilling with the staffs at a more "relaxed" pace while the injured were seen to by a healing mage. Only the worst cuts and bruises were to be treated. The rest built character.

"Build tolerance to pain, not succumb to it" was Piers's motto.

Only two warranted care, a chubby girl with auburn curls and a horrible gash on her lower calf. The other was Darren's friend, Jake. Apparently, he'd twisted his ankle while falling and broke the bone in a clumsy attempt to avoid hitting glass.

Alex whistled low as he and I traded blows. "Glad I'm not that chap right now."

"It could have been any of us."

"Never me. I'm slow and steady without a cut unlike the rest of you sprinting prodigies." He was in far better spirits than the rest of us, despite the fact he'd been wheezing just moments before. But he didn't have a single bruise, while Ella and I were dripping blood. I wondered if he'd healed himself, though Alex would be a fool to try in front of Piers.

"Oh pipe down, you big oaf." Ella shot him a look. "Those two could've been any of us. Even a pretty-boy healer."

"So you think I'm pretty?"

She groaned and continued down the line.

My brother winked. "I think she likes me."

"You steal my best friend, and I cut your throat."

His eyes were dancing. "Come on, Ry. She's not like other girls."

"I mean it." I pointed the staff at his neck and nudged a little harder than necessary. "Stop trying."

"Fine." He dropped his weapon in mock surrender. "I surrender."

"Good."

An hour later, Master Cedric reappeared with his assistants. My pulse jumped in my throat. It was time for casting in Combat.

"I wonder what he has in store?" Ella mused.

I bit my lip. Whatever it was, it wasn't going to be easy.

* * *

The next two hours stole every ounce of my will until all that remained was the empty shell of a corpse. I honestly had no idea how I carried on for two hours with Piers, but by the time Cedric's session ended, there was nothing left. No strength, no magic, no resolve.

This was why people left the Academy. Eloise and Isaac

took away our brains, Piers broke our bodies, and Cedric took what little magic we had and destroyed it.

The final session started simple enough. Cedric had us pair up and practice violent castings against various trees spotting the field. We were to experiment casting whatever we wanted so long as it contributed to the faction of Combat.

"Show me what you know. Test your limits! If you don't get the desired effect, cast again. Experiment with your magic—don't worry about the field. The staff is plenty experienced seeing to your messes!"

And I wondered why Barrius and the servants hated first-years.

By the end of the first hour, the pine Ella and I had been practicing on was a crackling tower of flames. I was ridiculously proud... until I saw the giant fissure Darren and Eve created. Ten pines lay crumbled in its center. *Dear gods.*

No wonder those two were the prodigies of our year. Even Priscilla wasn't far behind.

Silly girl, did you really expect to be at their level? I could practically hear the prince's voice in my head.

Afterward, Master Cedric had Piers return. Once again, we lined up to spar, one of us clutching a staff, the other empty-handed. The exercise forced one person to depend entirely on their magic to block the opponent's attack. I was tolerable at first, but after twenty minutes, my blocks were so weak that my partner's staff kept breaking the defense.

Bruises covered every inch of my arms. I couldn't be sure, but I suspected one of my ribs, too.

During the last thirty minutes, the training master had us casting individually with the barley sacks from earlier. We were expected to blast our targets from afar, by whatever means necessary.

In the first five minutes, I exhausted the last of my magic. I could barely budge a sack, let alone cast enough force to knock it backward into the air.

Half of the class stalled with me. We were still expected to try, of course. But without a magical reserve, they, like me, spent the remainder pretending as they watched the few still casting with unabashed envy.

The prince looked so self-assured, and had he even broke a sweat? Darren sent the giant sacks flying across the field with the flick of a wrist. I couldn't imagine the power it took to throw fifty pounds with the mind. I couldn't even do that with my hands, and I'd had those all my life.

Darren wasn't alone, though he did look the most at ease at the front. Some of the others were even smiling. From the looks the victors exchanged, it was clear they considered the practice a game.

They took turns trying to out-distance one another. Darren was good, but Eve, the quiet, pale girl I'd noticed the first day of class, stood out the most. Darren could cast the most power, but Eve was the most controlled.

Darren was hard to beat, but something told me I'd be a fool to think he had no competition. His friends were rivals—and hopefully I would be too, if I were to ever catch up.

When the lesson ended, that last impression stayed with me long after I finished the evening meal.

* * *

By the time I had retired to the library's third floor for the evening, I was fighting sleep with every page I turned. My eyelids kept falling closed involuntarily. At some point during the first hour, I must have fallen asleep, because it was only during the toll of the Academy's midnight bell that my reverie was broken, and I realized how late it had actually become.

It was time to head back to the barracks.

"In case you ever wondered, you snore like a drunken sailor."

I finished stepping off the ladder's frame and turned to face Darren. He looked pretty worn out himself, but not so much that I couldn't catch the wicked humor in his eyes.

I had no energy left for witty banter. "Not that it's any of your concern—" I tried to stifle a yawn "—but I wasn't asleep the entire time."

I started toward the door and paused as Darren jumped up, books in hand. Usually he snuck out a minute or so after I left, as a cautionary measure or to avoid conversation, it was anyone's guess.

Darren noticed my stare and shrugged. "It's been almost two months now, if you were foolish enough to get caught, it would've happened by now."

I attempted a frown, but I was too tired to give anything more than a slight grimace. "Thanks for the vote of confidence."

He twisted slightly to look at me, and for once, the air of condescension was gone. "I guess I never expected you to last this long," he admitted, "but you aren't nearly as hapless as I expected."

"Am I supposed to take that as a compliment?"

He smirked. "Interpret it however you like."

I rolled my eyes as we turned the corner of the hall. "I wonder if you have ever given someone a compliment that wasn't a backhanded insult."

Darren's grasp on the handle stilled, and he glanced back, eyes dancing. "I prefer not to. It gives people an unsettling impression of self-importance."

"Me?" I scoffed. "Self-important? Have you checked a mirror?"

He didn't look away. "You'll thank me one day for not filling your head with false compliments. Adversity teaches one more than flattery ever will."

"A compliment never hurt anyone."

He snorted. "The people who tell you what you want to hear are the most dangerous enemies you'll ever meet."

I stared at him. "You must've had a dark childhood if you mistrusted anyone who was ever kind to you."

Darren's shoulders tensed, and then he cracked his knuckles and gave me a wicked smile. "You'd rather I tell you what you want to hear?"

The prince took a step closer, effectively closing the gap between us, and my breath caught in my throat. "What do you want me to tell you, Ryiah?" His hand was still on the doorknob, leaving me pressed against the wooden frame as he leaned closer, his face only inches from my own. "Or is there something you want me to do?"

My face was on fire.

I could feel tingling from the top of my spine to the tips of my toes. I was lightheaded, shaky, thrown off by the dark, bottomless eyes boring into my own.

What are you doing, Ryiah? Some part of me, conscious of the disaster that was about to unfold, pleaded to return to sanity. But all my senses were in chaos.

I didn't like how Darren was able to turn my body against me. I wasn't a swooning convent girl charmed by spoiled palace brats, like the one in front of me now.

So why was I staring at his mouth?

"You should never trust a wolf in sheep's clothing." His voice was faint. "Because the only thing the wolf will ever want to do is break you." The prince reached down to catch a strand of my hair that had somehow fallen loose, twirling it with his finger and watching me the way a hunter regarded its prey. "Is that what you want me to do?" he murmured. "Do you want me to break you, Ryiah?"

Yes.

Wait...

What is wrong with me?

I snapped free of the fantasy to glare up at the prince. "I don't know what lines you feed the ladies at court," I snapped, "but they won't work on me."

He laughed softly. "Are you sure?"

I opened my mouth to protest, and Darren stepped aside. "Rest assured you're not one of my conquests, Ryiah."

I choked indignantly. "I would never!" That arrogant, egotistical—

"You have a long road ahead of you, my dear. If you want to join the victor's circle, you are going to have to stop taking offense to everything I say."

The prince opened the door and waved me forward. "I wasn't lying when I said you might have potential."

"Well, as long as it's been decided," I said sarcastically.

"That is a decision I have yet to make."

EIGHT

ON THE LAST day of Combat's orientation, no one had resigned, and Piers came into practice with a raging fervor.

"I told Barclae I'd cut this flock by five!" he roared. "And you have all remained to spite me. That ends *today*."

I exchanged nervous glances with Alex and Ella. We'd all known this was coming; the man had been threatening us for days.

"Master Barclae has given me permission to try something new." The knight pointed to the mountains just east of the Academy. There was a trail leading into the hills just past the stadium's track. The crags looked ominous in the afternoon light. "Master Cedric and I have a special course just for today. And there's only one rule: don't ask for help."

I gulped.

"There are healers, but the *only way* you'll receive treatment before you finish is if you forfeit."

Note to self: whatever you do, don't break a leg.

"At this point, you either have what it takes—or you resign. I don't care which faction you want. This may be orientation for Combat, but endurance and stamina are prerequisites for *all* lines of magic."

I couldn't help but notice Alex was looking a little green. I patted his shoulder awkwardly.

Piers and Cedric went on to explain the rest of the course.

In short, we were to race up and down a treacherous trail, dodging a random assault of castings and obstacles in hopes of snagging one of the hundred tokens hidden away in a chest.

There were one hundred and twenty-two of us. And the course was two hours in either direction.

Once we had a token, we were to return to the start. If we returned without one... well, it went without saying our fate wasn't good. Cedric had something special in store for the twenty-two of us left.

"And go!"

The class took off like a stampede, first-years sprinting across the field like it was a race for their lives. In some ways, it was.

There were two ways up the mountain: the side of a cliff or a gradual climb. I picked the first. Climbing didn't scare me; I'd had enough experience in the hills back home.

For once, I had an advantage over the rest of the class.

It was a great decision—until one of Cedric's assistants cast lightning. A bolt hit the dry grass to the west and a huge fire shot up from the ground, roaring to life. It spread in the blink of an eye. In seconds, it was blocking the head of my trail.

No.

There were large barrels of sand nearby, but there was no

way I could squelch the flames. I knew the masters had placed the props for us to put out the fire, but it was a futile effort. There were only a handful of students who could cast the magic needed, and I wasn't sure which route they'd picked.

I had no way of cutting a path across those flames. I started to turn—

And then I paused. At first I'd missed it with the smoke, but there was a cluster of students at my right. They'd cut across from the east. The prince and his friends had gone after the fire and a couple of first-years were tagging along, waiting for them to clear a path.

Darren and Eve tackled a barrel while the two brothers and Priscilla took the second. In no time, they had sand stifling a small trail across.

A desperate boy shoved his way past and sprinted toward the opening, not bothering to look back.

My muscles tensed—should I try too? I was close.

But I hesitated. There was something holding me back. The prince and his friends hadn't moved, and Darren wasn't the kind to let someone get ahead.

My choice was justified a minute later when the boy reached the trail's start. The prince gave a shout and the sand was gone. Ralph was trapped in a circle of hungry flames.

The boy couldn't move. Like me, Ralph did not have the magic necessary to cast an escape.

I turned away and started off after a group of first-years to my right.

A minute later, the boy cried out for Master Cedric. I could hear his scream through the flames.

One down, four to go. Maybe I wouldn't have to worry about those tokens after all.

First-years were starting to act mercilessly. It didn't surprise me in the least that Darren had been the one to lead the charge. I could hear him and his minions laughing as they started up the cliff with a new path through the fire. *Ugh.*

The trail I took was an easier climb, but it was also more traveled, and I was lagging behind. My first choice had cost me precious minutes in the course. I followed a horde of scrambling first-years up the rocky trail, ducking and diving as the constable's staff lobbed rocks at unsuspecting first-years on the ascent.

I had to be doubly careful. The assisting mages were hiding behind boulders casting arrows that rarely missed.

Eventually, we reached a dead end. There was a raging stream dividing the trail, easily ten yards across. Its waters were white, frothing, and fast.

If I fell in, I'd probably break my neck.

The masters were mad.

There was no other way to get around. I needed to cross.

Like the fire and its barrels of sand, this river was another obstacle. Instead of a tightrope and shattered glass in practice, we were facing a river. The only way to cross: bobbing logs and slippery rocks covered in moss. I shivered. It didn't look particularly promising.

I started my way across, one foot after the other, following the crowd of first-years in front. Seconds into my progress, the girl in front of me slipped. She just barely cast a recovery in time. A wobbling stick acted as a cane in the river's base.

As I approached the same spot, I reached out to grab the stake for extra support. It vanished the second my hand clasped the pole.

I should've known better.

All I heard was the girl's snicker before I was suddenly thrashing in the river, struggling to break the surface.

Cry for help and disqualify or fight and survive? I chose the latter.

But now I was fighting for air.

I kicked off the river's bottom and paddled for all that I was worth. It wasn't enough. The river's current pulled me back down and slammed me against a rock.

I broke the surface again and wrapped my arms around the next boulder I hit, struggling to rise. My teeth were chattering, and I was choking. My gritty nails clawed at rock covered in slime.

Come on, keep climbing.

My arms were shaking as I heaved myself up. I was close to shore, but I was afraid I'd be carried further away if I swam.

"Ryiah?"

I saw my brother running down the bank. He must've been one of the first-years ahead of me who turned around when they heard a heavy splash.

Thank the gods he even looked. The rest of the class hadn't bothered. It was every man for himself.

I made the lunge and Alex caught my wrist before the current could catch me.

"Thanks."

His eyes were wide as he helped me to shore. "Thank me when it's over. I thought you'd taken the trail west."

"I tried."

By the time I was out of the stream, we'd lost even more time. Another cluster of first-years had passed.

I started jogging up the trail. My boots squeaked with water and sludge.

"Ry, behind you!"

I spun just in time to conjure a shield. A rock shot out into bramble behind us; I'd used my staff as a bat.

"Blasted servants." I scanned the trees to find the culprit.

"Come on." Alex's fingers dug into my wrist as he dragged me forward. "We've got to get to that chest before all the tokens are gone."

He was right.

I stopped struggling and led the way, panting as we continued the rise. *So much for a gradual climb.* I was out of breath and Alex was wheezing by the time we reached a clearing at the top.

In the clearing ahead, a large group of first-years was engaged in a full-on assault with Darren and his friends. Both trails must have led to the same place. Alex started forward, and my hand shot out, blocking his chest.

I'd already seen the prince's tactics once. We would wait the battle out. There were close to forty students here, and I wasn't eager to test our luck.

They were certainly taking "no rules" to heart.

Darren and his friends threw punches and traded blasts of air and conjured daggers in the air. A part of me swelled with jealousy as Eve sent a powerful quake that shook the ground.

The other first-years held up their hands in surrender, letting Darren's group pass. It'd obviously been a desperate attempt to rid the competition from our pack. It was both foolish and brave.

Mostly foolish.

Alex and I didn't move, hoping to remain unnoticed. They'd just begun to leave when my brother sneezed.

No.

The procession stopped, and the prince spun, scanning the canopy behind us. A second later, his eyes caught on mine, and he smiled.

We didn't have time to run.

Boom.

Darren's magic shot across the clearing and the ground split in two. I leaped back, jerking my brother with me as dirt crumbled and caved beneath our boots.

Seconds later, there was a deep fissure in front of us, too wide to jump and too deep to climb.

It cut us off from our only route to the chest. We *had* to cross; there was no alternative.

When I looked up, Darren was gone.

That... I hissed. The prince had gone out of his way to do this to us.

I had the distinct impression, if it'd just been Alex, it wouldn't have happened.

"Why... why would he do that? He didn't do it to them!" My brother was scowling at the pack of first-years trailing behind the prince's group.

I didn't say anything. I was too busy studying the hole,

trying to find a way to cross.

"We can still make it," I announced. "We just need a running start."

Four yards is doable, right? It was a longer drop if I failed.

"And break both legs in the process?" Alex grabbed my arm. "It's not worth it, Ry." He motioned for us to turn around. "There might be another way around."

"And lose time?" We were already behind most of the year—there were still a few stragglers, but how many? Five, ten? If there were any less than twenty, we'd lose our chance at a coin.

I didn't want to be a part of Cedric and Piers's final elimination round.

"Ry, come on."

I stared at the gap, envisioning a thick tree trunk as a plank. It would be bigger than anything I'd ever attempted in the past, but that didn't mean it couldn't work. I'd been casting fire and wind for days, why not a stick? Albeit, a giant one.

"I'm going to get us across." I was going to cast. "Just hold guard in case anyone shows up."

Alex opened his mouth to protest and then thought better of it. He knew just as well how much time we would lose if we were forced to backtrack.

I set to work, concentrating on my breathing until it became a slow, even pace. I willed myself to lose the distractions around me: the buzzing of late summer insects, the sweltering sun, the dull and aching sensation of my limbs.

Slowly, everything trickled away until all that was left was the image of a sturdy, robust pine without its branches—sturdy and solid enough to carry me across. I breathed in the intoxicating scent of its sharp, resinous odor. I tasted the tang of bitter needles in the air.

I heard the trunk land, thudding against the dense clay earth. I imagined it spreading across the length of the fissure at our feet with a snap of will—like flint against steel. *Give me a tree.*

And finally, I opened my eyes.

There was a log laying across the gap in front of us. Alex gave a low whistle, returning to my side.

"You've been holding out, Ry."

I shook my head. "I didn't even know I could." Then again, I'd never tried to cast a tree.

Alex took a step forward, but I stopped him before he could cross. "I don't want you to break your neck if this doesn't work." I would go first.

Hesitantly, I put one foot forward, and then another, until both feet were firmly planted on the trunk. I was still on the part that covered the ground. Now came the hard part.

I took another step, testing my weight with arms spread out for balance. The trunk felt stable enough, and the coarse bark helped traction with my boots.

For a moment, I tottered, a bit dizzy, and then I sprinted the rest of the way across.

There was a dull throbbing in my head as I waited for Alex to follow.

He started to cross and the pressure grew, drumming inside like thunder, a heavy, rippling growl.

Uh-oh. "Alex!"

My casting shuddered just as my brother reached the edge—

The trunk vanished.

Alex stumbled forward, grasping at air.

I leapt and caught his hand seconds before he dropped into the dark fissure and broke both his legs.

I was stammering apologies as I helped him over the edge. "I don't know what happened." My head felt like it was on fire and my stomach was reeling.

"You didn't have... enough stamina," Alex choked. "Next time... we backtrack."

If there was a next time; we had to survive today first.

The two of us started down the rest of the trail in a dash. I kept up for several minutes—until the pain became too much.

Ducking behind a bush, I spilled the contents of my stomach until there was nothing left. A sour odor filled my nose. I wiped my mouth against my sleeve, noticing the headache was instantly gone.

So this is what happens when I push myself to the brink.

Alex was waiting for me when I emerged. He didn't ask, and I was grateful.

We didn't encounter another first-year for a while, but eventually we made out another group in the distance. Ella was with them, descending the steep switchbacks below. I hadn't noticed her at first because she was so far down, but now I did. Her black bangs and bronze skin glistened in the afternoon rays.

I didn't see Darren's group below, so I could only assume

they were ahead. A second later, I confirmed it. There was a cluster of first-years racing across the ravine following a winding stream to a dense cluster of trees. Was that the glitter of gold? I couldn't tell.

But the one thing I could tell was that the ledge we were perched over was an immediate shortcut to said trees. No one had attempted it because the fall was perilous. A gradual descent like the groups to our left was the safer alternative.

"Don't you dare, Ryiah." Alex had noticed my train of thought.

I was about to counter, and then he swore.

There was another company of students emerging from a hidden alcove at the bottom of the trail. They must have found another way to go around the overpass. There were about twelve or so in Darren's group, and this new hoard easily accounted for thirty. Add Ella's large group of sixty, and that left a shortage of tokens.

Somewhere behind us were bound to be fifteen or so stragglers, but it was not enough. Alex and I needed to get ahead of the first-years in Ella's group. Not all of them, but at least ten to be safe. I couldn't be too certain of the numbers ahead.

"It's the only way, Alex. We'll never catch up if we take the same route as everyone else." We were certain to catch up if we avoided the switchbacks and used the drop to cut straight down the mountain instead.

"You can't be serious." Alex stared at the granite ledge. It was easily a sixty-yard drop.

I lowered myself to the first foothold, digging my toes into the cracks along the side. "I climbed all the time in

Demsh'aa. You know that."

"I can't follow you, Ry." My brother had a crippling fear of heights.

"Only one of us needs to reach that chest in time." I adjusted my hold on the rock. "You follow the others, and I'll take the cliff. If either of us gets a token, we can grab an extra for the other. We'll meet back at the beginning."

He didn't look happy, but it was our only choice.

* * *

For the next thirty minutes, I scaled the side of the cliff. It was taller than anything I'd ever attempted back home, but there were also plenty of breaks in the rock for a foothold or catch.

My hands were cracked and bleeding from the constant friction of flesh against the sharp edges of rock. I had no way of measuring my progress against the rest of the class—I wasn't about to risk a look behind me—so I could only hope I'd made the right choice.

In what seemed like forever, I finally touched ground.

Sprinting over scattered brush and dense thickets of grass, I raced in the direction of a babbling stream.

No more than a quarter mile ahead, I could see a crowd of first-years rushing back. Flashes of red and orange—telltale copper coins the size of my palm—glittered from tightly clenched fists.

I shoved my way past the crowd, not caring to apologize as I made my way toward the chest.

I ran the two minutes it took to reach its wooden coffer and snagged two medallions. There was still a large handful left.

"Well, well, the lowborn is a thief."

Not her.

My elation broke as I came face-to-face with Priscilla. She must've separated from Darren's pack. Or perhaps I just missed him.

My fist closed around the two coins I'd taken. I started to push past, but Priscilla shoved me forward, back toward the crowd and the chest.

"There's enough for both of us!" I hissed. The last thing I wanted to do was draw attention. People would not take kindly to the fact that I'd taken more than my share.

Priscilla grabbed my wrist, and I jerked it away.

"She grabbed two!" she shrieked.

Angry faces crowded around me and the chest.

"Piers said no rules! It's for my brother—"

She turned toward the audience. "Does anyone think it's fair to sabotage the rest of us?"

"No, I wasn't..." I paled, inching backward, only to find myself surrounded by the hoard. *Where was Ella? Alex? Any of my friends from the study group?* I couldn't take on this crowd by myself.

"Give us your tokens, Ryiah."

I glowered at Priscilla, angry that she was playing the part of the people's savior when we both knew it was her furthest intention. Her only loyalty was to the prince. She was just using the students here in her personal vendetta against me. Our last encounter was coming back to slap me in the face.

I never should've baited her with the prince.

Out of the corner of my eye, I spotted Ruth and Jordan at the edge of the mob, but they both shook their heads. There were too many others for them to help.

The last thing anyone wanted to do was find themselves in the same position as me.

I had no way out. If it'd just been Priscilla, perhaps. Twenty-on-one was another tale.

I'm sorry, Alex. I tossed my brother's token to Priscilla.

"I said both coins."

"But I—"

"You should've thought about that before you got greedy." The beauty smirked. "Does everyone agree Ryiah should pay the price for her crime?"

A unison of nods.

"This is ridiculous!"

"You steal, you suffer the consequences. Give us the other coin."

Glaring, I hurled the second copper at her, hoping it'd leave a mark.

It didn't.

"Now, does anyone want to help me make sure she doesn't get her hands on anymore?"

Several hands shot up, and I froze.

"Wait," I argued, "I gave you what you wanted!"

She pursed her lips. "Really, Ryiah. You act as if we are doing this out of spite. Please understand we are only doing what we think is fair." She stepped forward and snapped her fingers.

The crowd lunged. In seconds, my hands and legs were bound, and a thick strip of cloth was secured around my mouth. My cries were muffled, and I couldn't cast—there was no magic left.

Priscilla leaned in close so that only I could hear her next words. "Darren told me where the two of you go each night. You're not as coy as you think. If you make it after today, I'll ensure you don't last the year."

* * *

I was tied up and bound to the base of a towering oak, a mere yard from the wooden chest and its now empty contents.

After Priscilla and her entourage left, there'd only been five medallions left, but in a matter of minutes, another cluster of first-years had appeared, snatching the last of them forever from my grasp.

I struggled for awhile, but that'd only left me with rope burning my wrists into shiny, red welts.

So there I was, tied to a tree with a giant piece of parchment above my head that read "hoarder." Thanks to the label, no one bothered to help. And why would they? One less competitor was one less competitor, much less a hoarder who had tried to cheat them out of a coin.

I wondered if the masters would have to send someone to recover me when they discovered a first-year was missing from their ranks.

Ten more minutes passed and my luck finally changed. I could see Ella and Alex out in the distance, jogging down the trail. Ella was limping—she must've gotten held up. I waited for their gaze to land on me.

In seconds, they were both sprinting toward the tree.

Ella set to my ropes as Alex read the sign above my head, running a hand through his messy locks, hanging his head. "I'm sorry, Ry."

The cloth left my mouth, and I gasped. "Not... your... fault... but—"

I pointed to the empty chest.

Alex swore as Ella hurled her dagger at the ground.

"We've got to... head back." I coughed between huge gasps of air. "Not over... yet." We still had our final test, whatever Piers and Cedric designed for the remaining twenty-two.

I stopped and pointed to the tunnel everyone had been using to return. It was almost hidden in the brush; I wasn't sure I would've ever noticed it otherwise. There'd been a third route to the coffers, but most of us hadn't realized it.

Another first-year appeared, saw the empty chest, and started jogging back toward the mountain. *At least we won't be last.*

I rubbed my wrists. "I saw some of the class use that tunnel." While they ignored me tied to a tree. "Let's take it." The alternative was trying to cast across an abyss with magic I no longer had.

"Well, if you're sure." Alex was understandably reluctant to enter, but as I pointed out, we had nothing to lose. Any students hiding out to ambush others for coins would have long since given up. No one this late had a token.

As we walked, I explained how I'd ended up bound to a tree.

"Priscilla really does hate you." Ella cast the light to guide us through the passage. Alex had apparently used his stamina up seeing to her leg. "What happened to me was expected. Everyone was fighting when we reached the base of that trail—but you and her? That's the second time she's gone out of her way to torment you."

I winced as I tripped over a small rock. "She thinks I'm after the prince."

"Why?"

I could feel both Alex and Ella's gaze on me despite the shadows. It was unsettling, and I knew it was because of my guilt. The secret wasn't doing me any favors. "The library."

My brother coughed. "What does that have to do with the prince, Ry?"

Ella knew right away. "*He* goes there with you, doesn't he?"

"No, not with me. We don't even study on the same floor."

My friend was silent, and I knew she thought I'd ignored her advice. I reached out to clamp a hand down on her wrist. "It's nothing else, I swear. Priscilla just thinks there's more."

My brother stalled. "When he cast that magic, the fissure... it was because of you, wasn't it?"

"He hates me." I scowled. "That Priscilla thinks there's anything else between us is madness."

"If they both hate you, Ryiah, that's even worse."

I shrugged. What was I supposed to do? I already had little chance of surviving the year, what were a couple more obstacles in the end? It wasn't as if I could change their minds.

After another hour in darkness, we finally reached the tunnel's exit.

"Now, that's more like it." Alex raised his hands to the sky, bathing in the red and amber glow. It wasn't that warm, seeing as it was almost night, but I suspected he was teasing for Ella's sake.

She didn't notice. "We've still got to get up that hill and whatever else is out there."

Ella was right.

Ten minutes later, a barrage of arrows came flying from our right.

"You just had to say it," Alex complained. "You couldn't say fluffy bunny rabbits and rainbows."

"What fun would that be?"

The three of us ducked and dodged, racing up the grassy slope as fast as our legs could carry us.

Eventually, we made it past the missiles' range and continued, cautiously, down the other side of the hill. It was barren—except for Sir Piers, Master Cedric, and a heavy burlap sack that sat between them, glimmering with the telltale tokens.

Piers twirled a coin in his hand, watching it spin and then falter, falling flat in his palm. He did this two more times and then glanced up.

"Do any of you have a coin?"

We shook our heads, shamefaced.

"There's still a handful of you left." He groaned. "Cedric, I think it's time."

The old man shifted his feet. "Shall I?"

Piers smiled, white teeth flashing. "I insist."

Cedric reached out to touch Piers's throat, standing as tall as he could to reach the full height of the knight. "Go ahead."

"Attention all remaining first-years." Piers's words screeched across the landscape. "Anyone who has not turned in a token shall report to the starting point now. Your final test will begin as soon as you all have arrived."

Cedric released his grip on Piers, and the commander turned to face the three of us. "Rest up, children," he said. "You might be here all night."

* * *

In the shortest fifteen minutes known to man, the remaining first-years made an appearance. A part of me wondered if they had hidden away from the entrance, hoping the masters would forget their earlier threat. Each one looked worse for wear than the last, and I was sorry to note Winifred among them.

Once the final student arrived, Piers turned to Master Cedric. "Is Tera ready?"

An assisting mage stepped forward; she was a short blonde woman with a heart-shaped face. "I am." In her hands, she held a flask the size of her palm. Its green contents seemed to glow in the fading light.

Alex gripped Ella's and my arm; he'd gone pale. "Whatever happens, don't let me be one of the five."

"It's four. We lost one at the beginning. Ralph."

"It's time, children. Gather round," Piers barked.

We drew closer, and Master Cedric motioned for us to take a seat in the same circle we'd assumed so many times before.

"Is anyone familiar with the basics of hallucinogens?"

Several of us looked around, but no one dared to speak.

Tera laughed and held her bottle high. "Well, the ones that aren't will certainly understand after they've had a taste of this." She crossed the grass to the nearest first-year and produced a small thimble from her pocket. She poured a little of the solution into the cup and indicated for the girl to swallow. She continued to do the same until each one of us had copied.

Gods. It was worse than any brew my parents had ever thought up back home.

"This potion is a powerful brew from mandrake root and nightshade. Distortive blends are what I was known for in my apprenticeship." The mage beamed. "You'll begin to feel the effects after a minute or two."

Master Cedric cleared his throat. "Draughts like these are used for interrogations. A trained warrior can withstand many things, but not a mental assault." His lips pressed together. "We usually don't use this type of thing on students, as it can induce madness if left untreated for too lo—"

Sir Piers jumped in beside Master Cedric before the rest of us could run screaming. "We *usually* don't, but good old Barclae has given us the go-ahead since this year's first-years are more resilient than our usual batch of halfwits."

Master Cedric rubbed a hand along his neck. *Does he pity us?* "The dose Tera gave you should be enough to induce a hallucination. The vision you experience will seem real, and nothing, not even the knowledge that you are dreaming, will stop you from believing its effects. Tera has worked her magic so that each of you will have a part of your subconscious reminding you of this fact and asking you to surrender. You'll be able to speak through the casting."

"And the moment you do, we'll administer the antidote." Tera smiled toothily at the rest of us. "The first four of you will be sent packing. The rest will pass."

But we would have no way of knowing when the others surrendered.

As Tera continued to talk, I leaned in closer to listen, my head unusually heavy as I strained to catch the rest of her words. Her speech was choppy and quiet, a slow murmur punctuated by sharp consonants that hurt.

Moments later, my eyes started to itch. Sharp, glistening blades of summer grass became a dull, almost hazy green. *The beginning of the hallucination?*

I glanced around the circle. Ella's pupils were dilated, more bug-like than human. I wondered if it was really her or a vision.

To my left, Alex sat staring intently at nothing, eyes just as wide, mumbling.

A cold shiver crept down my spine. Everyone else was muttering too, over and over. Nonsense words. Was I whispering too?

Dark tendrils of smoke snaked out of the sky like branches.

I didn't like this, but I didn't know how to stop it.

My hand began to twitch uncontrollably, and I was thirsty. So terribly thirsty.

Something is wrong.

That was my final thought before the sky went black.

I'm alone in a room I've never seen before.

There's a frosty chill that seeps down my arms like raindrops and ice. Everywhere I turn, no matter where I look, are giant, windowless openings. Just outside, a blood-

orange sky is painted with magenta clouds, sitting bright against the harsh emptiness of my tower.

Wind howls and I press my bare arms to my chest.

Bare arms? I glance down and find myself in a dress. Bright green silk, with frills and a sweeping neckline, it's something I would never pick out by myself.

Another cruel gust of wind blasts me, and I look up.

This time there's a long black bench at the room's center. Three strangers and Master Barclae are seated upon it. The strangers wear embroidered mage's robes in the stark colors of Jerar's three factions of magic.

I hasten to kneel, but my audience is too busy arguing to notice. I can't make out a word.

I lean in closer, but it's still impossible to hear.

"They are trying to decide if you're good enough."

I spin around but can't find the speaker.

"I'm standing right next to you."

I blink, and Prince Darren appears. He's no longer wearing the training attire of the Academy. Instead, he's dressed like that first day I passed him in the mountains.

"You're not good enough," he continues. "You shouldn't be here."

I open my mouth to tell him he was wrong, but no sound comes out. I gasp, clawing at my throat and looking to Darren with wild eyes. Help me, *I mouth.*

He throws back his head and laughs.

I lunge at the prince, but all I grasp is air, and then cold, hard marble.

Knees bruised, palms bloodied, I look up to see the prince is now on the bench with the others. He winks at me as he whispers something in the Black Mage's ear, and the man laughs.

"Don't trust him, and you can't get hurt."

Ella stands in front of me now, dark ringlets billowing as she gazes down at me in earnest.

I try to assure her I never will, but I can only offer silence.

Suddenly, the entire room spins, and I find myself outside my parents' house in Demsh'aa.

I immediately run to the door.

Smoke greets me as soon as I twist the knob. I can't breathe. I cough and hold a hand over my nose as I feel along the wall, trying to see through the haze.

"Mother?" I choke. "Father?"

My voice is back, but it does no good. There's only silence and smoke. I stumble forward, coughing and shouting as I pound on the walls.

The smoke clears the second I reach my parents' bedroom. I swing open their door and scream.

A pool of blood covers the ground and the rug, with my parents at the center. Their bodies are mangled and bruised, eyes glassy. Blood trickles along their skin like a web.

I sink to the ground. Why did I ever leave home?

Another boy's scream. And another.

My heart drops. Alex and Derrick are here.

I stagger out of the room, my parents' blood coating my hands and leaving bloody streaks as I feel along the hall. I shriek back, pleading for them to answer me.

Where are they?

I barrel from one corner of the small house to the next, but it's empty. My brothers' screams only get louder.

Where are they? Who is doing this? I slam my fist against a doorframe, hysteria tugging at my chest. I pull my knuckles away, watching the blood slide down my wrist.

"You brought death to this house."

My breath catches in my lungs as I turn slowly to face a dim figure shrouded in smoke. It's impossible to tell who she is.

"What did you do?"

"You can change this." The stranger ignores my question. Her voice is void of all emotion, and yet it tugs at my memory. There is something familiar. It's on the tip of my tongue. "You can change your future and never lose anyone you love."

"I don't know what you are—"

"Call out for Piers. Surrender. This is but a glimpse of what could come if you don't."

She's lying. This isn't my future... It can't be. Can it?

The stranger snaps her fingers, and an image shimmers in the air. I can see myself seated in a giant circle, sobbing quietly, eyes shut, as Tera paces along the edge. She holds two fingers up to someone else, laughing.

The vision ends, and I'm back with the stranger.

"Surrender now," she says, "and save the ones you love."

This can't be my future; I won't accept it.

"You picked Combat, Ryiah." Her voice grows cold. "Are you really so vain?"

A blast of magic hits me, slamming me against the wall.

"No." I struggle to right myself—even if she's telling the truth, I don't trust her, whoever she is.

"You fool!" the stranger rages. "You'd rather risk the

ones you love than give up your chance at an apprenticeship!"

I fold my arms. "If this is only a dream, then I won't lose them."

"You reckless idiot," she snarls, "you'll suffer, and so will they. There will be a day you regret this choice. There will be a day you regret everything."

Something turns in the pit of my stomach. Fear? Am I making a mistake?

All at once, I hang across the ledge of an endless pit, suspended midair with the stranger above. Her head is still hidden by a black hood and smoke.

Her magic is all that keeps me from plummeting to my death.

"Do you think you won't feel pain? Do you think you'll be able to tell the difference when every inch of your mind is screaming out for me to stop?" The stranger seethes. "These visions induce madness. You heard your instructor. How many times do you think you can die before you become mad as well? Are you so stubborn that you would rather lose yourself than give up a mage's robes?"

I remain silent.

"This is not a choice, Ryiah. Surrender now, or I will kill you. Again and again. You have five seconds."

"Please—"

"One."

Why is it so important for me to fail?

"Two."

"Who are you?"

"Three."

"Why—"

"Four."

I can't do it. Even though I'm going to die, I can't call out for Piers. I believe the stranger. I believe when she says I'll feel every moment of it, but I can't do it.

"Five." Her hood falls away, and gray eyes meet mine. It's the same face I see every day in the mirror. Her lips are twisted and cruel.

The stranger is me.

"Five."

A rolling boom filled the air, and then I fall into a long tunnel of black.

Wind whips across my face. My limbs twist and flail as I continue to plummet into the shadowy abyss. I never stop screaming. My flesh is being ripped apart by an angry storm; my stomach is lost in my throat.

I'm falling, falling, falling.

I shut my eyes.

So this is what it feels like to die.

I pray for it to end, but it never does…

And then I woke.

"Make it stop! Make it stop!"

Startled by the clamor, I opened my eyes. I wasn't falling, dying, or trapped in some bottomless pit. I was sitting on the grass beside my brother, Ella, and nineteen other first-years.

Across from me, a red-haired boy was shaking violently. Like everyone else, his eyes were clouded.

He cried out again. *"Please, just make it end! I yield!"*

I watched as Tera came forward and Sir Piers held the

first-year in place, emptying the contents of a clear vial into the struggling boy's mouth. A moment later, the boy was alert and hunched over the ground, heaving.

Sir Piers turned to Master Cedric who stood a couple paces away. "Well, that makes number four—five counting that boy at the start. I guess we can administer the antidote to the rest now."

Tera and Master Cedric began to make their rounds, slowly bringing each student back to consciousness. Tera was the first to reach me.

Her eyes widened. "How did you—?"

"I don't know."

"Did you even experience a state of delirium?"

I nodded and watched as Master Cedric joined her.

"She woke on her own, fully conscious." She was still staring at me as she addressed the master. "Her eyes aren't dilated, and she doesn't have any sign of residual effects..."

"That's unusual," the master said softly.

"But not impossible. It's happened before."

"And you're sure you gave her the same potion?"

She nodded.

Master Cedric studied me as I held my breath. "This one must be stronger than we thought."

Her jaw dropped. "You mean to say her magic did this?"

The master was silent for a moment, then: "Perhaps."

NINE

THE WEEK BEFORE we began our chosen factions was the first time off any of us had received since we entered the Academy.

Of course, it wasn't really free. Now that orientation was over, we were five students down and too anxious to do anything except recalculate our odds. In seven days' time, we would be selecting a faction, a decision that would dictate the remainder of our year. Nothing had driven that home more than that final day of orientation.

"Do they really think we need a week to choose?" Ella made a face as Alex and I joined her at the table for lunch. It was our second day into the week, and it was obvious all the first-years had already made up their minds.

"They are probably hoping our fear gets the best of us." Alex smiled weakly; all of us were less confident than our first day at the Academy. "Can't say they'd be entirely wrong."

I squinted at my brother over my second mug of tea. Even though we weren't expected to attend lessons, most of the class, my friends and I included, had continued the normal routine, which meant I was just as tired as any other day at the Academy.

"Do they really think we will resign after that day in the mountains?" I wanted to laugh. "If I didn't do it then, I'm not going to now."

"Hmm, but not all of us have your *potential*."

"Keep it down." I didn't want anyone outside of our group to hear. "My stamina is still less than most."

"For now."

"But what if it doesn't change? What if Master Cedric was wrong? Then it's just a painted target on my back, and we already know two of the Academy's favorite prodigies hate me."

Alex didn't deny it. Neither did Ella. All of us were brimming with too much nervous energy.

By the end of the week, seven more students had left. I would've thought that after two months of hard work and resilience, self-resolve would be contagious. But a week of reflection had taken its toll. Several young men and women weighed the price of a robe against their family, friends, and a comfortable career following the family trade. For some, magic lost.

I hurried to the atrium where the rest of our class was waiting. Today was not only the day we would be electing our factions, but also the return of the second through fifth-year apprentices and their faction leaders. We'd seen several new faces in passing, and the possibility of an introduction was too tempting to ignore. I had so many questions, and an apprentice would know firsthand how arduous year one could be, and maybe, just maybe, they could offer some advice.

Or so I thought.

"Today I have exciting news." Master Barclae marched into the ballroom with glee. "In two months' time, we have gotten rid of some of the dead weight that has been holding the rest of you back. As of this evening, two more first-years have decided to pursue opportunities outside of our school, bringing the total of deserters to fourteen."

I looked around the room, as did several others. All of us were silently hoping the two were part of the competition, but it was impossible to identify the missing faces from the crowd. There were still too many of us.

"I am happy to say Sir Piers and Master Cedric have not disappointed me in their latest endeavor—"

Piers let out a boisterous hoot and toasted the master of the Academy.

"—and I hope they continue to pull even larger numbers in the months that follow."

I swallowed nervously and glanced at Alex and Ella. They had the same uneasy expressions.

"I understand the majority of you were under the impression that I would be introducing you to the apprentice mages and their instructors today. *I will be doing no such thing.* You are worthless until you pass your trial year."

Any hope I had deflated in the pit of my stomach. I should have known. It was the reason they kept the apprentices sequestered to the eastern wing of the second and third-floor of the Academy.

"You are not to disturb them. They will only be here until the solstice, and then they will be setting back out to continue their training in the field. While they are here, they are not to be engaged. The apprentices are the future of our kingdom, and I will not have it squandered by overzealous first-years."

Master Barclae paused and then chuckled. "On a more positive note, I do have the pleasure of introducing the three masters who will be your faction leaders for the remainder of the year... Masters Cedric, Tera, and Narhari, please come join me at the front." Our current training master, the eccentric Alchemy assistant mage, and a tall, foreboding man of Eastern descent stepped forward to stand beside the master of the Academy.

A part of me wanted to whistle. The new master was... well, I could see why Ella preferred older men if they all looked like him.

"Masters Eloise and Isaac will continue to lead your sessions on magical theory, but your new faction will dictate what time of the day you report to the library to do so. The same with Sir Piers and physical conditioning."

Alex stifled a quiet groan. I knew my brother had been hoping orientation would be the end of those drills.

"Master Cedric here will be leading the magical application portion of your studies for Restoration. Due to a recent resignation, Tera has been promoted to Master leading the section on Alchemy. And, last but certainly not least, Master Narhari, is our returning master for Combat."

The master of the Academy gave a broad wave of his hand. "Make sure to report to the constable before curfew with the name of your chosen faction—without it, your time here will be considered a resignation."

I didn't even hesitate. I was already walking toward the

hall. Combat or nothing. I hoped it was something I wouldn't regret.

* * *

"Are you ready for the biggest mistake of your life?" Ella nudged me as we trudged up the training hill for our first session with Master Narhari. There were already rumors going around that the master of Combat sent first-years packing faster than Sir Piers and Master Cedric combined.

My reply was braver than I felt. "It's the only mistake worth making."

"I hope you still feel that way when practice is over."

I opened my mouth to reply, but the words got lost in my throat. Ella followed my gaze, and her jaw dropped.

"By the gods," she breathed.

Master Narhari was shirtless. He was as tall as Piers, with well-oiled black hair pulled sleekly back behind his ears, smoldering eyes of amber, bronze skin, and short, rough stubble that lined his upper lip and chin. He couldn't have been more than thirty-five years.

This was our master of Combat for an entire year, or whatever time we had left.

Ella and I stood dumbfounded on the side of the field. We weren't alone, more and more girls wandered across the field wearing ravenous expressions like wolves. None of us were about to complain.

When I finally regained my composure, I made it a point to count the number of students instead of the, errr, number of chiseled muscles in Narhari's chest.

Focus, Ryiah.

There were far less girls than boys, seventeen to the forty

or so young men. Most of the first-year girls had chosen Alchemy or Restoration. They'd been under the impression that we were disadvantaged for Combat.

Much as I hated to say it, Priscilla and Eve had proved exactly how wrong that theory was.

Master Narhari ordered us to line up with the barest attempt at introduction. He was one who believed in "train first, talk later."

If we thought the master would coddle us, we were thoroughly mistaken.

"This is Combat." The new master of Combat prowled the field with a scowl. "Try harder."

He had us casting at the same barley sacks from orientation.

After an hour, I had no magic left. My barley sack wasn't going anywhere. The prince's group was, of course, still going strong, but the rest of the class was faltering.

"You chose the hardest faction for a reason. Don't tell me you've used up your stamina. No one has unless they are face down on the ground. The *only* way you will build up your magic is if you challenge it. Easy will *never* be good enough." Master Narhari bent down to meet the darting eyes of a nervous boy to my right. *"Now!"*

The boy fumbled, and the rest of us tried to summon enough magic to make the sacks move.

Every part of me was in the moment, casting.

Nothing.

"Harder!"

I tried again, visualizing the force I needed to cast and launched the projection with all my might.

"You are fighting for your life. *Is this all you can give me?*"

My arms were shaking, and I was so lightheaded I was seconds from dropping. But I held on, feeling as if I were slipping away in the process.

A boy to my right fainted.

I ignored the burning sensation in my lungs and threw the projection of wind with every ounce of energy my body could hold.

There was a snap, like a string pulled too tight, and then I collapsed.

A second later, I woke on the ground, cheeks burning. I couldn't believe I'd lost consciousness... until I saw my sack across the way. It hadn't moved much, but its contents were spilled and it lay on its side.

"Take my hand."

I pushed off the grass to take Ella's outspread fingers. But the moment I tried to stand, my knees gave out and I dropped. I gasped and emptied the contents of my lunch just inches from my face.

Similar sounds were happening all around me, I realized. There were at least ten others on the ground, retching away. Ella touched my shoulder. There were dark lines under her eyes. Her palm shook as she held onto me.

We were certainly pushing ourselves to our limits. I tried not to think what we looked like to the prodigies still casting with ease.

"Now you see what it is to try." Master Narhari didn't look the least bit surprised at the rest of us. "If you have a problem with my approach, then resign now. You will not last a week in this faction if you aren't prepared to give your all each and every time."

Forty minutes later, we were dismissed. Ella and I could barely stand. It was all we could do to hold onto our staffs as we walked down the long training hill for our evening meal.

Between the increased workload from Eloise and Isaac, the new weapons drills with Piers, and practices with Narhari, we were miserable.

It became a daily occurrence.

After the first month of Combat, it was a daily joke between us that we would "last the day or die trying." No one talked about a year. We didn't dare.

Alex didn't seem to be faring any better in Restoration. According to him, Master Cedric had been holding out on us. Two hours of healing had turned into the stuff of nightmares.

"He had us animate a corpse the other day," James piped up. He was in Restoration with Alex. "Never want to see a dead man dance again."

Ruth snorted underneath a stack of manuscripts that took up the entire table. "Try Alchemy. Then complain about dead bodies."

"Tera can't be worse than Cedric," Alex countered.

Ruth shoved the pile of books and parchment toward him. "You try carrying every scroll on herb lore known to man and then recite it for me. *Backward.*"

James sniffed. "You have Master Tera. She was one of us a couple years ago."

Ruth rolled her eyes. "It just means she has more to prove. You know Cedric is an old softy. You're just afraid to admit you're beat."

Alex gave her a flirty grin. "You can trade stitching up animal carcasses with me anytime, sweetling."

Ruth made a face and went back to reading her books while Ella and I quizzed Jordan and Clayton about their own experiences in Combat. We never had an opportunity to catch up in class, so we spent most of our meals critiquing each other's performance.

It wasn't always the easiest conversation, having someone else point out your flaws, but it was a necessary evil if we wanted to improve.

Better to hear truth, a certain someone had said, than false flattery. I couldn't believe I was actually following his advice, but it'd made too much sense to ignore.

I had to admit it was helping, though I'd never be able to pinpoint the exact degree of success. I still struggled day to day in each and every drill, but struggle was a regular condition. If I weren't struggling, if I weren't keeled over in agony, if my muscles weren't screaming at the end of a long day... then I wasn't trying hard enough.

* * *

Master Narhari continued to test our breaking points. At first I'd thought his methods cruel and unrelenting, but as the weeks wore on, I acknowledged—albeit grumpily—he was just a man who saw the sky as our limit. Narhari expected the world of his students because he expected the same of himself. He wanted us to succeed, even if his definition included shattering our magical boundaries on a daily basis.

And it was beginning to pay off.

One month ago, I would have been thrilled to see my magic's stamina outlast the previous week by a couple of minutes or an extra block during my jousts with Ella. Now my castings carried on a half-hour most of the time. My stamina wasn't guaranteed, but even if it failed to increase right away, I was usually able to conjure more powerful castings in the weeks that followed.

First-years were beginning to slow down, or quit. By the end of the second month in Combat, eleven more had withdrawn from the Academy... Not because they'd run out of will, but because they hadn't increased their stamina in weeks.

A part of me pitied them.

All my life people had stressed the importance of "potential." It was the amount of magical stamina one was capable of building. We all had a limit. You could have some magic, but did you have enough? Only time would tell which of us did.

The hype was beginning to make sense.

The Academy gave me a year. I hoped it *would* be enough. I'd seen Darren and his close-knit following. Each one of them had yet to slow down. They remained at the top of each session and carried on long after the last of us fell.

Some of us were still improving, but we were all fearful of how much longer our stamina-building would continue. Sure, I had magic, but eventually I would reach the end of its limits. Would it be in weeks, or years?

As the third month of Combat commenced, some of the prodigies began to finally slow down, though I was loath to admit neither Priscilla nor Darren were one of them.

The two burly brothers, Jake and William, had stopped gaining in stamina, and they were beginning to struggle in the increasingly difficult tasks Eloise and Isaac assigned. The only area those two still excelled in were Piers's drills, but it was common knowledge that would not be enough. For a knight or a soldier, yes, but never a mage.

Ella and I had a wager going for how much longer the brothers would remain. Neither of us had a fondness for the brutes.

A week later, our friend Jordan resigned. A couple days after, one of the lowborn boys from Darren's group of twelve did as well. There was no shortage to the resignations taking place, and I wondered how many more would follow. Master Barclae had warned that half the class would leave by winter holiday. I had a nagging feeling he was going to be right.

* * *

On the third week of our fifth month at the Academy, I walked into my session with Master Narhari, expecting nothing more than the same routine that had been drilled into us for the past two and a half months.

Instead, I found Piers, whose session we'd just came from, leaning against a post in the fencing that encompassed the entirety of our training field. Masters Barclae and Narhari stood beside him.

The three of them looked particularly formidable.

I shivered and folded my arms, eyeing the masters with apprehension. The three of them together was not a good sign. Considering the last time Sir Piers had teamed up with a master, I feared for today's outcome.

"Don't they look just lovely?" Ella muttered.

"I feel like they put on those disturbing smiles just to mess with our heads," Clayton whispered back.

I laughed. My friends and I could not be more alike.

Moments later, the humor was gone when Master Narhari explained exactly why the visitors were present.

"They've come to check your progress," he announced. "We will be staging a duel between each of you and another student in this class. This will be a chance to demonstrate what you have learned thus far. This is not a test. There are no winners and losers today, and this will in no way influence your trials at the end of the year."

I breathed in a small sigh of relief and heard Ella at my right do the same.

"I know how hard all of you have been training," Narhari continued. "The next two hours should be the culmination of those efforts."

Ella and I glanced at one another. We knew who our partner would be. We had sparred so many times in class, as well as after. We knew each other's strengths and weaknesses like the back of our hands. Between the two of us, we could easily impress the masters without embarrassing ourselves.

Others shared the same conclusion. First-years began to pair up almost instinctively.

"Children, children," Sir Piers chuckled loudly. "You are sadly mistaken if you think Master Narhari will let you pick the same person you've been practicing with all these months."

My stomach dropped.

"I believe Master Narhari and I have a better understanding of your skill set than your pea-sized brains acknowledge. The two of us will choose the one who is…

shall we say, *best suited* for your abilities." His words made my skin crawl. Something told me Piers had been looking forward to today for far too long.

As the sets played out, one by one, I came to understand exactly why. There were only a couple of us left by the time my name was called, but I already knew exactly whom my opponent would be.

Piers had not forgotten that day with the staffs.

"Priscilla."

I took a large swallow as the raven-haired beauty took her place opposite mine.

"Begin."

The two of us circled one another, slowly.

Priscilla looked like a wolf honing in on a kill. She smiled, white teeth flashing, and laughed throatily as I stumbled, clumsily searching for an opening.

Her muscles gave away nothing, and since we'd not been provided any weapons, I had no idea how she planned to initiate her assault.

"You can always forfeit now." The girl's voice carried across to our entire audience. "Save yourself the humiliation, lowborn."

I ground my teeth but said nothing. The only way I would win this match was if Priscilla became too confident and slipped up. My magic was no match for hers. I'd seen her often enough in class to know that it would be a mistake to engage her directly. Maybe someday I would be able to beat her outright, but not today.

Not without luck.

"Go ahead and play the coward," she taunted. "I have no

problem leading the attack."

Priscilla raised her hand. I recognized the move from training right away. She'd always been a fan of extravagant gestures.

Immediately, I cast out a shield, clutching its arm holds with all the strength I could muster.

The air whistled loudly, and her magic slammed my defense, splitting my shield and knocking me to the ground in the same breath. My cheeks burned and I tasted blood; I'd underestimated the force she would use.

I quickly scrambled to my feet, just in time to spot a flying dagger headed straight for my face. I let myself fall to the ground, hands thrown instinctively across my face. A searing pain shot across my forearm, but the cut had missed any important veins.

Now.

I didn't bother to pull myself up before I threw a crowd of flames at her chest.

Priscilla ducked, but it still caught her sleeve. She cried out as the fire touched her skin, but a moment later, water doused the attack.

"Is that it?" the girl jeered. She was trying her best to disguise the pain in her arm. "Two seconds of flame? How about some lightning?"

Lightning? We hadn't learned weather attacks yet, let alone the deadliest of them all. That type of magic was reserved for the apprenticeship, not first-years. We weren't supposed to know such complicated castings. They were too volatile; we needed control.

Panicked, I glanced up at the sky, only to get the air

knocked out of my chest instead. It sent me sprawling back against the grass.

Priscilla was laughing as I doubled over, gasping for breath. "Really didn't think you'd fall for that one," she giggled.

I spat, blood and saliva hitting the ground as I stood.

What could I cast? Daggers were still so complicated. An arrow? Wind? More fire?

"You have no place here," she said lazily, circling around as she spoke. "*Trying*," she added, looking directly at Sir Piers, "is *not* good enough. The ones who *need* to learn are the ones *I* am least worried about—"

Priscilla's speech was cut short as she was sent flying against the fence. Arms flailed out widely in front of her as she emitted a loud shriek. Wood splintered and broke.

As she fell, I rose up, painfully, using a staff I'd conjured for support.

"You little—"

With my spare hand, I waved away her throwing daggers and redirected them at their former owner. A chill crept up my spine. I'd never tried the casting before, though I'd seen others use it in practice.

A sharp, gnawing sensation surged across my stomach, and I realized uneasily I was fast approaching my limit. Apparently, real battle and adrenaline depleted my magic much faster than two hours of practice.

Then again, I'd just used a large span of magical force to knock over a girl easily the weight of four barley sacks and attempted a new casting. So maybe my exhaustion wasn't all that abnormal, given the context.

With a violent gesture, Priscilla halted my blades and let them dissipate into the air. Then she stood, breathing a little unevenly, brushing off bits of wood and dirt.

"Time to end this little dance."

I braced myself for her attack, envisioning a shield as before, but this time her casting came before I could create a substantial projection.

Her force slammed my defense. My head spun wildly as I tried to maintain my casting's spectral form, holding the shield for as long as I could. For the longest ten seconds of my life, I held my ground, shaking violently and fighting the sharp, searing pain that was filling my head.

Then, all at once, the shield shattered. It splayed into hundreds of tiny shards as I staggered and fell.

I was supposed to be powerful. Wasn't that what Cedric had said after the hallucinogen?

I couldn't hold back my bile as I emptied the contents of my stomach, again and again. I'd reached my magic limits, and Priscilla hadn't so much as broken a sweat.

I couldn't look up. I already knew what the masters' expressions would say.

This girl does not belong here.

Half of our class had failed, same as I. That was to be expected. But I'd humiliated myself, and the knight who believed in me.

"Will someone help her back to her seat?" Master Narhari looked uncomfortable.

Ella and Clayton didn't hesitate. After, Clayton ran off to fetch some water while Ella pushed my hair back so that its strands no longer stuck to my face.

My "thanks" was barely a whisper. Then I took a long swallow and glanced up at Piers through the corner of my eye. As soon as the knight noticed me, he looked away, but not before I saw the grim line of his jaw.

So much for no consequences.

Swallowing the sinking feeling that had set in my throat, I watched the last two matches in a melancholy silence.

Ella won her bout against a boy who usually tagged along after the prince's crew. Their match had been a pretty even exchange until he engaged her in swordplay. Foolish boy.

The last pairing to duel was none other than Eve and Darren. Watching the two of them fight, I understood Ella's words when she described Combat as a dance... the dark, detached prince and the fragile, girl with so much power hidden away. Their exchange carried on for a long time. Each served a series of crippling assaults that the other deflected with easy precision. I'd seen the two of them practice often enough in class, and today was no exception.

A shower of flame was greeted by a wall of ice. A powerful exertion of force was met with a large metal-embossed shield that deflected and sent the other's magic careening into the forest beyond. The ground beneath Eve gave way, and she lunged with a set of knives, crashing across the dais. An exchange of blows played out between two spectral blades, until the two finally paused, conjuring their personal weapons of choice.

Clutching the hilt in both hands, Eve held a long sword that almost reached the entire length of her frame. We had briefly practiced with that type of sword during our sessions with Piers, but the way she confidently held the weapon now made me believe she'd spent a lot of time with it before the Academy.

Darren clutched a single-headed battle-axe in each hand.

The two of them circled one another wordlessly. Eventually Darren jumped in, swiping at his opponent to engage. The two continued to feign and parry, metal on metal thundering across the field.

Suddenly, Eve swung out, and Darren hooked her blade with his off-hand axe while his other hand's axe struck out, the barest of inches from her neck.

Eve dropped her blade, and Darren lowered his weapons.

The entire class burst into applause. Even the masters.

I kept my hands at my sides, seething with envy. Ella and Clayton were the only others not to join in.

We were all dismissed then, and as I limped back to the dining commons, I heard snippets of conversation all around me.

"...definitely not a mistake to let the prince join the Academy."

"...might as well announce the apprenticeships already. I think today was indicative enough of who the five for Combat will be..."

"...probably the best performance I've ever seen."

"...that girl, the one with the red hair, I heard her family runs an apothecary. She shouldn't have left home."

It was too much.

Fighting back unwanted tears, I broke free of the crowd.

"Ry?"

"Don't follow me." I spoke sharply so that Ella wouldn't hear the tremors in my voice.

My friend didn't argue; she seemed to understand my moods. She turned back with Clayton trailing close behind.

I couldn't face another person after what happened in class. I wanted to scream and cry and run and hit things. I was so tired of trying so hard and continuing to fail.

I started walking toward the field. There was a wave of self-pity I needed to embrace before I could breathe again, and I didn't want anyone to see.

"You should go back to your friends."

I turned, recognizing the voice of the person I least wanted to hear from.

My whole face was blotchy and red. "Why are you even talking to me?" I snapped. "Your kind doesn't associate with lowborns, remember?"

The prince didn't move. "I never said I don't associate with lowborns, Ryiah. I just said I don't associate with ones with little potential."

"Then you should be in the dining hall with your friends."

"You're not as a bad as you think. I thought you were, but you're not."

I stared out at the setting sun, holding back tears. "I don't need your hidden insults right now, Darren."

He stood his ground and continued to watch me in silence.

"*Please.*" My eyes were beginning to water again, and I did not want him to see me cry. I couldn't. "Please," I croaked, "just go."

I shut my eyes against the tears that were about to break.

There was a long, drawn-out pause, then the crunch of leather against grass, followed by silence.

I opened my eyes and found myself completely alone. I let

the tears fall freely then.

TEN

THE NEXT MORNING, I woke with the knowledge that yesterday's nightmare had not been "just a dream." I didn't feel any better in the early morning light; if anything, I felt worse.

In my first class, news spread that two more first-years in Combat had resigned before breakfast. They'd been part of the class to lose yesterday's duel.

"I would have thought you'd join them," Priscilla sneered when she caught up with me in the halls.

For once, I didn't have a retort. I was too busy wondering if she was right. Should I leave? What was the point in trying if I knew I was going to fail?

Ella shoved her way past me. "Go back to wherever it was you crawled out of, Priscilla."

The girl shot Ella a look of contempt. "I'm just giving her some friendly advice."

"Nothing out of your mouth has ever been friendly."

Priscilla laughed. "I'm tired of being surrounded by lowborn scum. As a daughter of nobility, Ella, I'm alarmed *you* don't share my thoughts. Let her leave now. It's not as if she actually stands a chance." Priscilla called out to someone who had been standing off to the side. "Darren, weren't we just saying how silly it is that the lowborns are here in the first place?"

The non-heir's eyes met mine, and I looked away. He'd had plenty of opportunities to criticize me in the past, so why stop now?

"No."

My head jerked, and I looked back to the prince.

Priscilla made a small sound of indignation. "But you said—"

"I said that they were foolish." Dark garnet eyes never left mine. "But that doesn't mean they shouldn't try." He turned and walked away, leaving Priscilla, Ella, and me in his wake.

I couldn't move. For a moment, all I could do was stare at Priscilla as she chased after the prince down the hall. She was raising her hands and arguing, but I couldn't hear a word.

"That was strange."

I didn't know how to respond. Had Darren just defended me to Priscilla?

"Well," Ella went on awkwardly, "that might be the first and only time I ever agree with a prince." She pulled me to her side and gave me a big hug. "You're better than the lot of them. Don't forget that. We both are."

I told myself she was right. And for the rest of the day, I didn't want to cry. I wanted to fight.

* * *

In the week that followed, three more students withdrew. Priscilla didn't say a word.

We were down to thirty-three in Combat, and Alex and

Ruth informed me their numbers had dwindled as well. The exact number was revealed during the final day of our fifth month at the Academy.

"Sixty-three gone." Master Barclae gave us a frightening smile over the evening meal. "We've met our goal and disposed of half the waste that was taking up our valuable resources and time."

That many? I glanced at my friends. They exchanged looks. None of us had realized how many had left. It was too hard to notice when you were focusing on yourself.

Fifty-nine of us left.

"In celebration of reaching our goal," the man continued, "the masters and I have decided to include you in our annual winter solstice ball the night before your weeklong reprieve. This festivity is for the apprenticing mages who depart for field training the following day."

Does that mean we can talk to them?

"As such, this will be your one and only opportunity to participate in activities with those you would not have the pleasure of speaking to otherwise. Do not waste it." Barclae raised his goblet and roared, "To fifty-nine!"

To fifty-nine indeed.

* * *

"Can you believe it, Ry?" Ella leaned over in her cot when I returned from the library much later that night.

"You're still awake?" The bell had just sounded for the second hour into early morning. I was already asleep on my feet.

She watched me pull off my boots and tuck my sack under the bed. "I can't sleep."

"I wish I had your affliction." The only reason I was here was because Darren had heard me snoring on the third floor of the library and shaken me awake. It was the first time he hadn't conjured water instead. I *still* wasn't sure what to think about his random act of kindness. Or was that the second?

Or a third?

Dear gods, how many times before I considered him my friend?

Ella tilted her head. "It's good to see you back at it."

I shrugged. The time for morbid self-reflection was past. "I've made it this far. I'm going to stick it out."

It was funny, but it took until I said the words aloud to realize I actually meant them. I was here to stay.

No one and nothing was going to hold me back.

* * *

It was the evening of the winter solstice and frost was in the air. Frost and excitement. We were all a bit mad with the prospect of a reprieve.

That and a night of festivities.

It was a disaster trying to dress with a herd of other girls competing over the mirrors. And some of the other dresses… I'd never seen so many laces and disturbing corsets.

My gown was a simple forest green with a cinched waist of golden thread and little else. There was no bodice or embellishments like the current trends. It was years behind the billowing sleeves and extravagant skirts. When my mother had passed the dress down, I'd been overwhelmed. It was the nicest thing that she owned. Now, next to Ella's dramatic flare, my dress was an heirloom.

"All part of trying to catch a prince," Ella grumbled after her turn at the mirror. I suspected she was right. Everyone wanted to look extra special for a prince. Priscilla had been stomping around all night, but for once it wasn't me on the receiving end of her wrath.

Lowborns, I supposed, *aren't an adversary in a dress.* Threadbare fashions decades old were nothing next to highborn extravagance. Ella was just kind enough not to say it.

We were one of the last to leave the barracks.

"You two are never going to believe what I just saw!" Alex called out to us as he raced down the snowy path to greet us.

It was dark, but the moon was full. It gave enough light for us to cringe at the mounds he was kicking up in his tracks.

"Alex," Ella scolded, "you just got snow all over us."

"Just you wait!" He snagged both our arms to drag us over to the Academy doors. We laughed and yelled, stumbling along the icy road.

"You big oaf!"

"Let us go!"

Ella and I stopped snickering as we took in the building in front of us.

Alex was grinning ear to ear. "I told you," he crooned. "I told you it was worth it."

All across the dark gray slabs of the Academy walls were hundreds of tiny twinkling orbs.

Every pillar and wall was covered in the tiny glass lights. They shone like beacons of violet. Even the roof and rafters glowed. It was as if the entire world had suddenly turned crystalline magenta and white.

It was the most breathtaking thing I'd ever seen in my life. A purple palace dripping with icicles.

"How did they...?"

"Alchemy."

The three of us jumped, having not noticed Ruth's soft-footed approach. She must've been waiting for us to make her entrance; like us, there were only a few people at the Academy she could stand.

"Master Tera taught us how to make the liquid glow last week. We brewed a whole batch of the stuff and handed it off to the constable's team to bottle and string."

Alex chuckled. "No wonder the servants were in such a foul mood." They must've been decorating the palace since dawn.

"It's so beautiful," Ella said softly.

"I know." My brother wasn't looking at the Academy.

I made it a point to kick him in the calf. He wasn't going to start that tonight.

But I didn't expect Ella to reach out and squeeze his hand. "Thank you for showing us."

"We would have seen it eventually," I grumbled.

"I wanted to be the one to show you."

The two were smiling, and I didn't like where this was going at all.

I pushed forward with Ruth. "Let's see what it looks like on the inside."

"Yes, enough of that awkward romance," she muttered. "It's making me uncomfortable." That made two of us.

We hauled the Academy doors open without a look back.

Like the outside, the inside was transformed.

Ruth whistled.

The servants had lined the sandstone walls with the same combination of lights. They made the passage shimmer against the black marble floor and the pattern continued all the way through to the atrium where the festivities were held.

Inside the ballroom, long transparent curtains hung almost romantically from pillars at each corner of the room. Falling snowflakes drew a crowd to the many-paned window at the center of the stairs, and the stained-glass ceiling shown magnificently against the soft violet lights of scattered globes. There was much less lighting in here. It made the room seem ethereal, less mortal and more gods-like instead.

All along the back of the walls were gold-clothed tables with platters of delicacies, cider, and tea.

With the exception of our first night, we'd only been offered the barest selection of dishes since first-years were not, as one of the kitchen staff had pointed out, "valuable enough to receive the finer stores." Lots of porridge, stew, and bread... It was fine as anything back home, but my tongue salivated now. The servants had been on orders to only serve the array of fresh meats and cheeses to the masters and their apprentices in the private dining room on the second floor.

"Oh, it's been far too long!" Ella dragged me with her to one of the tables. There was a long line of students ahead, but it passed quickly enough with Alex, Ruth, and Clayton following shortly behind.

Then we sat down to eat. I tried my best not to stare at the crowds.

"Is this what it's like at court?" I was feeling out of place among all of the decadence. Everything was grand and sparkling. Out of the fifty-nine first-years that remained, only a third came from backgrounds similar to my brother's and mine. Ella and Ruth came from outlying regions rather than a full life at the capital, but they were still highborn. It still showed.

My twin was dressed in simple beige trousers with an ill-fitted jacket that was too tight for his burgeoning frame. My father had told him to save it for the end of year ceremony. We'd thought it dashing, but now all I could see were the loose threads and patches worn bare... the same with my dress.

It was easy to see why someone would want a life at court. In the center of the room, Priscilla looked the part of a princess. Smooth material cascaded down her curves in rivulets. It glistened as it moved. Delicate lace fell freely from the girl's wrists. Even her hair was elegantly coiffed with a single gold chain wrapped gracefully around her forehead.

I sighed, envious. The cost of that Borean silk alone would be enough to feed my village for a year.

Ella followed my glance and then squeezed my wrist. "You look nice in your dress, Ryiah."

I sighed. Perhaps I did, but just then, I was too envious to note it. Tonight was just a reminder why I had to secure an apprenticeship. The coin the Crown gave to mages in service would be enough to help my parents and then some. Perhaps

I was vain, but I wanted more to life than the hand I'd been dealt.

The string quartet by the stairs started a new song. It was fast and jovial—something familiar to lowborns and highborns alike. I'd heard it plenty of times over the year.

My brother wasted no time in asking Ella to dance. The two of them hurried off onto the floor, spinning and turning into the crowd. I told myself it meant nothing, but I worried as I saw him blush. I wanted Ella and my brother to be happy, but Alex had a way of breaking hearts. Even if he felt something now, sooner or later he'd move on.

A part of me wondered if I should let them be. Who was I to stand in the way? Alex had never pursued someone this seriously before; maybe Ella was different.

But what if he broke her heart? What if she wanted nothing to do with me like so many friends before? The sister of the world's greatest flirt.

I looked away. It wasn't a decision I could make today; perhaps it wasn't my decision at all.

Others joined in the dance, including Ruth and Ella's shy admirer, James. The couples continued to grow, including some faces that I didn't recognize.

I sucked in a breath.

The apprentices had arrived.

Clayton sidled next to me. "Care to dance?"

I smiled apologetically. "I'd rather not."

"Would you like me to stay?"

"No." I waved him on. "Go ahead. Have fun with the others." I'd rather die before having another boy trample all over my feet. Last year, a particularly heavyset one had almost broken my toes.

A moment later, Clayton was gone, and I was left to myself with four half-empty plates.

I watched the dance play out in front of me, studying the apprentices and guessing their faction by their build. I'd made it a priority to talk to one in Combat by the end of the night—preferably a lowborn girl who could give me some advice.

"How is it that a beautiful girl finds herself alone on such a night?"

I started. To my right was a young man not much older than myself. He had short, curly brown hair and hazel-green eyes. They were crinkled with silent laughter.

Even though his line was beyond ridiculous, I found myself grinning. Possibly because he wasn't hard to look at. *Not hard at all.*

Was this how it was with my brother and all the girls in our village back home? No wonder they'd never stood a chance. A boy could spout the sappiest lines, and they'd fall all over themselves for a compliment.

Then again, this one was an apprentice and he could give me advice. I told myself that was the reason I flirted shamelessly back, batting my lashes.

"I find myself alone because no one has captivated my interest."

"Perhaps I can change that."

"I wouldn't know, but you can try."

"Fair enough." The boy sat.

"Are you one of the apprentices?" I already knew he was.

He gave me a crooked grin. "Year two. Are you going to

ask me which faction?"

I studied him, eyeing the white scar on his left cheek and the dark bruises on both his knuckles. "Combat."

He laughed easily. "That would make you beautiful and clever, not too many of those here tonight."

I swatted away his pretty words with the flip of a hand, though it was more a clumsy swipe.

He caught my wrist and leaned closer. "What's your name?"

I couldn't look away. There was something about him, something that made me want to smile and laugh and… and dance. I never wanted to dance. That was a warning, loud and clear. I didn't need or want pretty distractions like boys. There'd be time for those when I was serving the Crown's Army, casting spells in my black robe.

"Ryiah."

"Ryiah," the stranger chuckled. "Well, Ryiah, I'm Ian." He let go of my hand to gesture dismissively at our surroundings. "So what do you think of the Academy? Is it everything you hoped it'd be?"

I made a face.

"I thought so." He grinned. "It has that effect on all of us."

"Was it so bad for you?"

He nodded. "It wasn't pleasant, but then it never is. Nobody actually expects lowborns to last." So he clearly knew from my dress. "But I made sure to prove them wrong."

I sighed. "I'm still trying."

"Surely you're not *that* bad."

Ha. I arched a brow.

"A lot can change in the time you have left."

"Five months is not enough time to catch up." Not enough to pass the others. I had to be one of five to secure an apprenticeship. That was not the most favorable odds.

"You'd be surprised."

I laughed. "The only way I'll win this thing is by luck."

"May I?"

Before I could react, Ian had snatched my palm and brought it to his lips with a mischievous smile.

"I have been told my kiss brings good luck," he said wickedly.

I snatched my hand away, albeit regretfully. The boy was clearly the best part of my evening. "You must have kissed a lot of girls to get that kind of reputation."

"Maybe, but that doesn't make the gesture any less sincere."

"I—" For the first time, I was speechless, and I knew my cheeks were flaming red. "Don't do that!"

His grin didn't falter. "I never play at matters of the heart."

"I think you play at them all."

"Ian." A pretty apprentice appeared at our table with a teasing smile. "Are you going to pester the poor girl all night or are you going to ask me to dance?"

"Anything for you, Lynn." Ian stood, brushing off his pants with a look at me. "Unless you would prefer my company instead?"

"Go on." I was grateful for the reprieve. It gave me a chance to breathe.

Ian caught my arm as he passed. "This won't be the last

time we meet."

Lynn giggled. "The apprentices leave at dawn for Ferren's Keep, lover boy. Unless you forgot, we're a part of that."

"Ah." His dimple twitched. "But Ryiah is lucky now. The next time we meet, she'll be an apprentice of Combat."

"How...?" I gaped. I'd never told him my faction.

"Master Byron likes to know the top contenders for next year. The whole faction heard all about the mid-year tourney earlier this week, and since you're the only first-year girl with red hair that looks like she has something to prove, I had a pretty good idea of who I was talking to."

* * *

I stepped outside the Academy doors and slammed them shut with a huff. It was still early in the evening, too soon for anyone else to have left the celebrations behind.

At first, I'd only intended on stepping out for a minute. But after hearing how my humiliation had been the entertainment for every apprentice mage in Combat, I'd been overcome with the overwhelming desire to run away and never look back. Since that was not a viable option in the dead of winter, my next best option was to get as far away from the residents as I could.

I didn't want another charming apprentice to smile and flirt and then tell me I was a joke. Maybe Ian hadn't meant it—he'd been a lowborn with something to prove too—but that didn't take away from my mood.

It'd taken me all of a month and a half to forget that day with Priscilla, and only seconds to bring the emotions crumbling back.

I plodded through the snow, unaware of where I was

going, until I found myself at the entrance of the armory. The bottoms of my dress and cloak were dripping with slush, and my hair, which had been pinned neatly back for the ball, was now a wet, curling disaster. I should've been upset that I had ruined my mother's dress, but in that moment, I would've gladly ruined a dozen of the same if I'd thought it would bring me any peace.

I tried the handle on the armory door.

It was unlocked. *Good.* I needed to escape, and I wasn't ready to go back to the barracks or the Academy's halls.

I conjured a bit of light in my left hand as I entered the building quietly. All around me shadows danced. My casting's flame reflected off the silver blades lining the armory walls.

I discarded my cloak and let it slip to the floor as I approached the back of the room. Near the wall was another door leading to a second room that first-years had used for practice once or twice when the snow got to be too much.

The second room was composed entirely of mirrors. I could see myself everywhere I turned, an angry girl unfit for Combat. Ian was right. I *did* look like I had something to prove.

Going back to the main room, I grabbed a candle and a broadsword off its rack and returned to the mirrors. I lit the sconce in the second room and then turned to face the glass.

Almost unconsciously, I started the swordsman drills I'd practiced so many times in class. One by one, my steps gave way to an intricate dance of blades. I slashed and cut in rhythm, never striking the same spot of air, while I watched my form in the mirrors.

It was strangely soothing as I picked up my pace and continued the assault. Forward and back, striking left and feinting right, I parried each attack until I became familiar with its replication in the mirrors.

Then, I cast an opposing blade to deflect my broadsword's assault. I continued the dance, metal and magicked metal meeting at every turn.

Each time I struck, my casting blocked, again and again.

I wasn't sure exactly how it happened, but as the exchange continued, my magic no longer needed me to direct it when and where to go to parry each blow. It just moved. I didn't have to concentrate to cast.

"Very good."

Startled, I dropped my blade and the casting disappeared.

The prince stood, leaning against the doorway, watching me.

Did he follow me?

Darren looked particularly disconcerting tonight in a fitted leather vest and dark pants. After seeing him so many days in training breeches and tunics, I'd forgotten how morose his attire usually was.

"What are you doing here?" I wasn't sure whether to be pleased the prince had given me a compliment or mad that he interrupted me. I wanted to be angry, but it was hard when the prince didn't have the usual condescension that was always written across his face.

Darren took a step forward, ignoring my question. Instead of answering, he motioned for me to pick up my blade.

Does he intend for us to fight?

I reached down to grab the hilt of my sword, and by the

time I had pulled myself back up, the non-heir was holding a blade of his own.

"Begin," he said.

I didn't know what to do. I'd never sparred with the prince. Priscilla, yes, and once Jake, but never Darren. He was the best there was, and Piers only ever paired him with the top of our class, which I was certainly not.

Darren saw the hesitation in my eyes. "Ryiah, I'm trying to help you."

I clutched the sword and widened my stance. *You can do this*, I decided. *You've got nothing to lose.* No one could see us; no one would notice when I lost.

Darren began to circle, and I imitated his pattern. The mirrors were distracting, but I forced myself to concentrate solely on the dark-haired prince instead. He was almost cat-like in his movements, lunging in and out with a surprising grace that bespoke of years of practice and control.

After a couple of minutes, it was painfully obvious the non-heir was holding back.

"Just get on with it." I gritted my teeth and blocked an easy strike with one of my own. "I know you're better than this."

Darren frowned as he countered and cut. "This is not about me beating you, Ryiah."

"Then what is it?" Because it clearly wasn't practice for him.

"I want you to cast out your magic again, like you were doing before you noticed me. You shouldn't have to think before you use it now. When you fail to defend yourself with the real sword, I want your casting to engage me instead."

I sucked in a breath and tried my magic again. The blade came along easier than the last. I willed it to hold its own defense, as Darren suggested, and continued to strike and parry with the sword I held in my hands.

Darren began to pick up the pace.

The prince's blade struck so fast my muscles could no longer react. The cut should have reached my shoulder, but my magic and Darren's sword collided instead.

Wow. My eyes widened as we continued to spar. I didn't realize I could do that. Not like this.

"Magic learns over time," he panted. "Keep challenging it, and the casting becomes instinct. The projection is already stored up in your mind."

Each time Darren caught the best of my physical defense, my magicked sword parried in defense. The prince's cuts, unlike Ella's and most of our faction, didn't give me enough time to visualize how my casting would guard. My magic had to rely on instinct, something it'd never done before.

"I think that's enough."

After ten more minutes of sparring, my castings had faltered. I was now covered in welts. Darren lowered his blade, and I followed. He was breathing a little harder, though nothing like the heavy gasping of my own.

"That was incredible." I leaned against the mirror, letting the glass panel cool my back. I didn't want to admit it, but a part of me felt faint from all of that casting. Apparently, my magic cost more stamina in that sort of always-present defense.

Darren vanished his sword with the flick of his hand. "You've come a long way."

When he looked up, there was an odd expression in his eyes. Was I being appraised? I was immediately conscious of what I must look like.

My cheeks burned. So many girls had dressed up for the prince tonight, and here I was at my worst.

Not like you care about impressing him, I chided.

"Why did you come here?" There was a strange feeling in the pit of my stomach, and I wanted it to go away.

"I followed you."

"What do you mean you followed me?"

"I mean—" his mouth twitched "—that I was on my way to the barracks when I saw you storm off angrily toward the armory. I was curious if you'd set the building on fire."

I flushed. "That was one time, and it wasn't a building!"

"What can I say?" Darren smirked. "We all know you have a temper."

I glared at him. "Only where you're concerned. The buildings are safe."

Instead of scowling, he laughed. "It's good to see you're back."

I guffawed. "What does that mean?"

"You were sad."

I couldn't reply. There was a lump in my throat, and now I was confused. Why did he even care? And why did I care that he'd noticed? Was he looking at me? I couldn't find it in myself to meet his gaze.

Darren shifted, looking uncomfortable. He started toward the doorway and then turned back. I snuck a look and saw him clenching and unclenching his fist, his expression torn.

"For what it's worth," he said suddenly, "a shield is not

meant to be hit head-on."

Huh?

"It's meant to be held at an angle so that you can deflect or, at the very least, lessen your opponent's blow. If you do it right, it gives you the chance to lead a counterattack, something that most opponents are unprepared for in the heat of the moment." Darren paused to meet my eyes. There was something there, and a knot twisted in my chest. "You should try it next time, Ryiah."

Before I could reply, he was gone, leaving me alone with a series of unanswered questions.

What in the name of the gods was that?

* * *

It was much later that night, after I'd already fallen asleep, that I woke up with a start.

"You should try it next time."

At first, after the prince had left, I'd been irate. His remark had been just another critique, one that insinuated I didn't know what I was doing, all in the guise of advice. I'd tossed and turned, punching the pillow and fisting the sheets.

But then my nightmare had come and gone. And in it, just as each night before, I relived that horrible day on the field, the day Priscilla had made me a fool in front of our entire faction.

The duel haunted me each time I closed my eyes.

Only this time, I noticed something new.

My shield.

Each time Priscilla had led the assault, I'd held my casting directly in front of my body. I'd assumed the best defense was one that left no part of me exposed—but, by doing so,

I'd let the full force of her magic hit my shield head-on. Not only had her casting destroyed my defense, it'd sent me sprawling to the ground.

What would've happened if I'd held the shield at an angle instead? According to Darren, it would've deflected and lessened the blow, maybe even have left Priscilla open to an attack of my own.

I was so used to fighting with weapons directly, I had never stopped to consider how I used my defense.

And that's when it hit me.

The prince had been trying to help me.

Against Priscilla.

ELEVEN

"WHAT IS IT you want me to do again?"

"I want you to hit me with your magic."

"Are you sure?" Clayton gawked. "It's going to hurt, Ryiah."

"If you won't do it, I will." Ella gave me a wink. "You know I'll never hold back for you, Ry."

I grinned right back. "Nor would I for you."

"You cast even harder than me!" Clayton shot Ella a look. "You'll break Ryiah's ribs."

Thanks for the vote of confidence.

I held my hands to the air. "I don't care who does the casting, I just want to practice a blasted shield."

"But the healers are off duty. If you get hurt—"

"Then we'll send for my brother." I folded my arms defiantly. "I'll survive, Clay."

"Why do you even want to do this?"

"You both saw how badly I performed at the mid-year duels." Neither spoke. "I'm good with attacks, but I need a better defense." That, and a little something the prince had said the night before. But I wasn't about to mention *that*.

"The duel was weeks ago, Ryiah. You've got to let it go."

"Ella?" I was sick of arguing. Clayton had a little sister and was too easy on the girls in our faction. I hated to say it, but I wasn't sure he'd snag an apprenticeship at the end of the year. If he went up against Priscilla, Eve, or even Ella, he was done. Hopefully me too at some point, but I had work to do first.

Darren's advice had been plaguing me since I awoke, and now that we had a week of reprieve, I intended to make the most of it.

"Clayton, if you can't keep your opinions to yourself, go bother someone else."

"Maybe I will." He marched off with a huff. "You two are mad!"

"Well, we wouldn't be here if we weren't." Ella nodded. "You ready, Ry?"

"As I'll ever be." I backed up ten yards and spread my legs shoulder-width apart, hands braced at my sides.

Ella released her casting with the flick of her hand, and a second later, there was a flurry of snow tearing across the field.

I can do this.

A shield appeared in my hands. This time I angled the casting to the side instead of holding it directly in front of my chest.

It felt strange, being exposed. I tucked my left shield arm inward so that my wrist almost brushed my ribs. My right foot shifted forward, knees slightly bent.

Wham!

Ella's casting hit me at full force. Magic slammed into the shield with a crash.

There was the sound of creaking wood, and then the shield cracked.

The next thing I knew, I was lying face down in the snow.

Dear gods, was I trying to kill myself? It felt like someone had taken a hammer to my side.

"How do you feel?"

I waved Ella off with a feeble groan. Today I'd master Darren's advice, even if I broke every rib in the process. If nothing else, I would give Alex a reason to put his lessons to work. I just prayed the masters had given him enough tools to heal bones shattered to bits.

"Are you going to tell me what this practice is *really* about?"

I brushed off the splintered fragments from my shirt and smiled. "You wouldn't believe me if I told you."

Her expression faltered. "The prince?"

Was I that obvious? I nodded.

"You sure he was trying to help?" Her lips were pursed. "It could be sabotage."

"Why?" I laughed. "I'm hardly competition."

"He went after you and Alex in orientation."

How could I explain that was a lesson too? Twisted, yes. But that was Darren... Nothing was ever what I expected.

Funny, because he'd said something similar about me.

Why am I still thinking about the prince?

"Let's just try the casting again." I didn't understand Darren or his help, and I wasn't sure I ever would.

Ella sighed. "He's not a good person, Ryiah."

I didn't argue. The prince was someone else's enigma; I just cared about his advice.

Liar.

I returned to my starting stance as Ella braced for a second attack. "Ready?"

I widened my legs and cast a new shield at a greater angle than the last.

"Go."

Her magic slammed my defense.

I gritted my teeth and dug my heels into the ground. My head roared from the sudden blow to my casting, but the magic held. *It's working!*

Then, suddenly, the pressure fell away.

There was a loud, splintering crack yards away.

I spun.

One of the beams in the fence had split open behind me. I'd redirected Ella's casting. There were fragments of wood scattering the ground.

And my shield was still intact.

"I did it!" I let out a screech, jumping up and down like I was five years of age. *"I did it!"*

"You've got this, Ry!" Ella cheered me on. "The next time you duel someone, you're going to wipe the ground with them!"

"Even if it's you?"

"Don't be greedy." She laughed. "You'll never beat me. Now get ready."

"Ready," I said.

So she cast out her magic again. And again. About a quarter of the time, I gripped my shield at just the right angle and my defense held. The rest of Ella's castings, I missed completely and her force sent me staggering back with the broken fragments of a shield along the snow.

Ten more times and I fell to the ground, vomiting the contents of my breakfast onto the freshly fallen snow.

Ah, practice.

At just that moment, a pack of first-years cut across the field. Among them was the prince, dark eyes averted and mouth pressed in a permanent frown of contempt. He didn't see us—he was too busy listening to a boy at his right.

Darren looked like a stark, black wolf against the frozen landscape.

I swallowed as I watched him pass. A part of me kept remembering his words in the armory. *You were sad.* Why was that residing in my chest?

Why did it even matter? Why did I care?

My gaze trailed after Darren as he and his group continued their trek to the top of the hill. Like half the faction, they were training during their week off.

It would've been too much to hope that the prodigies grew lax. Gods only knew they'd never let someone like me catch up.

"Ryiah?" Ella was watching me with a frown.

I looked away and focused on the ground. For the first time, I was torn. The prince played the villain in my story. He played the role in every conventional sense.

So why was I still so confused?

* * *

The week of reprieve came and went too fast for comfort. I wasn't sure I even accepted the passing of days. Everything was an endless cycle of routine. Drill and cast, study and fight. The only noticeable change was the absence of masters; everything else remained.

Before I knew it, it was the final day of our break.

Half of our year sat over dinner, too exhausted to eat. Clayton and James were a part of the other half; the ones who'd slept in and wandered around the seaside for most of the week. Even Ella, Ruth, and Alex had given themselves an hour or two's rest in the evenings with the absence of assignments. I'd declined every time.

What did that make me? Was I too ruthless? Too competitive? Did I want this faction too much?

My parents had always joked I was a dog with a bone, that once I found something I wanted, they'd have to pry it from my teeth to get me to let go.

I wanted to believe my drive was a gift. But was it too much?

No. Darren hadn't stopped training either. And he was the best in our year.

He hadn't been in the library, but I'd seen him in the snow, walking back from the armory each night to the barracks.

Was he avoiding me? Was he hoping I'd return to the armory?

I told myself it didn't matter. But every day in practice with Ella, I'd been reminded why it did.

I didn't trust him.

But he'd also helped me more times than I cared to admit.

I set my glass down with a bit too much force. Water flew out across the table, and my friends guffawed.

"Watch yourself, Ryiah!" Ruth pulled her books off the table and dabbed at their covers with the sleeve of her tunic.

"Everything okay?" Ella had been watching me closely all week. She hadn't said anything, but I could see it in her eyes. She wasn't going to voice her opinion again unless I asked.

I avoided her gaze. "I'm fine." *I think.*

"You haven't eaten," Alex observed.

"I have a lot on my mind." I stood, banging my knee against the underside of the table. "I'm going to study. Find me when you're done." I needed to get away from their questions and Darren's looming face in my head. Away from everything.

Books and drills, they were the two things I could depend on to clear my mind. Anything else was a mistake.

I was about halfway to the library when I spotted the source of my frustration. I'd mistakenly assumed he was somewhere in the dining hall with the rest. Instead, he was in the midst of conversation with Jake and William, the two burly brothers who always seemed to be everywhere he went. They were debating the merits of the crossbow in the center of the hall.

Just like them to stand there oblivious of anyone who needed to pass.

I cleared my throat, and all three of them turned to stare. I avoided Darren as I fixated on my least favorite of the brothers. Jake's sour expression returned my own; neither of us had forgotten the rope incident during orientation.

After Priscilla, Jake was my least favorite of their group.

"Are you going to continue to block the hall or are you going to let me pass?"

The boy snorted without budging an inch. "Where are your manners, lowborn? I think the word you are looking for is 'please.'"

"Get out of my way before I grind you into a pulp." Or myself, whatever came first. I wasn't going to cower or fall over myself pretending like he was my better. We were equals here at the Academy—maybe not outside of it, maybe I was cocky from all my conversations with the prince, but I wasn't about to let the brute walk all over me.

Or maybe I was just bristling for a fight. Maybe I was wondering why the prince had been avoiding me all week.

"You really think you can take me?"

"Jake, let her pass."

Gah. That voice. My eyes involuntarily shot to the prince. He was watching me with the hint of a smile playing across the corner of his mouth.

"Go ahead, Ryiah," he said, "we won't stop you."

And now he was being kind. It was too much.

I shoved past the two brothers, not bothering to apologize, my hand grasping the door handle as I told myself I didn't care.

But I did. *Blast him.* I couldn't walk away. Not before I thanked him, even if it cost me my pride.

I spun around and croaked his name.

"Yes?" Darren's eyes were dancing.

"Can we talk?"

He arched a brow.

"Alone."

The brow arched higher as William growled, "You have no business talking to a prince."

My teeth gnashed together as I snarled, "Whatever business I have is none of yours."

Jake and William exchanged speculative glances. Darren motioned for them to leave, and the two of us were left standing alone in the hall. *Is it always this dark in here?* I was suddenly nervous.

"What do you want, Ryiah?"

I stared at the ceiling; I couldn't meet his eyes.

"I want to apologize." Gods, was it always this hard to talk to him? "I've been doing a lot of thinking lately, and I realized that I've been making the same mistakes I accused you of." *Keep talking.* "You're not a very nice person," I admonished, "but you aren't the horrible one I made you out to be either. And for that, I'm sorry. You helped me when you had no reason to, so thank you."

Silence greeted my admission. I felt foolish standing there when it was clear he had nothing to say. *It doesn't matter*, I told myself. *You've made your peace. You're conscience is clear now.* Rather than stick around in awkward silence, I gave a curt nod and turned toward the door.

"Ryiah, wait—"

Darren's hand shot out to grab my wrist. I barely caught a glimpse of the strange expression on his face before his fingers closed around my arm. I went from flushed to a raging fire in seconds. I couldn't think. Sparks had flooded my chest.

My eyes snapped to Darren, who looked as if someone had stuck him with a red-hot poker. He was staring at me with a look stuck somewhere between wonder and abhorrence.

What in the gods was that?

The prince dropped my wrist in an instant, but it was too

late. We'd felt... something.

I waited for him to speak, but he seemed unable to in the silence that followed.

Should I leave?

"I helped you because you have potential."

He was watching me with an odd light in his eyes. There was nothing hostile, nothing condescending in the way he was looking at me now.

Stop staring at him. But I couldn't.

"You are meant to be here, Ryiah." Darren ran a hand up his neck, and for the first time, he looked out of sorts. "You are... You are possibly the one good thing about this place."

I didn't know how to respond. All I knew, during that moment, was that his eyes were the most interesting shade of garnet I'd ever seen. I'd always thought they were so dark they were almost brown, but now I realized they were ebony, somewhere between the pitch-black of night and the mahogany of a rich wood.

Gods, how was I just now noticing how disturbingly attractive Darren really was? Why did it have to be him? Why was I feeling lightheaded and weak, like I wanted him to say something more? Why was he still watching me, and why was I incapable of looking away?

"T-thank you." I swallowed, again and again. "For what you just said, even if you didn't mean—"

"I meant every word."

Darren took a step forward. I took a step back. And then he took another.

This time I didn't move.

We were standing too close. I knew it. He knew it. And

we just didn't care.

"Rest assured you're not one of my conquests, Ryiah."
He'd said that once. But what if I wanted to be now?

There were shadows dancing across the prince's face. "I am going to do something against my better judgment," he said softly. His eyes were like two embers as he reached down to put one hand against my waist and the other underneath my chin. "You can scream obscenities at me after."

And then he kissed me.

It was a long, slow kiss, one that sent chills from the stem of my neck to the very tips of my toes. It burned hot and then cold, making me dizzy and weak.

My knees buckled and I gasped.

Darren chuckled softly as his hand steadied me in place, pressing the two of us against the rough sandstone walls.

I started to pull away, but then he increased the intensity of his kiss… and I lost all will to move.

After a minute or so, the flood of emotions receded just long enough for me to react with a startling fervor of my own. I found myself kissing Darren back, wrapping my arms around his neck and letting myself fall into the moment.

He was consuming me, and I couldn't breathe. It wasn't enough.

The prince jerked back, sooty lashes shading his eyes as he regarded me in surprise. His chest rose and fell against my own, and for a moment, neither of us spoke.

Gods. Was this why all the girls chased after a prince? For the first time, I understood.

And then the moment came to a halt. The library door

crashed open to reveal an oblivious boy and a pile of scrolls.

Darren released me and staggered back as I steadied myself against the wall. My cheeks were burning and neither of us could look at the other.

I was too afraid of what I would see if I did.

There was a growing collective of voices coming from down the hall.

"Ryiah, is that you?" My brother turned down the passage with the rest of our study group.

I flushed and looked to Darren, but he was gone. The door to the library swung shut with a loud bang. The lanky first-year and his scrolls were all that remained.

"What happened?" Ella's eyes shot between the nameless boy and me. Her scrutiny didn't miss my red face.

"I… I have to go. I'm sorry." I couldn't say anything else. I stumbled past my friends to the barracks without another look back.

What in the name of the gods just happened?

* * *

I arrived at the barracks to find the one person I least wanted to see.

Priscilla.

She shouldn't have caught me off guard, but the memory of what had just happened in the hallway minutes before was still too fresh in my mind. Seeing Priscilla, the girl who everyone believed was intended for the prince, left a bitter taste in the back of my mouth.

What does he see in her?

Priscilla smirked when she saw me enter the room. "You still haven't left, what a shame. I'd have thought a week would change your mind." She was braver when we were alone. "We already have our five apprentices," she added. "You're just wasting your time."

"I'm not going anywhere." My fists were clenched at my sides. She had picked the wrong night to pick a fight.

"You should." The girl held up an elaborately designed dress to her chest and looked at her two friends. "What do you think? My father had the seamstress make this for me. It's perfect for the post-trials ceremony... Do you think Darren will like it?"

The girls fell all over themselves with compliments.

My jaw clenched. I couldn't believe the prince would care about a dress; she was just doing this to provoke me.

Priscilla gave me a sly smile. "Don't worry, Ryiah. No one will see you wearing another ratty hand-me-down for the ceremony. Only the apprentices are noticed."

"The masters would never be daft enough to give an apprenticeship to a girl like you." I was growing angrier by the second. "We both know you are only here to play a part."

One of her friends laughed unexpectedly, only to quickly cover it up with a cough as Priscilla glared at both of us.

"For a commoner, you certainly think highly of yourself. Don't get any delusions, Ryiah. Sir Piers may have believed in you once, but that was before the mid-year duels. You're worthless now."

Her words had a truth that bled, and for a moment, I was tempted to tell her what her precious prince had done. She already hated me, so what was stopping me?

Don't be a fool. You know perfectly well that would be a mistake.

Rather than continue the unpleasant exchange, I headed to the baths.

By the time I returned, Priscilla and her friends were long gone, leaving me alone to the silence of an empty barracks.

Good. The last thing I needed was more time with that witch.

Everyone else was still out, studying, dining, or enjoying one last night of freedom with friends. I should've been doing the same, but I wasn't ready to face the prince. What if I ran into him in the library or the armory? What could I say?

I'd been kissed before.

In Demsh'aa, there'd been a boy... but there had never been a spark, no sense of worlds colliding when his lips had brushed up against mine.

Darren's kiss tonight had everything Jayson's lacked.

It'd made my legs weak and my lungs burst.

I didn't even know I could feel so many things.

Jayson had held me gently, as if I were a doll he hadn't wanted to break. Darren had acted impulsively, kissing me like he couldn't stop even if he wanted to. He hadn't asked permission. He'd taken it, and for some inexplicable reason, I'd let him.

And then I'd kissed him back.

The mere fact that I had liked Darren's kiss was upsetting enough. That my body had betrayed me and acted on its own accord was unfathomable.

There were a thousand reasons why kissing the non-heir, or letting him kiss me, was a mistake. He was a prince. He was fickle. He was rude. He was arrogant. I knew better. I was lowborn. He was *wrong*.

I didn't even like him.

Or did I?

And what about Priscilla? Almost everyone in the Academy, including myself, assumed she and the prince were set to be betrothed and that it was only a matter of time before the engagement was announced.

What was Darren thinking now?

Was I just another conquest? Was that what I wanted? Gods knew I hadn't pulled away or asked questions.

Had Darren been testing me?

I'd seen the look in his eyes when he realized I was kissing him back: *shock*.

What if the kiss was a joke? A horrible, cruel, sadistic joke?

I slammed my fist into my pillow. Blast the prince for being so unreadable. I never knew when to take him at his word, let alone his actions.

Don't trust them, and you can't get hurt. Wasn't that what Ella had told me that day after she saw me arguing with Priscilla and Darren? She'd never told me what happened back at court, and now I was unable to think of anything else.

It doesn't matter what Darren meant by that kiss. I marched out of the barracks and into the snow. I was far too restless to sleep. *You are here for one reason. That reason was never a prince.*

I would fight for an apprenticeship and forget everything else.

TWELVE

THE ACADEMY HAD a longstanding tradition of hazing. I found this out the hard way.

It started three days after our break.

The first time it happened, I didn't think anything of it. If more first-years were taking trips to the infirmary, it was because the pressure was more intense. We were into the second half of our year and Combat was cutthroat. It wasn't uncommon for someone to need a healer once or twice a week.

But then it became an everyday occurrence.

A fire casting sent in the wrong direction? An accident. A not-so-dull blade ramming through flesh and bone? Another accident. Jake and William casting a fissure during our daily runs so that a younger boy pitched forward and broke both arms when he hit the ground? Definitely not an accident.

A first-year spent twelve hours with a healer, and then he resigned the next day. That wasn't an accident.

A couple days later and there was a similar incident in Alchemy. Half a week later in Restoration.

By the second week, we'd lost a couple more and I'd

finally had enough.

"I'm going to report it." Hazing was a tradition, and I could understand its appeal. The first-years left had withstood the Academy's rigorous demands; they wouldn't be swayed by our training or the masters for the rest of the year; they would need an extra push to resign now.

But that didn't mean highborns like Jake and William should be the ones to set the terms. It didn't take much to see that the best in each faction were targeting the ones that threatened their rank. For the most part, that meant the ones with the private schooling and tutors were hazing the lowborns advancing faster than the rest.

I wanted students to leave too. It would better everyone's odds. But I wanted it to be on their terms, not the privileged.

A part of me wondered if the prince was involved, but I couldn't bring myself to check. Darren and I had avoided each other since that night in the hall, and I wasn't sure whether I should be upset or relieved. Ella claimed she'd spotted him with Eve the times the others struck, but that didn't mean he didn't play a part.

"Reporting it would be a bad idea, Ry."

"Why?" I turned to Ella in a huff. "If the victims don't report it, they'll just continue until there's none of us left. The masters need to do something."

"Trust me, they know." Her expression mirrored my frustration. "They just don't care. It's been going on for years. They have a similar practice in the other war schools and even the girls' convent in Devon."

My brother guffawed. "It's not right."

Ruth slammed her book shut with an exasperated groan.

All of us were studying in our usual nook. "If you tell, the others will call you a snitch. Do you really want to be their next victim?"

"I don't care what the school thinks of me. It's not right!"

Ella nudged me with her boot. "It's a supported tradition for a reason, Ry. Mages don't ask others to solve their problems, and hazing is just another way to weed out the weak. Don't give the masters a reason to think you don't belong here."

I hated to admit it, but she had a point. Still... "So I'm just supposed to watch?"

"I wouldn't say that." Ella grinned. "We can definitely give them a reason to think it's more trouble than it's worth."

Excitement bubbled up. "What do you have in mind?"

"Let's give them some accidents of their own."

"I love the way you think."

"I love the way *you* love the way I think."

Alex snorted. "You two are going to get yourselves caught."

"They are going to target you next," Ruth added. "Is that really what you want?"

I thought for a moment, but the answer was already waiting on the tip of my tongue. "I'm lowborn, and Priscilla hates me. It's only a matter of time before they try."

"Well, I don't care if they go after me." Ella wrapped an arm around my shoulder. "Because I've got this one to help me retaliate."

"I hope you two know what you're doing."

"We don't, but that's part of the fun."

The next day, the two brothers tried another "accident"

and ended up in the infirmary instead. Their victim, a brawny lowborn who'd beat William in an earlier sparring match, never even knew she'd almost found herself on the receiving end of their newest attack.

Turns out, I liked leading the hazing a lot more than I thought.

A couple days later, Ella and I redirected another highborn's casting from the back of the library. She'd been trying to sabotage a younger boy. We enjoyed watching her wonder why her magic wouldn't obey.

After two more incidents, the hazing changed. Perhaps the others had grown weary of hurting themselves, but they'd resorted to more appropriate pranks.

Ella and I were almost disappointed.

A boy in Combat woke up screaming to a hoard of snakes hiding out in his bed. One of Priscilla's friends, the girl who had laughed at her expense a week before, found all her belongings drenched in what I could only assume was a slimy mass of fish guts.

"You know it's going to be us soon." Ella eyed Priscilla as we sat down for the evening meal. Two more weeks had passed, and Combat was running out of first-years who hadn't been hazed. Only one of their victims had left since their practice changed, but it didn't mean the hazing was any more pleasant.

"I miss the older hazing. No one is leaving now." Ruth pushed some braised vegetables around her plate. "I need the best odds I can get."

"You're highborn." Clayton scratched his neck. "It's different for the rest of us. We deserve to last the year."

She narrowed her eyes. "If you are afraid of a bit of trouble, you shouldn't have joined the Academy."

"Hey, hey." Alex spread his arms out on the table. "Let's not fight."

The pressure was getting to all of us.

James ducked his head. "Odds are what brought on hazing in the first place."

"You have no room to talk." Ruth rolled her eyes. "There are only ten of you in Restoration left. We've more in Alchemy."

Ella groaned. "I wish we had ten. Those are much better odds than thirty-three in Combat."

"True enough." Ruth sighed. "I hate to say it, but I'm glad I'm not Ryiah. They are probably saving the worst for her." She gave me a look. "No offense."

Ugh. I groaned. I didn't want to think about a bunch of snakes in my bed. I'd already lost enough sleep over the prince. Now I was keeping both eyes open in the barracks for pranks. I could only imagine what Priscilla or Jake had in store for me. I'd seen them watching me in the last couple of days.

"Why do you think they are after her?" Alex blinked. "They never found out what she and Ella did."

"Because Priscilla hates your sister." Ruth stared at my brother. "*How* have you not noticed that?"

Alex shrugged. "I thought it was the prince. He went after her during orientation."

I stared at my plate, using my fork to stab small indents into a slice of roasted potato.

"Ryiah?" Ella prompted.

I glanced up. "Right. Probably them both."

I excused myself, promising to meet up with Ella for our nightly practice outside the armory. I needed to stop by the barracks first; I'd left one of my books behind.

The last thing I wanted to do was discuss the prince. Even the mention of his name brought back memories of that night, and I didn't want to remember it.

Yes, I'd enjoyed that kiss, but I was mortal. It wasn't a crime, just a lack of judgment on my part.

"Ryiah?"

I almost jumped out of my skin. Leaning against the wall was Darren. I hadn't seen him until he spoke.

My heart began to beat wildly as blood rushed my face. I'd done a good job of avoiding him for weeks, and now in seconds, I was undone. I didn't like this effect.

Was I excited? Petrified? Was it possible I could be both?

Best to appear unaffected and aloof.

"H-hey." Well that failed.

"Can we—" The prince's eyes darted across my face and then to the wall; he looked guilty and pale. "—can we talk? Outside?"

"I... n-no. I have s-somewhere to be." I was headed to the barracks, but if he was headed there too, I was going to find a new destination inside. Was a book really that important? Not if it meant going somewhere with him.

There were too many risks. The worst one being I would let him kiss me again.

That I might wish he would.

I bit down on my lip as I stepped back the way I had come.

Darren reached out. "Wait!"

My eyes caught on his, and he pulled back a second before our skin touched. There was a flare of recognition that stopped him from taking my hand.

For a moment, the two of us just stood there in silence.

Gods, a part of me wanted to ask him about that kiss. He was staring right back, and I could see questions written across his face. He wanted to ask me too.

I parted my lips.

"What did you—?"

"Go back to your friends, Ryiah."

What?

First he wanted to talk, and now he ordered me away. He looked away. Was he really that ashamed of me?

Suddenly I was furious.

He was the one who kissed *me*, not the other way around.

I only kissed him back because… because, well blast it, it didn't matter, because he kissed me first.

Darren should apologize for not asking *my* permission. He had no right to act like I was an embarrassment.

"Really?" I jerked my chin up angrily. "First you assault me. Then you avoid me for weeks. And now you send me on my way like I'm a mistake?"

"You think I *assaulted* you?" Darren bristled. "You kissed me back, Ryiah."

"I didn't kiss you back." It was a blatant lie, but I didn't care. "And take note, you are supposed to *ask*."

"Well, you certainly didn't protest."

"I tried to push you away, but you were too wrapped up in—" My cheeks burned hotter as I stammered an explanation. "—in assaulting me!"

His eyes flashed. "Girls don't complain. And believe me, there've been plenty."

How dare he!

My voice dripped with spite. "Not every girl welcomes the advances of a weakling prince with no chance at a throne, even one so lowborn as me."

It was cold and untrue, but I wanted to hurt him in any way that I could. His dismissal stung more than I cared to admit.

"I could have any girl in this Academy." Darren's words were clipped and cold. "You were just a mistake."

It was a punch to the gut, and I should have expected it, but for some reason, he still caught me by surprise.

I took a hitching breath and swallowed, hard. I couldn't even come up with a retort and tears were threatening to break.

I wouldn't give him the satisfaction of seeing me cry.

"G-get out of my way." My voice caught as I started to push past.

"No, Ryiah, don't—"

It was too late.

The moment my hand twisted on the knob, a sea of red dropped from the sky.

Buckets of gore covered every inch of my clothes.

Rivulets of scarlet dripped from my hair, my face, my arms, and my legs... everywhere.

"Go back to where you came from, lowborn."

Jake, William, and Priscilla were standing just outside the door with empty buckets in hand. Between that and their malignant smiles, it didn't take much to ascertain their roles.

My skin burned beneath the plaster of repugnant red.

"Go home, Ryiah," Priscilla repeated Jake's earlier taunt. "This school was never meant for commoners."

I swiped at the blood on my face. "I might be a commoner, but at least I don't resort to petty hazing to eliminate my competition." The blood and the guts shouldn't have bothered me really. They were harmless, and I'd been expecting an attack for days... But for some reason, I was seething.

No, not some reason. Because of *him.*

Darren stepped out from behind me, eyes averted, to stand beside his friends. His clothes were immaculate. *No blood.*

I could not control the shaking of my fists. He'd known exactly what was waiting for me beyond that door. Hadn't he asked me to follow him outside?

He'd planned this. After... after I'd finally started to—

"I have to say, the pig's blood was a nice touch." Priscilla smirked. "When Darren first proposed the idea, I was reluctant. But seeing you now, well, it obviously worked. You should see the look on your face."

There was a loud pounding in the back of my skull. All I could hear was the *boom, boom* of my heart thumping away, echoing right into my bones.

I was seconds away from flinging that condescending traitor as far as my limits would go.

I couldn't care less about Priscilla or the hazing. This was *personal.*

"Don't be a fool, Ryiah." Darren's eyes were locked on the fists at my sides. "Plenty of first-years get hazed."

"But never you, right?" If he thought I was reckless before... I locked eyes with the enemy. "Time to change that."

In that moment, I didn't care that he was a prince or the most powerful first-year in the Academy. All I knew was that he was a boy who hurt me, tricked me, kissed me, betrayed me, and somehow won my trust against every instinct and piece of advice I'd ever received.

I was a fool, but Darren, he was something else— something twisted and cold. Gods, I couldn't believe I'd ever imagined him any differently.

Don't trust a wolf, he'd warned me, and yet, here I'd done exactly that.

"Dueling will only get you expelled, Ryiah."

"Are you afraid you'll lose?" I taunted. "Because I'm not." It was a lie, but lighting that prince on fire would sure feel good while it lasted.

Even if I spent a day in the infirmary after.

"Give the wench a lesson!" Jake urged. "If you don't—"

"I will!" Priscilla leaped forward and our castings shot out in an instant.

Before the attacks could clash, a wave of power crushed them both. I watched our powers explode in the air in shimmers of violet and gold.

"Let her be. No one is dueling today."

I glared at the prince as Priscilla pouted. "Why not?"

"She's not worth it."

The words cut like a knife.

I wasn't worth it? I was worth a *thousand* of him. I didn't toy with people because I was some sadistic, brooding prince.

The four of them started toward the barracks, leaving me dripping blood onto the stone walkway.

"Fight me, you coward!" I lunged forward and sent a blast rattling the ground. My magic barreled forward, straight toward the prince's unguarded back.

Darren spun around.

With the flick of his wrist, my casting rebounded harmlessly into the forest.

His dark eyes met mine, unreadable.

"Fight me!"

"If I fight you," he said quietly, "they'll send you home. Is that really what you want?"

It wasn't, but I couldn't look at him without fire singing my veins. All of my senses were bursting, screaming at me to cast.

I looked away and clenched my fists harder.

"That's what I thought."

I needed to say something, but he was already turning to leave.

"It turns out I was wrong." I raised my voice and called out after his group, watching as they walked away. For a moment—just a moment—the prince's shoulders tensed. "I never made a mistake. You are *exactly* who I expected."

Darren didn't bother to reply.

But then again, I never expected he would.

* * *

An hour later, Ella found me in the barracks, furiously scrubbing the stain of pig's blood from my skin.

"Oh, Ryiah, I'm so sorry."

I didn't respond. I just kept washing.

She grabbed a cloth to help rinse the red from my tangled hair.

"You never showed up for our practice," she said quietly. "Was it Priscilla?"

"Darren too."

"The prince?" She gnawed on her lip. "Not that I don't put it past him, but he hasn't been involved in any of the hazing. Why you?"

I watched the crimson haze twist and curl around the tub's drain. "Why not?"

"Ryiah." She placed her hand on my wrist. "What happened between the two of you?"

"I should have listened to you," was all I meant to say, but instead I found myself spilling the secret I'd been holding onto for the last month.

When I was finished, my cheeks were burning with shame. I couldn't believe I'd gone against my best friend's advice. She'd been warning me about the prince all along. It was like my old friends in the village back home. I used to tell those girls to stay away from my brother, but inevitably they'd been drawn to him like flies. Each one had thought that somehow she was special and he wouldn't break her heart like the last.

Darren hadn't broken my heart, but he'd broken our friendship, and somehow that was worse. All these months of building my trust and helping me just so he could play me for a fool. He was probably having a good laugh.

"I think it's time I told you what really happened in Devon." Ella's gaze was apologetic; she hadn't spoken a word until I was done. Even now, there'd been no judgment, just pity. "There's something I think you should know..." Her eyes clouded and she took a shaky breath. "I would have told you sooner, but I was ashamed."

* * *

That night, I stared up at the ceiling, long after Ella and the rest of our barracks had fallen asleep.

How could I have been so naïve?

For some reason, I'd really thought there was something genuine to the prince, something likable and kind, something that could justify the reckless attraction and confusion I'd felt in spite of all his sarcasm and condescending talk.

Now I knew with certainty there was not. What Darren had done to me was terrible, but what he'd done to Ella was worse.

No wonder she hated the prince.

Ella and her family had lived in the capital for years, in one of the palace's many rooms. She'd grown up playing with the children of court, though the two princes had usually not been a part of that group.

"Blayne and Darren were too important to mingle with most of the court... It was only as they got older that they started paying attention to the rest of us. Darren was private and aloof, much like he is now. He spent most of his time with the knights. I hardly ever saw him. Blayne was the older, more sociable of the two. He was handsome, popular, self-aware. He was also charming, and he could do no wrong."

Ella had only been twelve when the crown prince had lured her away and attempted to rape her in the midst of a ball. She'd tried to fight him off, but Blayne had muffled her screams.

"But Darren heard me anyway. When he came to investigate the shouting, he found his older brother on top of me. He could see there'd been a scuffle. It was obvious from the rips in my dress and the long scratches on Blayne's neck. Darren looked me right in the eyes, Ryiah. He knew exactly what was happening."

But Darren had just walked away.

"At first, I thought maybe he'd gone for help... but no one ever came. He left me there, Ryiah. That's the kind of person he is."

The only reason Blayne never succeeded in his mission that day was by accident. In the heat of their struggle, the boy had slammed Ella's head against the wall and her powers had knocked the crown prince unconscious.

Until that day, I hadn't even known I'd had magic. I tried casting for months afterward, but it took another two years to learn.

Her family left court the very next day.

Ella had warned me repeatedly. She'd said it since day one. Don't trust Darren. Don't trust the non-heir. Don't trust a prince.

The overwhelming hostility had never made sense.

Now it did.

Darren had willingly stood by as his sixteen-year-old brother attempted to rape my best friend.

Prince Darren, second son to King Lucius III, was the most base, amoral person I'd ever met.

He wanted to try and send me home by pig's blood and an

embarrassing kiss? Did he really think that would work?

He'd just guaranteed my stay.

I was not going anywhere.

Someone like that would not *win.*

If the prince was to be an apprentice, so was I.

The whole blasted school thought he was a prodigy and the next Black Mage. Maybe he was and maybe he wasn't, but the gods would have to stop me from trying to steal that away.

* * *

If I wanted the prince's head on a stick, it was nothing next to my brother.

"The prince did *what*?"

I grabbed my brother's wrist in an attempt to quiet him over the morning meal. "Please, Alex," I begged, "don't make a scene."

Much to my dismay, rumor had spread around the compound in the span of a night. Ella hadn't said anything— she was too loyal to me—but Jake in particular had made a big show about regaling the men's barracks with the hazing while my brother was present.

I'd had no choice but to fill Alex and our friends in on the rest. I'd kept out certain details. As far as I knew, Darren hadn't told anyone about that kiss, but my brother heard the gist: prince befriends and betrays girl; then he and his friends share a good laugh.

Alex was the levelheaded twin, the pacifist... except when it came to me. Then brotherly instinct took over, and no one, not even me, could calm him down.

The last time I'd seen him this upset was when his best

friend Jayson called an end to our courtship. It'd been amicable, but that hadn't stopped my brother from ending a ten-year friendship and swearing that he would gut the trader's son, should he ever come calling again.

Alex had broken many hearts in his wake, but the gods should fear if anyone ever hurt his sister. I had tried to point out as much the last time, but it hadn't gone over too well.

My brother broke free of my hold and took off toward the front of the room.

I scrambled over the bench. "Alex!"

Ella stood up. "No—"

It was too late.

The two of us raced after my brother, calling his name, but Alex had already shoved his way past Jake and William and grabbed the non-heir by the neck of his tunic.

The entire room went silent, all eyes trained on Alex as he sent a fist flying into the prince's face.

Alex had only a split-second of advantage. Moments later, my brother was airborne, plummeting into the table behind him, as Darren stood brushing himself off angrily. There was blood dripping down the prince's face.

"You spineless predator!" Alex roared as Jake and William held him down. "All you do is prey on the weak!" He swore as Jake's fist collided with his nose.

No, Alex! I started to run.

"You think you're the next Black Mage." Alex spewed blood and saliva through his teeth as William kicked him hard, and again. "All I see is someone too insecure to let anyone with potential try. You think you can bully everyone into leaving. Well, my sister Ryiah—"

At my name, Darren started, his knuckles grazing his platter as he jumped from his seat.

"—is staying and so will anyone else you haze, if I have anything to do with it!"

I reached Alex's side just as Jake raised his knee. Magic was pulsing in my palm—I didn't want to fight, but that was before they laid a hand on my brother.

"Stop."

Jake lowered his leg to glance at the prince.

"That's enough." Darren shoved the boy aside to offer Alex a hand as he struggled to rise.

My brother spat at it. "I might not be a mage of Combat," Alex croaked, "but at least I'm not a tyrant."

The prince's eyes were still locked on my brother as Ella thrust her way forward, offering Alex her shoulder so that we held him up by the pit of his arms.

"Healers don't win wars," Darren said.

"Neither do monsters."

The prince stared at Alex and then me for a long moment, anger burning in the dark recesses of his eyes.

Then he turned and left the room without another word.

My brother's words echoed long after.

* * *

In the weeks that followed, my brother became a bit of a hero.

Hazing stopped. There hadn't been a single incident since my bout with the pig's blood, and the whole school had been witness to my brother's confrontation with the prince.

None of us had any doubt who was responsible for the change.

Alex, for one, was enjoying his newfound fame. We'd gained a lot of new faces to our study group. Many, like the rest of us, had been upset by the hazing but unwilling to speak out... The other half, of course, was a pretty new fan base.

For a while, we were accepting of our new members. The larger our group, the better our defense, and so on. I was still wary the prince might retaliate, but nothing happened as the weeks flew by, and it quickly became apparent that the latter was more trouble than they were worth.

"If I hear giggling in the library one more time..."

I glowered over at the cluster of girls—and a couple boys—who held on to my brother's every word.

"Just look at them fawning over him!" Ella sawed away at a defenseless piece of cabbage over our evening meal; we'd been restricted to the back end of the table in light of our new flock. "They're treating him like he's a god... Gwen and Kylan wouldn't have looked twice at him a month ago!"

"You sound jealous." *Please don't be jealous; please just be annoyed that they are crowding our table.*

Ella glowered. "I'm not jealous. I'm disgusted." She eyed my promiscuous brother, who was now seated a good five spaces ahead, surrounded by a cult of his newfound admirers. If we got any more, we'd be exiled from our own table.

"It'll pass." It had better.

"And if it doesn't?"

"A bloody massacre?"

Ella didn't comment. She was too busy watching Alex to hear my joke.

Does she like him? There was a sharp twinge in my side. Had my best friend started to fall for my brother over the course of our year and I'd failed to notice? All those nights I'd gone away to study, had he been walking her to the barracks and charming her all along?

You're not the only one who likes someone you shouldn't.

I swallowed hard and forced myself to chew, swallowing the tasteless gruel that seemed to make up so many of our meals. Blast it, Ella wasn't supposed to like him! She was *my* friend.

"He'll break your heart." The words slipped out, and I couldn't take them back.

"I know." Ella shook her head with an exasperated sigh. "I know it so well."

At least she was fighting it. *There's my girl.*

Still, as soon as my friend looked away, I could feel my brother's eyes on our section. It didn't take years of practice to recognize those crinkled lines in the corner of his eyes.

Alex was enjoying this. He was *enjoying* making Ella squirm after months of her turning away his advance.

Idiot boy.

I stabbed at my bowl, letting the metal clatter against the stone surface. Alex was going to ruin everything. It was worse because I could see a part of him cared.

Idiot brother.

My eyes shot to the front of the room in spite of myself, to the object of so many confusing thoughts. He didn't look my way once.

Idiot me.

THIRTEEN

"I'M SURE ALL of you have been wondering what the trials are going to be like." Master Eloise entered the giant library, bearing a mountain of scrolls in her arms.

Everyone stopped talking at once. There were two months left to our year, and those of us left were restless and tired, an odd combination but one that fit. We'd been asking the same question for weeks. There were rumors of past trials, of course, but we needed to hear it for ourselves.

Ella's nails dug into my arm; she was just as nervous as me. The final threshold meant *everything*; if we failed, there was no second chance. The school admitted a first-year only once.

"Some of you might already be familiar with how the end of year works—through family or friends who attended our Academy in the past—but I can assure you it's a completely different experience when you are the one undergoing the trials. Students tend to forget everything they knew."

Master Isaac joined his counterpart at the podium. "To a contender of Combat, brute strength is everything. I can hardly deny this. You've spent countless hours learning how to fight and to cast, but potential and training are not all that make up the great faction of Combat, and they will not be all the judges look for in your trials.

"The judges want to see a warrior, not a soldier." His lips thinned. "Soldiers follow other soldiers into battle—they obey orders, fight valiantly. A warrior can do the same, but he is also a commander, an independent mercenary, and a strategist. The warrior fills many roles, and the capacity to do so requires an intelligence that ordinary soldiers are not trained to possess."

The room was filled with absolute silence as everyone quietly mulled over the masters' warning.

"In the course of your study, Master Eloise and I have attempted to impart the groundwork that would behoove a warrior's learned wisdom. You've been introduced to the principles of climate, Crown and Council Law, geography, strategic planning, diplomacy... and, most importantly, the history of Jerar. Each one of these disciplines will play a pivotal role in an apprenticeship, should you be so fortunate. Because of this, there are two trials for each faction."

Two? Something churned in my gut. I thought we'd only have one.

"The first test is a replication of the mid-year duels, but the second is an application of your studies in this classroom." Master Eloise shifted her grip on the stand. "Each of you will be given a twenty-minute audience alone with a panel of judges. They will provide you the scenarios, and you will be expected to give an appropriate response. They *expect* to hear citations from Academy lectures, but what they *want* is to understand how you would make that knowledge a part of your own approach. The tactics of warfare are forever changing. The more creative your answer is, the more they'll take notice."

A couple of students groaned, and I thanked the gods I'd made it a point to carry out my nightly studies.

"If you feel unprepared at this point, it's too late." Master Isaac's reprimand for the crowd was harsh. "We've already entered the final course of your study. Regrets will only get you so far."

In other words, *welcome to the beginning of the end.*

* * *

If I thought my peers were motivated before, it was nothing to the final stretch.

If a first-year wasn't in the library, they were on the field, practicing drills or conjuring spells out by the armory until the servants dragged them back to the barracks kicking and screaming. Most of us weren't even aware of the passing of days. We were far too consumed with our studies to take notice.

It was a daily occurrence to find my friends vomiting onto the field and crawling on their knees.

The only reason we took time to eat was to line our stomachs enough to get through the next round of drills. The staff had taken to handheld goods—anything a student could eat on the run. And we were running, always running. To the barracks, the library, our lessons, even in sleep.

We smelled like something that crawled out of a swamp, even the highborn girls.

After a couple more days, the servants stopped trying to enforce curfew entirely. There was no point in trying to uphold a rule when the entire student body was in chaos. It wasn't uncommon for half our year to show up bedraggled at the barracks first thing in the morning with only a quick change of clothes. Ella even started joining me for late-night sessions on the third floor to escape the noise.

I almost forgot I had a brother. Alex and the rest of Restoration were huddled in the infirmary practicing their magic, desperately pouring over scrolls on healing for hours on end. I saw him in passing with some of his admirers, but that was all the time we got.

There was too much on the line to slack during the final sprint.

There was too much on the line for all of us.

* * *

Ella turned to me with a quill sticking out of her hair; there were ink stains all over her sleeves. "I don't think I'm ready for this."

"Are any of us?" I stifled a yawn, twisting in my seat. It was a new trick I'd learned—never stop moving if you wanted to stay awake. The last month had sucked every last drop of enthusiasm out of me, and if I wasn't careful, I'd find myself sleepwalking straight out the Academy doors.

Why did I want a robe so much? Surely the Cavalry wasn't *that* bad. I didn't need to be the best. Life as a soldier would still bring me an escape.

Or maybe I could be a knight? That was a nice compromise, right?

I didn't have to go back to Demsh'aa and take up the family trade. There were still options if I failed the Academy trials.

If I fail, ha, more like when.

"Half the faction is sleeping." Ella's eyes were red like mine and there were dark circles underneath.

I repeated our month-long mantra: "Sleep and fail."

"It better be worth it." She gripped the leg of the bench. "I'm dozing off even in this blasted chill."

It really was colder on the third floor, but it also kept us awake. Now that we weren't in hiding, we could take up space on one of the other floors, but that would mean proximity to *them*. Besides, I liked my little alcove; I'd grown fond of it over the year.

I jerked my chin to the second floor. "The other half is here, like us." Three tolls past midnight. *They* were still pouring over a mountain of scrolls for the hundredth time while Clayton snored loudly on the study's couch below. As long as they were awake, we would be too.

"Do you think they are threatened by us?"

We'd improved a lot over the course of the year; I shrugged. "Jake and William, maybe. But not Priscilla or Eve, they still outperform most of the year."

"And not him."

Never *him*. I bit down on my cheek, fighting to keep focus and not return to the questions best left untouched. Ever since the hazing, we'd avoided one another like the plague.

"For a while, I really thought he wanted you to succeed." Her weary eyes met mine. "I know what happened to me… but I thought… well, I suppose it doesn't matter either way."

No, it didn't.

"You know," she said, "that's only three."

Ella was implying that there were still two spots for an apprenticeship; I sighed. "There's also Ray, Myron, and

Torrance. That's six at the top of our faction."

"No one is a guarantee. Those last three… we've beaten them in practice."

"Once for every three times they beat us in drills." I didn't like those odds.

"Once is all it takes."

Gods, I hoped so. Because after everything, I needed to win.

I gave Ella a weary smile, and the two of us returned to our books.

Throughout my entire stay, I'd been able to tell myself the trials were months away, that I had plenty of time to become the greatest Combat mage the school had ever seen. Now ten months had come and gone, and I had no more room to pretend.

I was as good as I was going to get. I only hoped it would be enough.

* * *

"Welcome, proud families, friends, visiting mages, and nobility. Today marks the beginning of our first-year trials. I am Master Barclae, the current master of the Academy, and I will be your guide to all that encompasses the competition for the next seven days…"

Master Barclae continued on as I scanned the rows of high-rising benches across the training field. I knew my family was somewhere in the audience, but with the sheer magnitude of people and the dramatic costumes of the spectating nobility in front, I couldn't make out one face from the next.

Right now, all forty-three of the remaining first-years,

myself included, were lined up facing the stands so that the audience could get a good look at the surviving applicants. It was a bit degrading to be introduced by each of our factions' training masters while the first couple of rows whispered amongst one another.

I had no idea who most of the spectators were, but they all had opinions about us. Which one looked the strongest. Who was the weakest. Who would be apprenticed. And who would fail.

Barclae had gathered all of us that morning before the visitors had started to arrive. He and the rest of the staff had explained exactly what we could expect to see in the next few days.

The trials were to be a weeklong affair, and our families were not the only ones to be present.

There were also graduated mages and the Crown and its ensuing court. Until that morning, I hadn't even realized the king and his court came *every* year. Since the Crown was funding the Academy, the trials were an opportunity to check on its progress, and the trials made for entertainment for the court. Nobility contributed donations just for the privilege to attend. They made sport of the event, taking bets and wagers on the rest of us.

A part of me was appalled, but Barclae was quick to note that extra coin helped fund the training of the apprentices. First-year study was financed by the Crown, but the training of apprentice mages and the salaries of the Academy's prestigious staff, *those* were financed by the trials.

Sjeka also made more than half of its yearly income from a week's worth of board. The village raised the rent on all of its housing, which the nobility and visiting mages easily afforded. The king and his family, apparently, had rooms in the Academy. A part of me wondered why Darren had slept in the barracks, but that thought was squandered as quickly as it came.

Further south was cheaper board, much less accommodating and nearly a two-hour walk from the Academy, but that was where many of the visiting lowborn families, including my own, were expected to stay during the trials.

So now here we were, forty-three fumbling first-years for all the world to see. Fifteen of us would become mages. The rest would be a courtier's joke for a month or two until the shame was finally forgotten.

Before a sea of hungry faces, at their own private bench just beyond my row and facing the audience, were the Three. In glistening, many-layered silk robes edged in gold, the Black Mage of Combat, the Red Mage of Restoration, and the Green Mage of Alchemy sat patiently awaiting the end of Barclae's welcome. Our reigning Council of Magic, the three Colored Robes, was to serve on the panel of judges for our first-year trials alongside the master of the Academy.

When they'd first arrived, the stands had gone wild, and for good reason. The Three were the most important and powerful mages in Jerar. Fame like that followed you for years to come.

When Barclae was done giving his speech, the crowd had still not gotten over its initial excitement. Half the stands rushed after the departing three, while the rest of the mass, undoubtedly the visiting families, stumbled across the field, attempting to greet the students they had come to see.

I didn't bother to move. The crowd was a sea, and I had a much better chance waiting for the commotion to pass.

"*Ryiah*!" a high-pitched yelp was all I needed to hear.

My younger brother was near.

I barely had time to turn before a mass of gangly limbs crashed into me. Derrick squeezed my ribs so tight I could barely breathe.

"I missed you too!" I choked out.

"I can't believe... you and Alex... still here." Derrick's words were muffled by my tunic. "Never thought... this far!"

"Neither did I." I was still drawing large gasps of air.

"Derrick." There was a throaty chuckle. "Let your sister breathe."

Derrick released his grip, and I winced. I couldn't believe how much he'd changed in one year. He'd outgrow me soon. My little brother was not so little anymore. Three years no longer seemed like a lifetime apart.

My parents wore ear-to-ear grins as they stood just a short pace away. They'd patiently waited their turn.

"Mom, Dad." I hugged each of them fiercely and then stepped back so I could take them in... My vision started to blur, and I blushed. Was I really crying? It'd only been a year.

"Has it been that terrible?" My father looked alarmed.

"No," I stammered, "it's been..." Amazing? Terrifying? Somewhere between? "I just missed all of you."

And it hadn't hit me until now. I'd been so wrapped up in the Academy, I'd lost sight of anything else.

Derrick circled me, taking in the changes to my appearance. "You're so fit now," he crowed. "You look like a *knight*."

I snorted. "Not even close. Wait until you see Sir Piers. Or my master of Combat, Narhari."

"You chose Combat?" Derrick whistled. "I *knew* you would."

"Not Alchemy?" My mother arched a delicate brow. "But you and Alex are so well-versed in herb lore and tonic making!"

I grinned. "Alex chose Restoration, Mom."

"You two." She sighed. "Always one to rebel."

"I'm choosing Combat next year," Derrick volunteered.

"And there goes our third." My father shook his head. "Choosing the easiest path has never been a part of our children's destiny."

"Where's Alex?" Derrick had finally noticed that our brother was nowhere to be found.

"Where else?" I gave him a look. "Probably off with a parade full of admirers."

My mother scowled. "He's still at it?"

"He never stopped. He—"

A familiar voice coughed loudly behind me. "Are you going to introduce me, Ry?"

I turned to find Ella and her family grinning broadly behind us.

"This is Ella." I dragged my friend forward by the crook of her arm for introductions. "She's the reason I'm still here."

The boy at her side chuckled. "She seemed to imply it was

the other way around."

"Ry." Her grin widened. "This is my brother Jeff. You know, the one who *didn't* last a year."

"Why subject yourself to that torture?" He gave a mock shudder, eyes dancing. "I leave that to my little sister."

Ella and Jeffrey went on to exchange insults, and then our parents finally stepped in to finish the round of introductions we'd all but forgotten. It was *nice*. Her parents were a lot less decorated than most of the highborn families here, and they didn't seem to care that their daughter befriended a lowborn girl.

"Is that Ruth's family?" I nudged Ella's arm. Our friend was standing off the field with a formal looking pair. They looked uncomfortable and stiff.

"Don't bother," Ella murmured under her breath. "They are one of the old families of court. They wouldn't even look at me because my father was lowborn before he took up the sword."

"Ah."

My eyes locked on a familiar mass of curls in the distance. "And there's Alex. Finally ready to abandon his little cult."

Jeff looked to Ella with a smirk. "The one you were talking about?"

My friend stared out at my twin, lips pursed. "He's trouble, that's what he is."

Jeff turned his attention to the other half of the field, unperturbed. "Is that Priscilla?"

Ella elbowed her brother, hard. "She hasn't changed one bit."

"Priscilla is not half as beautiful as your lovely sister here." Alex had finally arrived.

Ella flushed, and I kicked his shin, hard.

Alex wasn't perturbed. "Mom, Dad, how are you?"

"How are we?" My father arched a brow. "Better, now that our son has finally decided to grace us with his presence."

"What about me?"

Alex ruffled our younger brother's hair. "I missed you too, squirt."

Derrick gave him a look. "I'm taller than you were at twelve."

"Still little."

"And this is why I like Ry best."

"You two just enjoy picking fights. Some of us prefer to *heal*."

"Enough." My father interrupted their squabble before Derrick and Alex could go head to head. "Let's have a tour of this Academy, shall we?"

Ella's parents cut in that they would like to see it too, and then we were off. We got five steps into the atrium before Derrick's jaw dropped to the floor.

"Is that the king?"

I squinted up the stairs. Sure enough, leaning against the second-floor railing was Darren, another boy of similar features, and an older man with stark white hair and a dark countenance who I could only assume was their father, King Lucius III.

The king of the realm held himself much the way his sons did, composed and almost disconcertingly aloof. The man wore his hair short like his heir, but with a meticulously trimmed beard that was his alone. Both father and eldest bore the same piercing blue eyes, and I wasn't sure what was worse, the sharp cobalt of ice or the bottomless fire of Darren's garnet brown.

Each of them was dressed in the same stiff, fitted brocade that was associated with the Crown. It was a severe, heavy material that gave off little movement. While the king and his heir wore their robes with thick embroidery and chain adornments, Darren wore his simply, though he still bore the hematite stone pendant around his neck.

So this is his family.

I knew I needed to stop staring, but I couldn't. There was something about the three of them together that made me wonder what it had been like for the youngest before the Academy. Their air was stifling and cold.

Prince Blayne shifted on the stair and caught sight of the crowd of us staring. His lip curved up at the side as his gaze locked on Ella.

"He's looking at us," Derrick whispered, awed.

But awe was the last thing on my mind. My friend had tensed at my side, and apprehension crawled up the back of my spine. Not even her parents knew the reason she'd insisted on leaving the palace years before.

"Let's get out of here." I tugged Ella forward as Prince Blayne leaned into his brother to whisper something in his ear.

A second later, Darren was turning and frowning over at Ella. His eyes caught on mine, and that frown turned into a glare.

"What was that?" Derrick must have noticed the look that passed as we exited the hall.

I finished guiding our families to the front of the Academy. "It's complicated."

We said our farewells to our families at the entrance and promised to catch up the next day during the breaks of the tourney. Our parents got along enough to share a dinner in a nearby pub, and a part of me was proud to see how easy a friendship could be. The Academy was a trial in every sense, and I was grateful to Ella to have one thing that was steady and easy in the chaos of everything else.

Alex, Ella, and I headed back down the corridor in the direction of our barracks. We'd only just crossed the atrium when we found ourselves face to face with the crown prince. While I couldn't be sure, I had the distinct impression he'd been waiting. A second later, my thoughts were confirmed when Prince Blayne stepped out directly in front of us, cutting off our exit.

"Lady Ella—" Blayne ignored my brother and me. "—it's been too long." He reached out and snatched my friend's hand.

Ella instantly paled, and I could see fear written all over her face.

She was usually so outspoken, but now she was as silent as a rock.

I took Ella's other arm, seeing as how Blayne still hadn't let go of her first.

"Let's return to the barracks," I said loudly. I didn't bother to acknowledge the prince—and tugged at my friend's arm. "We need to get back."

The crown prince sneered at me. "Ella will leave when she's ready." His grip hadn't lessened, and I could see white marks on her arm.

Alex put himself directly in front of the prince. "Let her go."

My brother was probably confused by the strange encounter, but even he could see something was wrong. I instantly forgave Alex for all his previous transgressions.

"Get out of my way, lowborn," the prince snarled. "This is none of your concern."

Alex opened his mouth to reply with some chosen words—and I right there alongside him—when Darren appeared, seemingly out of nowhere.

"Let them be."

"Darren—"

"Blayne."

The two princes glowered at one another before the elder finally dropped his brother's stare. A second later, Blayne dropped Ella's arm.

"We will catch up some other time, my sweet," he promised.

My fist was clenched as the crown prince sauntered down the hall without another word. If he tried anything with Ella—

Darren turned on us and fixated his anger at me. "Get out of here," he snapped. "Why are you still standing there?"

I bristled. "You don't have to—"

"Come on, Ry." Alex's fingers dug into my wrist. Even he knew better than to antagonize two princes; I just saw red wherever the non-heir was concerned.

And just like that, we were gone. There was no point in sticking around.

You pick a fight with Darren now, you'll find yourself hanged for attacking a prince. I sighed. *The king is here. Do you really want to throw away everything for him?*

I didn't.

Ella turned to me as soon as we had entered the barracks and my brother was gone. "Thank you, Ry." She had refused to discuss Blayne in front of Alex, and as far as he knew, the prince was like that with all highborns. He'd been especially upset for her; it had been almost sweet. "I... I don't know why I..."

I put my hand on her shoulder; she didn't have to explain. "I won't let him come near you again, I promise."

Her smile was timid. "I'm lucky to have you as a friend, Ry."

"I think you and I would have found each other, one way or another," I said, grinning. "How else would we have survived a full year of Piers and Narhari?"

She laughed, and the two of us relaxed into a comfortable silence.

"That was nice of your brother, too." Her words were timid. It was the first time I'd ever heard her sound somewhat nervous. "Alex... he really cares about his friends, doesn't he?"

I sighed, not sure I wanted to encourage my friend, or my brother. Things were complicated enough as it was. "You're my best friend, a sister he wants to protect." I was such a liar for letting her down, but I couldn't bear the thought of Alex breaking her heart.

"Oh." She sounded crestfallen, and a part of me flinched. I was a terrible friend.

Ella finally managed a tight smile. "Did you see Ruth earlier? Poor thing, I don't think she'll be sleeping at all tonight."

Thank the gods Combat doesn't go first. A small part of me wondered if it'd be better just to get our trials over with sooner, not that we had any choice in the matter.

"Our turn will come soon enough," I finally grumbled.

"We made it this far." Ella faced me from her bunk, black curls tumbling from her face. "We'll make it to the end, Ry."

I prayed she was right.

FOURTEEN

PARENTS ARRIVED EARLY the next morning, looking better rested than any of their children. Since the first four hours of the Alchemy trials were not for public viewing, my family and Ella's took a tour of the village instead. Most visiting families did the same, and this time, Alex and I were able to tell our parents and Derrick a bit more about our experiences at the Academy. When we returned to the school around noon, a quarter of the nobility, including the Crown, was noticeably absent.

A servant tending to the afternoon meal was the one to offer up an explanation to the rest of us. Apparently, the first half of the Alchemy trials actually *was* viewable—for a price.

Usually first-year trials were held in the stadium to accommodate a larger audience, but for the brewing stages of Alchemy, students needed certain accommodations. As a result, seating in the upstairs laboratory was awarded to the highest bidders. Nobility paid handsomely for the experience; it usually helped them win wagers in the second half of the Alchemy trials.

In a little over an hour, the rest of the school was gathered at the raised seating bordering the Academy stadium. I'd always wondered why there were so many stairs; now I knew.

As we settled into our seats, I noted the rest of the school was there as well. No first-year wanted to miss the trials, even if we were better off studying for our own. There wasn't one face missing from the crowd. Watching the culmination of everyone's struggle was the highlight of our year. We were terrified and fascinated in the same breath.

The crowd drew silent, and I glanced across the field. Master Tera and the twelve students of Alchemy had arrived. Each first-year carried a small wooden crate filled with flasks of differing colors and sizes. Some liquids were translucent and bubbling. Others were thick and pasty.

I spotted Ruth near the end of the row. She looked as pale as a ghost with trembling hands and bloodshot eyes. Not a one of her factionmates looked any better. A couple even looked sick.

Master Barclae addressed the audience from his bench with the judges. "Welcome to the Alchemy trials. We will now see the application of the potions our first-years brewed during the first half of the day."

The audience broke into cheers. A couple highborns screamed their wagers and waved gold coins in their fists, spitting on them for luck.

Do they even realize how hard we fought to be here today? Whether any of us won an apprenticeship or not, the forty-three students left had beaten incredible odds. We had carried on at all costs. A wager was a cruel way to measure that sacrifice.

Barclae continued. "Our students brewed potions this morning, and now the judges and I will evaluate each first-year's draught, apply the necessary remedies, and then continue on to the next. No scores or remarks will be given aloud for any of the trials. Only on the seventh day will our victors be made public during the official naming ceremony."

The judges shifted along the bench, quills at the ready with rolls of parchment in a small table in front.

Master Tera cleared her throat from across the way. "Paralysis." Her voice boomed and crackled across the stadium.

Twelve nervous first-years reached down into the crates they had carried in and pulled out a small vial no bigger than my fist.

How are they going to measure paralysis?

A second later, my question was answered as the first student uncorked the vial and took a quick swig, wiping his mouth with his wrist.

The rest of the row followed.

"Gods," I whispered. No one had told me the first-years used the concoctions on themselves.

I wondered if they wanted their results to be the most effective, or the least. Either way, they lost.

Minutes ticked by. The faction stood underneath a cloudless sky, sweat beading along their brows as they waited for the potions to take effect.

Nothing happened at first, but then some of the audience began to murmur amongst themselves.

A loud thud sounded. And then another. And another.

Slowly, in the course of five minutes, each first-year of Alchemy dropped to the grass, shaking spastically, almost uncontrollably, while their eyes rolled to the back of their heads.

I watched in horror as twelve bodies continued to twitch, and then I held my breath as the spasms stopped completely.

Twelve motionless bodies were sprawled out across the field.

Paralysis complete.

Excitement rose in the audience. The first two rows began to point and shout, confirming their bets.

Ten minutes later, a first-year began to shake violently in place. The boy coughed, and then his tremors abruptly ceased.

Slowly, he rose. Tears came silently as he took in the immobile first-years around him.

Two nobles in the second row violently tossed their wine skins to the ground; their candidate had lost.

The boy had placed last in the first round of the Alchemy trials. His potion was clearly the weakest of the bunch.

Five more students rose unhappily within a ten-minute span.

After a half-hour, the judges came forward to examine the remaining young men and women. Ruth was one of the six who had stayed in the effects of her potion's enchantment.

Barclae raised a hand to motion the first test was complete.

The Green Mage, leader of Alchemy, tipped a small flask of purple liquid down the throats of the four nearest first-years. The Red Mage, leader of Restoration, knelt down to touch the throats of the two remaining students.

In seconds, the faction was cured.

Immediately, the four students who had been cured by potion sat up coughing and spewing blood and the remnants of their brews. The two first-years cured by touch began to tremble, vomiting and pouring sweat as their body emptied itself of poisonous toxin.

Ruth took the longest to stand. Some of the audience was whispering excitedly, and I wondered if my friend had won. Maybe she had, but without the judges' commentary, seven more rounds, and then the oral exams later on, I had no way of knowing whether Ruth would be one of the five to earn an apprenticeship. Only time would tell.

I hoped she would.

The Alchemy trials continued for the next three and a half hours. There were two more self-inflicted draughts, one for aging and another for sleep. The aging potion's effects were unnerving to watch: twelve first-years took on sagging skin and hair loss, taut arms became feeble and weak, and everyone sunk into their bones.

The sleeping draught was uneventful. All I heard were snores. The peaceful look on the participants' faces left many in the audience yawning for the half-hour we watched.

The last five concoctions were intended for battle: liquid fire, a coating to fortify metal—they were given blades for that demonstration—toxic sludge, exploding earth, and choking gas. The judges stood close by to rectify the results as first-years occasionally collapsed from their own doing.

At times, it was hard to watch the students throw down their bottles, knowing that something dreadful awaited them once the fumes released. The only casting I was left with questions after was the oil they had used to reinforce their swords. The judges had collected the weaponry for further examination later on, and there was no way to judge on appearance.

Overall, most of the students did very well. Ruth had stood out in five of the eight tests. I wondered how she was feeling.

Master Tera came forward to escort the twelve first-years off the field. The class had looked terrible when they started, but now after the completion of their first trial, they looked like walking death. It left a sinking feeling in the pit of my stomach.

I wondered how I would feel in two days when it was my turn instead.

* * *

The following day, I watched the nine remaining first-years of Restoration live out eight hours that were, if possible, worse than the previous day's trial. Alex, James, and the others had drawn from the same marble statuettes that Ella and I would be using to decide the pairings for our faction's trial. The first-year that did not have a matching figurine was given Master Cedric as a partner.

Restoration's trial was a healing demonstration of sorts. Students took turns healing one another of projected ailments inflicted by Master Cedric.

It was all I could do not to cringe.

Alex cured difficult maladies, ranging from swelling to deep, gushing wounds that were impossible to watch. He stumbled a bit during the healing of black frost burn, and his session ended with his performance on par with the three pairs of students who had come before.

His partner, a quiet boy with black braids and a hard jaw, proved to be my brother's undoing. Alex had been good, but the boy was better—*much* better. The boy's turn had barely begun, and within twenty minutes, Alex suffered severe cuts, blackening frostbite, intense burns, a concussion, and a heightened state of paralysis. His partner continued to cure as fast as the ailments were cast by the judges. The dark-haired boy never faltered, and he was cut off at the end of his forty-five minutes without so much as a blunder the entire act.

Alex's partner was as out of breath and exhausted as the others, but he had also doubled the outcome of everyone else's casting in the allotted time.

Half the audience stood after the boy finished, roaring his name, over and over. *"Ronan. Ronan. Ronan."*

Poor Alex looked miserable beside the new champion of Restoration. Unlike Alchemy, it was easy to spot the winning apprentice.

Still, Alex was lucky. He had a one in two chance that he would make his faction's cut of five.

The final pair to present was James and Master Cedric. Sadly, Ella's shy admirer did not fare so well. While he clearly tried, James could not cure beyond the fourth ailment. It was a surprise the boy had lasted as long as he had.

The Restoration trials ended. Master Cedric escorted the faction off the field, and Alex gave a weak wave of his hand as they passed.

Derrick turned in his seat after our brother had left. "Tomorrow is you, right?"

"Yes." My stomach curdled at the prospect. I felt faint just thinking about it. Suddenly the stadium looked five times as large.

"Combat duels?"

I nodded.

"You'll win."

If only.

Ella and I bid farewell to our families shortly after, and when we returned to our barracks, we both glanced at each other wordlessly.

We had done everything we could to prepare ourselves for what lie ahead. It was a hard truth to admit, but there was nothing more we could do.

"Good luck, Ryiah." Ella's eyes were unusually bright.

I swallowed. "You too."

"It'll all be over soon."

Not soon enough. I spent a listless night wondering who my opponent would be.

Ella? Darren? Priscilla? Someone else?

I never slept.

* * *

All twenty-two of us stood in the grand atrium of the Academy. Each of us held a small marble figurine that decided our fate. Master Barclae and the Three Colored Robes were explaining each statuette's order in the tourney. We made eleven pairs.

I glanced around the room, wondering if anyone else had gotten any sleep. All of our families, the king and his visiting court, and even the realm's mages were waiting outside to watch us duel for the chance at an apprenticeship.

In the palm of my hand was the tiny carving of a red fox.

Master Barclae called each token's name forward, starting with the rabbit and ending with the wolf. Ella and Jake were to duel first, having each selected a rabbit. Eve and William were next, the serpent. Ray, the talented lowborn boy from Darren's following, and I had the fox. Next went the fish, the lion, the bird—Priscilla and one of her friends, Jade, a tall girl with blue eyes and endless lashes—the boar, the dog, the buck, the horse, and, finally, the wolf: Darren and Clayton.

A part of me wanted to laugh. *Of course* Darren was the wolf, was he ever anything else?

At least I don't have to duel my best friend. A part of me could admit I was fortunate in that. I wouldn't have wanted either of us to be responsible for sending the other home.

Our faction lined up in pairs and followed Master Narhari down the long corridors and beaten trail that led onto the Academy field to wait our turn. As we took our place at the far end of the grass, Jake and Ella took their designated spots at the center of the field.

The crowd began to chant. "Combat! Combat!" And then shrieks and hollers filled the air as Master Barclae declared the start of the match.

The trials of Combat had begun.

* * *

I watched helplessly as my best friend twisted and dodged a giant cyclone of flame.

Jake held a devious smile as he lodged another and another. This time Ella wasn't quite so fast, and part of her tunic caught fire as she scrambled to get out of the way. She barely managed to put out the flames when Jake sent a fourth fire careening her way.

Ella threw out a blast so strong it knocked the flames to her left. She sent the fire spiraling back, and without hesitation, she cast out a storm of blades, launching them with all her might.

Jake only just managed to throw up his shield. A second later and he would have been mauled.

The two had been exchanging crippling blows for a half-hour. With every second, I was growing more and more anxious. Any anxiety for myself had been displaced in the onslaught of my friend's duel.

It was exhilarating to see all that Ella had learned in a year. At the mid-year tourney, Ella had not used half the castings she was using now. She was faring well, and even though she was quickly reaching the end of her stamina, she was still putting up a fight that Jake was struggling to put out.

BOOM! A blast of Ella's magic split open the ground beneath Jake's feet and he dropped.

There was a sickening crunch, and then I saw my friend run forward, holding a casted bow and arrow in hand as she circled the hole, ready to shoot should Jake try anything at her approach.

But he didn't. His leg was broken and his magic gone. Ella had effectively expended the boy's limits and left him with no defense.

The look Jake shot her as he surrendered was worse than any Priscilla or Darren had ever given me.

"I yield."

The crowd went hysterical. And above the madness of it all, I could hear Alex screaming her name in the stands.

"Ella! Ella! Ella!"

My best friend had won.

* * *

Next up were Eve and William. The match wasn't even a fair fight. Within twenty minutes, Eve had exhausted her rival's stamina and become the second champion of the day.

The crowd was even more hysterical than before. Eve's victory had been astoundingly quick.

As they exited the field, I saw the prince catch Eve's arm and congratulate her on the match. William's eyes flashed dangerously, but Darren didn't seem to care. Then again, he'd always seemed closer to the girl than anyone else.

"Ryiah."

I turned to see Master Narhari waiting for me. Ray was already walking onto the field in anticipation of our match. My stomach sank.

No going back now.

I followed my training master, trailing behind Ray until I was in my starting position, two hundred yards apart.

The sun was bright in the sky, not a cloud to help ease my vision as I squinted at Ray across the way.

I'd never had any qualms with the boy standing before me. One year my junior, Ray had come into this place like me: an untrained lowborn with a dream and ten months to prove it. He'd never taken part in the hazing and never tried to act as though he was better than me, even though he was a part of the prince's following. He was just a tall boy with olive skin, dark curls, and serious amber eyes.

And right now, he was the only person standing between me and an apprenticeship. A shame. I'd rather take a victory from someone who didn't deserve it.

"Annnnnnnd begin!"

All I saw was red.

Before I even knew I was doing it, I cast out two tunneling trails of flame. I watched as the twin fires bit across the landscape. In seconds, they reached my opponent and cut him off from escape at either side. He was trapped.

As Ray attempted to quench the fires with an outpouring of sand, I threw all the force I could muster at Ray's feet, willing the earth to crack open just as it had done for Ella.

The ground moaned loudly and collapsed, but I'd been too slow. Ray was gone.

Suddenly, I couldn't see anything.

A thick cloud of smoke appeared out of nowhere, and I was surrounded by thick, gray fog anywhere that I turned.

Coughing, I tried to summon enough wind to rid me of the heavy vapor, but before I could blow it far enough away, the sharp "zzzzzing" of metal slicing through the air alerted me seconds before Ray's sword came slashing through the haze.

I had the barest instant to throw up a shield to block the overhead blow, and then Ray's sword slammed my defense. My arms buckled and quaked—but I held on.

As soon as Ray withdrew his blade to try a different cut, I slammed my shield into his chest and charged. I threw myself into the blow, effectively knocking the wind out of my opponent as the impact threw the both of us backward and out of the blinding smoke.

We both fell.

I tucked in my chin and knees, letting the impact hit my bottom as I held my arms out at each side and rolled. Then I pulled myself up at the same time as Ray.

We faced each other warily.

I braced myself, keeping my stance limber as I awaited Ray's next attack. I'd used up a lot of my magic in that first—and now useless—attempt to entrap him. I'd have to be careful to conserve the rest for my defense.

Ray had always done well in our class, but I had never paid much attention to his training. I'd been so consumed with watching Darren and Eve, I'd never stopped to think about the others in their group. Now I wished I had.

A minute passed, and then I saw it in the way Ray was holding his arms. I threw up my shield, widening my stance and angling my guard arm so that I wouldn't receive the full impact of his casting.

His magic hit me much harder than Ella or Clayton's had ever in practice. I had to dig in my heels to keep the magic from taking over my defense.

There was a shattering vibration, and then Ray's magic rebounded. Magic shot off the shield and into the woods behind me. A moment later, there was a loud crack as a pine split in two.

I swallowed, realizing how close I had come to losing the match. That shield trick had just saved me from an instant defeat.

Ray's mouth fell open in shock.

He recovered quickly, but it was just enough for me to realize that, while I hadn't noticed him in practice, he'd clearly paid attention to my duel with Priscilla. That attack had been no accident. He'd been planning to capitalize on my weakness.

Thankfully, it was a weakness I no longer had. The prince's advice had just saved my neck.

Ray narrowed his eyes, and I readied myself for another casting. When nothing happened immediately, I squinted, trying to see what could possibly be delaying his attack. A second later, I noticed the glint of steel and the strange curve of metal in my opponent's hand. It was similar to the battleaxes we'd practiced with in class, only smaller.

Why did he pick such a small weapon?

The answer came moments later when Ray hurled the object at me with staggering force. I threw up a shield and took off at a run, sprinting as fast as my legs could carry me.

If Ray had been a knight, I would have been able to dodge the axe easily. But we were mages, and Ray was using his magic to steer the weapon. It crashed down on the shield on my back.

The blade was heavier than I expected. The impact sent me staggering to my knees as the shield splintered in two. The axe's thick iron-tipped edge dug into my right shoulder before falling away. It cut a deep gash that was felt all the way down my arm.

I bit my lip hard, and forced myself to stand. Blood was pouring from the wound, and it was costing me everything not to cry out in pain. I glanced to Ray and saw another throwing axe appear in his hand. My heart stopped.

If he kept throwing those axes, he would be able to wear out my stamina much sooner than he did his own. Normal long-range weapons couldn't break a shield. An axe could, but up until now, I had foolishly assumed that it wouldn't be a problem in distance encounters.

The second axe came hurtling toward me. I made a swift decision to change tactics. Instead of running away, I ran toward the axe. I threw my shield as hard as I could, causing his axe and my shield to totter off harmlessly to the left of the field.

I hadn't wanted to engage Ray directly. He was tall and stocky, and I knew he would be able to outlast me in any weighted exchange. *Especially with an open wound.* But as long as he kept throwing those axes at me, I had no choice... unless I used my magic for something big, and I wasn't sure I wanted to do that again, seeing as how my last two attacks had done little else than drain my stamina.

Summoning two blades, a hefty broadsword for myself, and a spectral blade for an additional attack, I lunged at Ray with everything I had.

It was a mistake. As soon as I engaged him, I realized how reckless the decision was. Ray only needed to wait for me to bleed out and make a mistake. I shouldn't have rushed him.

It was too late though, and I tried my best to ameliorate the situation. As predicted, Ray made no attempt to expend himself. I felt like a fool as we continued to exchange blows. Piers had spent months lecturing us about the realities of blood loss in battle, and here I was a self-fulfilling prophecy: *"Nine times out of ten a knight dies not because of a direct wound, but minor ones that amass over time. The smart enemies don't strike to kill. They just wait for you to do the work for them.*"

This can't be how it ends.

I continued to lead the assault. Ignoring the throbbing of my right arm, I clutched the sword in both hands and delivered blow after blow. I tried to will my second casting to do the same, but Ray was prepared with a spectral blade of his own.

Our match transformed into a flurry of swordplay.

I knew I would lose if I kept the contest going, but I was out of ideas. We were thirty minutes into our match, and Ray still looked as composed as when we'd started. Meanwhile, sweat was stinging my eyes, my limbs were aching all over, and my shoulder smarted terribly whenever I shifted weight.

My spectral blade faltered. Just as it deflected Ray's oncoming blow, I felt the casting shudder. I slammed the broadsword I was holding as hard as I could into Ray's left side. He blocked easily, as I had known he would, but the impact gave me just enough time to jump back before my second casting vanished completely.

I began to run toward the armory.

All I had left was the sword in my hand. My magic hadn't been able to hold onto both. I'd exhausted most of my magic trying to float the spectral blade and wield it on its own. I was beginning to feel lightheaded, and the searing pain in my forehead had begun. It was only a matter of minutes before my magic expired completely, and then I'd be defenseless.

I had to get my hands on a real weapon.

Midsprint, I released the broadsword casting and used the last bit of magic I had to summon a shield at my back. I was too open to attack, racing across the grassy field.

Not even a second later, there was the sharp whistle of arrows and then the repetitive thuds as they lodged themselves harmlessly against my shield.

The ground beneath my feet began to tremble, and I dove to my right.

Glancing back, I saw a fissure where I'd been headed just moments before.

I was close to the armory door now. Just another minute and I would be safely inside. I suspected it was off limits, but I didn't have a choice. I couldn't just let Ray win.

I had to put up a fight any way I could.

We were supposed to rely on our own magic, our own prowess. Well, I had, but now there was a resource I couldn't ignore, a room full of weapons. It was either forfeit now or bend the rules and hope the judges overlooked my decision.

I chose the latter.

I grabbed the wrought iron handle, ready to throw open the door—

Ray's hand shot out after me, snatching my injured shoulder and jerking me back, sending me sprawling into the grass instead. This time when I fell, I didn't land the right way.

There was a sickening snap and then *agony*. A piercing, blinding pain jutted up my arm while I blinked away tears.

I didn't need to understand Restoration to recognize that my left wrist was broken.

I pushed up on my knees.

"You know you're not supposed to enter the armory." Ray shook as he panted. The last couple of castings had cost him dearly. I wasn't the only one running out of magic.

"Surrender, Ryiah." His eyes held pity as a sword hovered seconds away. "Don't make this any worse than it already is."

He was giving me a chance, I realized. Ray didn't want to hurt me any more than he had to, but he would should I continue to stand between him and an apprenticeship.

Using my right arm to push myself off the ground, I gritted my teeth and stood. The shoulder pain was excruciating, and my surroundings were hazy at best.

Ray let me stand, but after a couple seconds of silence, he became impatient. "Surrender *now*, Ryiah, or I'll have no choice but to make you." His blade pressed just above my collarbone, into the deep wound on my shoulder.

The pressure of metal against swollen flesh and bone was so overpowering that my stomach roared, and I was seconds away from a scream.

I tried furiously to conjure a sword, a shield, any sort of defense to put between myself and the blade at my shoulder, but I came up empty-handed.

Ray pushed down with his blade.

The agony in my head was so terrible that I could no longer discern anything except the pain and the heavy breathing of my opponent.

This was it. This was how I would be remembered: just another first-year who had tried. I'd done well, but not well enough.

No!

The thought came raging through me as Ray increased the pressure of his cut. There was nothing I could do about the pain. He had me there. He had me trapped, defenseless... the perfect ending to a perfect victory.

But there was one thing Ray couldn't plan for, one glimpse at hope he might not have suspected in his careful approach. It was dangerous, and until today, I had never bothered to consider it... but now... I had nothing left to lose.

I threw myself onto Ray's sword, letting its metal pierce my wound as the blade severed and cut, piercing straight through flesh.

My vision went black, and I fell forward, shrieking and dragging Ray down with me as my pain casting lashed out in earnest.

Somewhere in the midst of our screams, thunder rolled.

There was a bone-shattering blast, and then something heavy collided with my skull.

I lost all consciousness after that.

* * *

"Do you think she'll wake soon?"

"I don't know. She's been through a lot."

"I can't believe she did that—"

"Mad! That's what it was. If I—"

"She could have killed them both!"

Slowly, I became aware of the voices surrounding me; they weren't happy.

I opened my eyes to find Ella, Alex, and the rest of my family standing next to my bedside in what could only be the infirmary. Two mages in the red robes of Restoration were scowling.

I was immediately filled with a hundred questions.

I tried to sit up, only to gasp and clutch my ribs as the immediate pain sent me doubling over in agony.

"She's awake!"

I tried to shift more comfortably and groaned. There was an almost unbearable ache in my shoulder. Every muscle burned. My left arm throbbed as if someone had hammered it repeatedly with a mallet.

"W-what happened?" My mouth was gritty and dry like sand.

My mother handed me a glass brimming with water and motioned for me to drink. She couldn't speak; she just kept shaking her head, lips pursed.

"You destroyed the armory." Derrick's eyes were dancing as he leaned forward. "You should have seen it, Ry!"

"The whole structure fell, toppling on both of you," Ella told me seriously.

"You almost killed yourself!" My father was furious. "All so that you could take down an opponent!"

"Master Barclae is beside himself," Alex added. His lips were a hard line like our father's. "What were you thinking, Ry, pain casting like that?"

"I was going to lose." My whole face burned with shame. "I had no stamina left... I... I knew it wasn't s-stable, but I thought maybe it'd be enough to d-disarm Ray and g-give me the lead." I hadn't realized I'd be collapsing an entire armory or almost burying us beneath it. "At least I won," I rasped. "Right?"

Silence.

And then: "Ryiah, honey, you lost." My mother brushed a strand of hair from my face. "I'm sorry."

My heart stopped. I lost? But that meant—

Alex took over for my parents. "Ray cast a defensive sphere that saved the two of you when the building came down. If it weren't for him, Ry.... Even Restoration has its limits."

So Ray had the final casting after all.

And that was it. He'd won.

Not only had I broken the tourney rules and destroyed a valuable building in the process, I'd risked both of our lives. My opponent, *my noble opponent,* had saved us.

I couldn't even hate him. I had only myself to blame.

The air was suddenly stifling, and it was all I could do to fill my lungs with air.

I was the reckless girl who lost control of her magic and almost killed herself and her opponent on the battlefield. I should have lost gracefully, but I'd wanted more. I'd taken a risk.

Why couldn't I have just lost with dignity?

Ray had given me an out. I should have taken it.

While a lost match wasn't ground for disqualification, the last first-year to secure an apprenticeship with one had attended the school more than a decade ago. And in my case, with the stunts that I had pulled, it was pretty clear what my outcome would be.

Why bother with a second trial? I'd already failed the first.

* * *

"I would have done it too, Ry." Ella faced me long after my family had left the infirmary. They'd stayed on a bit to make sure the healers were giving me the best treatment they could, but after that, their disappointment had been too much to take. Now only my best friend remained.

"I almost cost us our lives."

"We are Combat. That's a part of the risk. They are only upset because you're their daughter."

"Alex was furious."

"Not Derrick. Your little brother is like us." She adjusted the pillow at my back. "He wants to join Combat too. Trust me, he gets it."

Or maybe he was just excited I'd blown something up, but I didn't mention that aloud. Ella seemed determined to cheer me up no matter what.

"You and Ray lasted the longest, Ry. I think you were the most evenly matched. The judges will take that into account."

My hands twisted in the covers, but I was too tired to argue. I knew I'd be spouting the same nonsense if our roles were reversed.

Ella continued on like she hadn't noticed my mood. "Priscilla won her match with the same strategy she used to beat you in the mid-year duels. You missed that, of course. And the prince and Clay."

"Who won?"

"Take a wild guess."

"Darren."

"It was the shortest match the Academy has ever seen. The Black Mage gave him a standing ovation."

I picked at the food one of the healers had brought in from the dining hall. On the day I humiliated myself, the prince would be a shining prodigy to worship. The gods really hated me.

Why did I even bother with this school?

I was on orders to spend the entire night in the infirmary, and the walls were closing in. I wanted to run and scream, and instead I was stuck. I couldn't even stand. My stomach was queasy and hollow, and I was seconds from puking into a bucket.

I had only myself to thank for the pain I was in right now.

Ella leaned in to refill my water. "Master Barclae announced the order of the second trials."

I pushed peas around my plate, sighing.

"Ryiah... you are one of the first-years taking them tomorrow."

My grip on the fork tightened until my fingers were white. "So soon?"

"It was a random drawing for all of the factions." Ella swallowed. "Combat has the most students, so some had to go tomorrow."

Was I really ready to walk away from Combat without trying? I set my plate to the side.

"I should just leave." There was no point entertaining this fantasy; I'd held onto an impossible dream far longer than I should. I needed to accept what could never be. "They'll never let someone like me get a robe after what happened today."

For once, Ella had the decency to duck her head. "You could still win an apprenticeship, Ry, if your answer—"

"How many have been apprenticed after losing a duel?"

She didn't answer. We both knew the truth.

Two. In close to a century of the school's founding,

there'd been only two.

"You're a fighter, Ry. I know you will take this to the end. It's what my best friend and a Combat mage would do."

"And if I don't?" My reply was bitter. "Will you fault me if I walk away now?"

She met my eyes, and her expression was fierce. "You won't."

* * *

Blast her, Ella was right. I couldn't leave this place. Not yet.

I woke that morning and snuck down to the barracks before the first toll of the morning bell, determined to pack my bags and leave before dawn.

Instead, I found myself strolling onto the Academy field and staring up at the stands, finding them oddly barren without thousands of bodies lining their seats. I sat there on the highest bench, looking down at the field and what remained of the armory, a mountain of lumber and dirt.

I tried to imagine a different ending to that duel, but I couldn't. A part of me knew, if faced with the same choice, I would have made the same choice again. Pain casting had been reckless, yes, but I'd been backed into a corner, and it had been my only out. Ella had said she would have done the same. Was she just saying that to be nice?

Would a warrior surrender to certain terms, or just take a risk? I'd taken a risk, and it hadn't paid off, that much was certain. I'd destroyed a building and almost killed a fellow student.

Still, there'd been too much sweat and blood to walk away now. I would stick it out.

I'd given most of my youth for a chance to be a part of this place. Every waking dream of childhood, every hope I'd ever held—they'd all centered around a robe and the adventure on the other side. All those storybooks about those brave knights and the mages of legend—I couldn't leave that little girl behind without completing this one final test.

This girl was a fighter. She could never be anything else.

I would stay for the ceremony, too. I would watch as Darren, Eve, and the others received something I hadn't been fit to earn. I would stay so that I could close this final chapter and leave my magical aspirations behind.

There was always the Cavalry. Or maybe I could make it as a knight.

Rather than heading to the library to spend the next six hours studying until my eyes bled, I followed the training field to the hill to where I had sulked so many months ago after my mid-year duel with Priscilla.

It was time to take a deep breath.

The exams were held in a tower to the west of the Academy, just overlooking the cliffs. I'd never been there. The building was disconnected from the rest of the castle's structure, and it stood a good hundred feet taller than any of the roofs surrounding it.

Each toll of the Academy bell and another first-year walked toward that gray beacon. I already knew from Ella, I was to be one of the last for the day. I stayed on the hilltop, watching the small green specks of first-years enter and exit the tower doors at the edge of the grounds.

By the time the late afternoon sun set, my turn was fast approaching. I left my post and started the descent. When I reached the tower's base, my count rang. It was time.

Too late to turn back now.

For ten minutes, I climbed the stairs with increasing apprehension. The inside of the passage was dark, and I had to be careful where I stepped. A small flicker of light from the wall sconces was all I had to guide me in the shadowy nook.

After five more minutes, I heard the shutting of a door above and stepped aside to let the returning first-year pass. It was only after the footsteps froze that I bothered to look up and see whom it was.

Darren stood two steps above me, shadows covering all but the barest lines of his face.

My pulse leaped against my throat. *Why is he just standing there?*

"Excuse me." Darren made way to pass, averting his gaze.

I started to step to the side, and then I stopped myself. The trials were almost over and we'd never cross paths again. This was my one opportunity to ask.

"Why did you do it?"

After everything, it shouldn't have mattered. It didn't, really, but I needed to hear the words. Because as long as we kept this distance, as long as he avoided me, there would always be some small part of me wondering why. Because of that kiss. That stupid, irresponsible kiss, and the way I had felt because of it.

Darren's jaw locked. "You were always so eager to think the worst of me. Would it really make a difference what I told you now?"

No, it wouldn't. "I suppose not." I glanced away, furious

that I wanted his answer anyway. *Let it go, Ryiah.* I clenched my fists, wishing I could make myself as cold and unfeeling as him.

The movement didn't go unnoticed.

Darren studied me in the shadowy passage, his head crooked to the side instead of continuing on his way.

The warning bell chimed, and the prince's shoulders grew tense.

"The judges won't take kindly to you being late, especially after yesterday's trial. You should hurry."

My laugh was incredulous. "You and I both know my fate has already been sealed."

"You shouldn't discount yourself, Ryiah. The trials aren't over yet."

I stiffened. *No.* He couldn't say something like that now, not acting like he actually cared about my welfare after everything that he'd done. Darren was an enigma, and I was done trying to unravel him. "You are truly something. Still playing at those mind games after everything!"

"Mind games?" Darren's expression turned incredulous. "Are you really so daft?"

"Not enough to fall for false flattery twice."

"For the love of—" Darren slammed his fist against the wall and glared down at me. "I guess I should congratulate myself," he declared, "on helping the world's biggest idiot—"

"Helping?" I spat. "*Helping*? What part of your actions was helping?" I climbed the remaining steps so that he couldn't escape. "Was it when you were sabotaging me in the mountains? Insulting me at every turn? *Or when you kissed me just so you could play me for a fool in front of your friends?*" I grabbed the non-heir's collar, forcing him to meet my cold, angry eyes. "Really, Darren, which one of those should I be thanking you for?"

Our faces were inches apart, and Darren's livid gaze was burning me alive. "You really want the truth?" he snarled.

I refused to cower.

"Priscilla, Jake, and William were going to go after you whether I led the hazing or not." He watched the full impact of his words hit me like a ton of bricks. "They found out that you and Ella were sabotaging their hazing, and they were going to try and have you expelled. Eve overheard Priscilla and she told me because she knew I..." Darren faltered and then continued on as if nothing had happened. "She knew it would work."

What had they been planning? "I could have handled them on my own."

"Maybe—" His eyes flashed. "—but I thought if I avoided you, Priscilla would drop the vendetta on her own and I could talk the boys around." He'd tried to stop them? "But it didn't work, so I talked them around to the pig's blood instead."

"You betrayed my trust." I choked. "You humiliated me after we... after you..." No, I couldn't say it.

"Everyone knows hazing is a tradition. It's practically a rite of passage."

"I didn't care about the hazing!"

"I knew you could take care of yourself." Darren still didn't understand why I was so upset. "Plenty of Jerar's mages have gone through the same."

"I didn't care about the act. I cared that you played a part in it!"

A long silence followed my confession. I couldn't believe I'd spoken the words aloud.

Finally, he replied. "I tried to stop you, Ryiah. That night, I changed my mind."

What?

Darren had to be lying. *He's just trying to manipulate me again.*

What had he said right before I went outside that door? *No, Ryiah, don't—*

And then to Priscilla when she was about to attack me: *"She's not worth it."*

Had he been protecting me? He couldn't have... But then why had he only deflected my casting when I tried to attack him? And why had he ceased brawling with my brother the second Alex had mentioned my name? And stopped his own brother that first day of trials after the encounter with Ella?

Millions of questions were clouding my head, and none of them were making any sense. Or rather they were, I just wasn't sure I wanted to trust their answers.

"Still can't make up your mind about me, can you?"

I glanced up and Darren's garnet eyes met mine. He seemed tired, and I wondered if it was because of me, or the trial he had just come from.

"You are probably wondering why I went through the trouble."

I held my breath.

"I've asked myself the same question many times, and I've come to the conclusion that somewhere along the lines of this year, I went mad." The prince gave me a wry smile. "Luckily for me, it seems to only pertain to things that involve you."

"But..." I couldn't think, and my heart was beating impossibly fast. I wanted to believe him. I didn't understand why I needed to trust him. I didn't understand why I even cared.

But there was still something missing, something pressing at the back of my mind that I couldn't forget. Something important that could void all the explanations he had just put forward.

And then I remembered.

"What about Ella and your brother?" The words tumbled from my lips. "What was your excuse then?"

Darren stopped smiling. "My brother and Ella?"

"When she was twelve, you left her alone with him. You saw what he was doing and just left—"

His expression was dark. "That's what she's been thinking all these years?" He glowered. "Why don't you try asking your friend whose magic saved her?"

"But she said it was hers."

The prince made a frustrated sound and started to push past me.

"Darren, wait!" I didn't know what to think, but I knew I didn't want to leave us like this again. If it were true and he had been helping me all this time, if he had helped Ella too...

Darren turned to face me. There was an emotion I couldn't read in his unfathomable gaze. "You need to decide whether I am the evil tyrant in your head, or a friend, Ryiah.

I can't make that decision for you. It's something you'll have to decide for yourself."

I looked away. Trust and Darren? The two were opposite ends of a spectrum.

The bell tolled loudly, and I jumped as I realized I was now late to my test.

What does trust matter? I wondered. I wouldn't be around long enough to find out anyway.

I reached out for Darren's arm before he could start his descent.

My breath caught as my fingers brushed his skin.

"If we were friends—" I swallowed. "—what would you say to me right now?"

He didn't hesitate. "I would tell you that you could still win this."

"Thank you." I released his wrist and took a step back.

Something odd flashed across the non-heir's face. "Good luck, Ryiah."

I gave Darren the barest of nods and then proceeded up the stairs. It took me until I reached the door to realize I was smiling.

FIFTEEN

"FIRST-YEAR, YOU are late."

My cheeks burned as I bowed my head, nervously peeking out from under my bangs at the panel of disgruntled judges before me.

There, just as in my dream, sat Master Barclae and the Three Colored Robes. This was the first time I was really able to get a good look at the three mages who ruled the Council of Magic. Each of them looked almost unearthly as the gold trim of their robes shimmered brilliantly against the rays of a fading sun.

The Black Mage of Combat had been the one to address me. His head was shaven, and there were two golden hoops dangling from his right ear. He had burnt amber skin and piercing green eyes, the kind that seemed like they could see straight through to your soul. He was younger than I expected, no more than thirty-five years.

"What is your name, child?"

The second person to speak was the wearer of the red robe, a beautiful blonde woman with violet eyes and full red lips. She was older than the Black Mage, but not by much.

"Ryiah."

"Ryiah," said the third, a formidable older man with long brown locks and startling yellow eyes. The Green Mage of Alchemy. "You are the talk of the Academy. Never in the history of the first-year trials has a student inflicted so much damage to our sacred Academy."

I swallowed uncomfortably and Master Barclae shifted in his seat. "What do you have to say for yourself?"

All eyes narrowed, and I willed myself to speak, despite the wave of nausea that was fast approaching. This would be my one chance to explain in my own words.

"I never meant to destroy that building. I only went after the armory to try to get a weapon when my regular stamina ran out." I made myself hold their gaze despite all instinct to look away. "When Ray stopped me, I still wanted to win... I knew pain casting was unstable, and I wouldn't be able to control the magic if I tried, but I had no stamina left to cast anything else.

"If I didn't try, I would've had to admit defeat and... and I couldn't do that." My tone was pleading. "If you want something as badly as I do, you can't give up. I'm sure each of you have had a moment like that, where you had to make a choice, and you chose your robe, no matter the consequences—"

"You impaled yourself on a sword," Master Barclae said dryly.

"I would do it again, a thousand times over if I thought it would help—so long as I didn't harm Ray." I couldn't help feeling less confident than my words. "It was the only way I could access my magic." I thought of all the stories in history. "Better to lose a limb than a battle."

"You are a fool." The Red Mage was unimpressed. "It wasn't a limb you almost lost. It was your life and the life of that boy you were with. And you still lost the duel."

"A *powerful* fool," the Black Mage corrected, smiling behind the palm of his hand. "She's lowborn and fairly untrained, but her potential could rival the prince's someday. She's a pain caster too. Those are rare."

"But you heard her." The Red Mage was appalled. "She'll kill herself the first chance she gets."

"At least she takes risks. She's willing to die for her cause."

"Well, the trials aren't the right cause."

"True enough."

The Three glanced to Master Barclae, and he cleared his throat. "Very well. We shall now begin the second portion of your trials, Ryiah. You will have a half hour to address three scenarios, all concerning the art of strategy in Combat..."

* * *

I returned to my barracks much later that evening feeling confident, confused, half sick and half mad. The trial had only lasted a half hour, but the questions the judges had asked left me reeling in self-doubt. *Were my answers good enough?* I thought they had. I'd cited several battles for each scenario they'd given me. I'd weighed the resources, the weather, the landscape, and the politics of each situation to provide the best approach.

I'd considered all the right questions: Was it a full-scale invasion, or was it better just to send a small regiment to conduct the mission? Was it on our homeland, or in a neighboring country?

For each question they asked, I'd had a million queries of my own. I'd been desperate to show the product of my endless nights in the library, and even more frantic to prove I was more than the reckless first-year they had seen during the first half of my trials.

"What happens if the enemy is someone you care about?" they pressed. *"Someone you would never expect?"*

I folded my arms. "My loyalty is to the Crown and Jerar."

"But what would you do?" They wanted more.

The ugliest war in history was two centuries ago between a pair of kings who'd been lovers. I'd spent hours pouring over those scrolls; it was fascinating. "A true warrior puts her country before everything else. It's a sacrifice everyone should be prepared to make."

"You would put Jerar before everything else? Your family, your friends, even your lover?"

"I would. I would press that advantage and do whatever needs to be done." I would give myself to the people and be the hero I'd read about as a child, the kind of mage who slays dragons and saves kingdoms from slaughter.

The girl who saves the world.

Darren had told me I could still win this. So had Ella.

Was an apprenticeship such an impossible goal?

I pretended it wasn't.

* * *

The next two days were the longest of my life. I spent the time in restless wonder, following my friends around the small town of Sjeka and trying not to think about what lie ahead.

"It's in the hands of the gods now." Alex looked sick as

Ella and I tore into a sticky bun from a nearby stall. Some of us ate when we were nervous and others—like my twin—puked all over the village square. Repeatedly. "I should stop torturing myself, but I can't."

We had five more hours before the naming ceremony. All of us were trying to pretend the trepidation didn't bother us as much as it did.

Ella scanned the rest of the crowd. "I'm surprised your adoring fans haven't tended to your injured pride." She'd intended for her comment to come off lightly, but the slight resentment in her tone destroyed any pretense of indifference.

"I sent them away days ago," he mumbled. "There's only one that I want."

Ella scowled. "Well, I hope she's got half a brain to push you away before she gets hurt."

"Oh, she's got a brain. That's the problem."

"Good," she huffed, "I hope she doesn't lose it!"

Oh, Ella, she didn't even realize—no, it was better this way.

Alex shot me a pleading look, and I just shook my head. I mouthed the words, *"Don't you dare,"* but he was too busy staring after the oblivious girl he liked.

What would happen if he courted my best friend? Could I handle the fallout? Would it even matter if we failed out of the Academy? Alex and Ella would never cross paths again.

For a second, I considered sticking my meddling nose in the sand. Alex and Ella had been dancing around one another for months, and I'd seen how he looked at her when he thought I wasn't looking. It wasn't just a game to him anymore. Somewhere in the course of the year, my brother had actually started to admire Ella for more than a pretty face.

Come to think of it... Alex hadn't courted a single girl since we'd arrived.

And Ella... she was charmed by him; she was just too stubborn to admit it. She was probably also afraid of me. I'd made my stance on my womanizing brother perfectly clear.

Blast it, I was a terrible friend. People deserved to make their own mistakes.

"Alex, don't move."

My brother froze, swatting at the air. "What is it? Last time you told me that, a spider—"

"It's not a spider, you dolt. Just stay there." I ran after Ella and pulled her to the side of the street, away from my brother's hearing.

"What's wrong?" Ella's lashes fluttered in alarm.

I sucked in a sharp breath and let it out with a sigh. "My brother likes you. He *really* likes you, and I think you like him too."

"I..." Her skin darkened in a becoming blush. My best friend was too pretty for her own good; no wonder Alex chased after her for a year.

"I don't think it's a good idea. I can't promise you won't get hurt, but I—" Another deep breath "—I promise to stop meddling. I think you two deserve a chance. If you are interested. I won't hold it against you because I love you both—"

Ella's arms went around my neck. "Thank you, Ry."

"He doesn't know." My face was red with embarrassment.

"I thought I'd tell you first. In case you didn't—"

Her smile was hesitant. "Do you really think he's changed?"

"I think he's trying." It was as much as I could give.

"Well, well, isn't that just precious." A sneer tore the two of us apart.

Groaning, I released Ella to face the bane of my existence. Or at least a *very* unpleasant thorn.

"Oh, please don't stop on our account." Priscilla smirked with one arm wrapped tightly around Darren's waist. "This will be our last chance to see your touching friendship before we go on to our apprenticeship. Darren and I need a good laugh, don't we?"

Darren's eyes met mine, and my throat became unbearably dry.

Neither of us spoke. I was too busy remembering the encounter in the stairwell. I couldn't summon my usual hate.

"Go haunt somewhere else, Priscilla." Gods, I loved Ella in that moment. "Surely there's a drafty wing in the Academy for harpies like you."

The beauty laughed, but her eyes flashed with heat. "Come, Darren. We've got to return to the castle in time for the ceremony." She put her hand lightly to his chest as she whispered loudly: "I have something special to wear for this evening. I had it especially picked out with you in mind."

Her eyes fell to me, and she smirked. "It will be the perfect opportunity to announce our betrothal."

My eyes flew to Darren as something kicked at my gut.

The prince was a stone, not one emotion flickering across his face as emotion whirled up around mine.

The prince and Priscilla left the square without another word. I stared at the spot where they'd stood long after they disappeared.

Had I really thought I was special after one reckless kiss? Darren was a *prince*. I'd known all about the upcoming engagement for a year.

I'd never wanted him, so I wasn't sure why everything burned. I was better than this.

"Ry?"

I felt as if someone had ripped my lungs right out of my chest. I shook my head, unwilling to speak.

"After you came back from your trial, you asked me about that night when I was twelve..." Ella cleared her throat. "I tried to pain cast like you, but I couldn't."

What was she talking about? I stopped staring and turned to her.

"If I can't pain cast after all this time, then it couldn't have been my magic the night his brother attacked me." Her voice was soft. "That's why you asked, wasn't it? It was him."

Gods, I needed to hate the prince.

But just now, I couldn't.

* * *

Much later that evening, Ella and I were standing before our reflection in the looking glass of our barrack's quarters. She had lent me one of her many dresses for the occasion, a deep blue gown that would "capture the gray-blue of my eyes." It was even more spectacular than her dress at solstice. I tried to tell her that it didn't matter what I wore, but she was of a different opinion.

"This is a night to be proud." Ella helped brush out my scarlet locks into something more manageable. "Whether our names are called or not, we completed a year where others failed. That is not something anyone can take away from us."

We finished dressing, and I linked my arm in hers as we exited the barracks. Outside, Alex was waiting for us, looking handsome in the same clothes he had worn for the solstice.

"Ready?" His eyes shown unusually bright as he took Ella's other arm.

"There's no going back now."

The three of us began our slow march down the path to the Academy. We greeted our families at the door and continued ahead of them as we made our way to the atrium. The place was packed, and as one of the last groups to arrive, we were forced to wait at the back of the room.

Standing to the right of the enormous stairway were Master Barclae, the Three Colored Robes, Sir Piers, Masters Eloise, Isaac, Cedric, Tera, and Narhari.

King Lucius and his two sons stood expectantly at the base of the stairs, all dressed in their choice colors and fitted brocade. Priscilla linked arms with Darren, looking resplendent in a red and gold dress fitted in rubies that flared dramatically at its base.

I swallowed at the sour taste in my mouth and forced my gaze to remain at the top of the stairs.

Minutes later, Constable Barrius squeezed his way through the crowd and up the stairs to stoop beside the master of the Academy. He whispered something, and the man cleared his throat expectantly.

A hushed silence fell over the room; this was the moment every one of us had been waiting for.

The master began his speech. "Ten months ago, one hundred and twenty-two naïve, young faces stood in this very room. I told them that half would not make it past the first few months. I told them they were foolish. I told them they were wasting my time.

"I did everything I could to encourage these students to pack their bags and leave the very next day. When that did not work, I had Sir Piers and Master Cedric take them out to the mountains with the sole purpose that they were not to return until we lost the first five. I celebrated with a ball when half the year resigned. I have continued to parade their loss until we were left with the forty-three standing in front of us now.

"The forty-three first-years in this room are the culmination of everything a true mage should be. While they may not have the potential necessary to continue their studies, these young men and women represent the best of Jerar. Should they not go on to become mages, I am sure they will make fine knights or soldiers." His voice drew gruff. "With that, I'd like to call forward the fifteen who will be continuing on to the exalted apprenticeships that the Council and Crown are so proud to bestow…"

Master Barclae pulled a tightly rolled scroll from his robes, and Barrius held his torch close so that the formidable man could read from his list.

"For Alchemy, I call forward Piper, Julian, Thomas, Ruth, and Damien."

The five first-years rushed forward. I barely caught a

glimpse of my spritely friend as she raced up the stairway and shook the hand of Barclae and the other masters, one by one. When the commotion finished, Master Barclae had the five new apprentices of Alchemy stand along the right rail of the ascending staircase.

"In the faction of Restoration, I would like to invite Ronan, Alexander—"

My brother is going to be a mage.

Ella had to gently nudge Alex to let go of her hand as he staggered forward, pale as a ghost.

"—Kiera, Muriel, and Kaylein to the stand." Barclae and the rest of us watched as five fumbling first-years found their way up the steps to shake hands and then stand at the left spiral of the stairs.

"And finally, for the faction of Combat, among the twenty-two young men and women that beat out all odds... I welcome Prince Darren..."

The crowd went wild.

"Eve."

The small girl pushed her way through the masses to join the prince at the top of the steps.

"Ella."

My friend screeched and ran toward the stairs. There were a couple of laughs among the audience.

"Ray."

My opponent from the first trial nodded solemnly and found his way to the center of the dais.

"And finally, for the last apprenticeship of the evening..."

My heart stopped.

I knew it was foolish to hope, especially when Master

Barclae still hadn't called *her* name, but I still held on. More than anything, I wanted the master of the Academy to say mine.

"Lady Priscilla of Langli."

I watched as the girl ascended the steps. I watched as her dress glistened across the dais. I even watched as she accepted Master Barclae's outstretched hand.

Priscilla smiled prettily, shaking the hands of the masters to her right, and that was when the piercing jealousy split across my lungs. It continued to splinter as Priscilla took her place beside the prince.

Hot tears started to pour down my face, but I was powerless to stop them. For once, I didn't try to hide them; no one would see me when they were looking at the apprentices instead.

The final five stood just below Master Barclae, facing their audience on the center stair.

A slow clapping started. It continued, on and on until the room was a thundering storm of applause.

Derrick said nothing as he slipped to my side, his hand grasping mine. My brother just held my fingers tightly, letting me grieve silently amongst the clamor of so much applause. There were other first-years like me, with tears in their eyes and a bitterness to their smiles, but we were only twenty-eight in a sea of so many broken dreams.

I would be happy for my friends, for my brother, but this moment was too soon. Alex, Ruth, and Ella were somewhere up there with the other twelve apprentices living out their wildest dreams.

I was not.

And it hurt more than words could tell.

For a couple of days, I had actually managed to convince myself I had a chance.

Master Barclae motioned for everyone to settle down so that he could start a speech. "Let us all congratulate our newest order of apprentices—"

I could not stay any longer. It was too much.

I turned to leave, letting go of Derrick's hand to exit the crowd.

"Master Barclae." The voice of the Black Mage was urgent.

The master of the Academy sounded irate. "What is it, Marius?"

"The Council and I would like to invite one more to take an apprenticeship tonight."

"We would?"

I turned, slowly, to see the other Colored Robes giving the Black Mage a strange look.

"Yes."

"We already have our fifteen!"

The man refused to back down. "I am enacting my right as the Black Mage to include one more apprentice for Combat."

"It has *always* been fifteen—"

"In the school's founding, it was more." The Black Mage stepped forward to address the audience and the king. "It was too many at the time. We lost more lives than we gained... Yet, it has always been acknowledged that the number could change, should others arise with the potential we require." He pulled back his hood so that everyone could hear his next words clearly. "I believe today to be that day."

I couldn't breathe. It was too much to hope. I'd never considered the possibility—

"My dearest Ryiah." Marius found me in the audience with a grin. "Will you please join me as the final apprentice of Combat?"

I stood motionless. I was too afraid that, if I moved for even a second, the dream would end.

"Ryiah." Derrick elbowed me in the ribs. "Ryiah, you've got to get up there."

This is real.

The audience fell silent as I walked forward, and the sea of people slowly parted to let me approach the steps. As I drew forward, I caught sight of Alex's grin. Ella was beaming.

I could also see the loathing in Priscilla's eyes.

As I passed the prince, Darren gave the slightest nod, the barest semblance of a smile on his lips. His eyes danced as they met mine, and I realized suddenly that the answer to his earlier question was yes. Yes, the non-heir was a friend. It didn't matter that he was betrothed. My feelings didn't matter one bit. Because there'd been no shock in his eyes when I had climbed the stairs just now—Darren, Prince Darren, had put faith in a future that even I had never bothered to foresee.

Trembling, I took the hand of the Black Mage and then continued across the line. Eventually, I finished shaking the masters' hands and made my way to my spot at the end of the row, right beside Ella.

Master Barclae strode forward to address the audience, again. "Ladies and gentleman, I give you the fif—the sixteen apprentices of our Academy. Please give them the applause they deserve."

This time, when the clapping and shouting started, it never stopped.

And now an excerpt from

APPRENTICE

THE BLACK MAGE BOOK 2

ONE

I WATCHED THE two figures dance, twisting and turning as they exchanged matching blows in the stifling morning heat of the desert sun. The sand shifted and clouded beneath their feet, small swells of dirt temporarily blinding my vision as the two continued to reposition their lightning-quick blows.

I studied their forms. Lissome, dangerous. I couldn't help but notice how the sweat glistened off their tanned skin, highlighting the contours of taut arms and shoulders. It was an observation I'd partaken in many times but had yet to grow tired of watching.

The two fighters continued their match. The taller of the two, a young man with sandy brown curls and laughing green eyes, seemed the most at ease with the procession. He countered his partner's rapid attacks with an almost lazy defense that spoke of a lifetime of training. The second young man was the opposite, trying to hide his building frustration in every blocked attempt. Garnet eyes flared underneath black bangs, and my heart skipped a beat. The shorter of the two might have been less skilled in hand-to-hand combat, yet my eyes clung to him just a second too long.

The bout carried on for several more minutes. I fanned myself with my hand, desperately wishing our faction had been assigned a cooler terrain to train in. I certainly hadn't expected the desert, and I had yet to grow accustomed to its sweltering heat. Many of the other apprentices seemed to share my opinion; there was not a full water skin to be found anywhere in the audience.

The tall boy caught the second off guard with a swift, sweeping kick that sent his partner sprawling into the sand. The second shot the older boy a look of pure venom that would've sent most people to their knees. The tall boy just chuckled, offering the second his hand, which the second blatantly ignored, as the rest of the class hooted and cheered.

A man in stiff black robes stepped forward with a scowl. "That will do, Ian." Then he addressed the young man on the ground in a much friendlier tone: "Darren, that was very good for a second-year. You have no reason to be disappointed."

The expression on Darren's face didn't change as he stood, brushing sand from his breeches and belt. His eyes stated very clearly he did not share Master Byron's confidence. I hadn't the slightest doubt that the prince would be training in private for weeks to come. Though we couldn't be more different, it was amazing how similar the two of us were when it came to performance. The master had been praising him for weeks, but until he was the best, Darren wouldn't be satisfied.

"Ryiah. Lynn. You two are up."

Nerves tingling, I made my way to the front. A young

woman with dark bangs and amber eyes gripped my elbow as I passed. "Good luck, Ry," Ella whispered.

Standing where the two boys had fought just moments before was a girl of Borean descent, who I had sparred with many times before. Lynn gave me a reassuring smile. I tried to return the sentiment as I took my position across from my mentor.

Palms sweating, I waited for the master of Combat to start our drill.

"And begin."

Lynn was the first to make a move, ducking into my circle with a low jab to the ribs. I held my guard and countered her strike with a low block of my own. The girl pulled back, long ponytail flying, and I quickly launched a high kick, narrowly missing as she fell back out of reach. My fingers itched to send a casting, but I quickly squelched the urge.

No magic, Ryiah.

Refocusing on the task at hand, I studied my opponent, seeking any tell in her stance that might foreshadow her next attack. Lynn's hazel eyes met mine, sparkling with a delicate innocence that matched her doll-like features. It was a lie. She might be petite, but I had long ago learned the truth. The olive-skinned third-year was lethal in hand-to-hand combat and anything with a pole.

I exhaled slowly. I'd lost every single match to my mentor since we'd started these duels, but like Darren, I wanted to win. I was the sixth apprentice to join Combat months before, and I still had something to prove.

Every time I lost, I wondered if the others were questioning the Black Mage's decision to admit me to their ranks.

A snicker came from somewhere in the audience. I didn't need to look to identify the girl. Priscilla of Langli was impossible to mistake.

Lynn shifted her hips, weight transferring ever so lightly to her right heel.

I jumped in with a hasty outer block and sent my right fist to the girl's abdomen. Lynn pulled back just in time, my hand barely grazing the thin cotton of her shirt.

I launched a low, rounded kick, and she parried it with an easy blow of her own. I fell back and instinctively angled my hips so that I was just out of reach, fists raised and ready to counter Lynn's next offense. When it didn't immediately come, I sprung forward, feigning a two-fisted punch while my real attack came in the form of a high kick aimed at her ribs.

My mentor wasn't fooled. She easily countered, stepping into the kick the second she saw my knee rise, and rammed my body with the full force of her weight.

I stumbled.

Lynn rushed forward, kicking and punching in a quick succession of blows. I struggled to block, but I was still off balance from her previous attack. A hard-packed fist collided with my stomach and another with my face.

Lynn sent a quick kick to my shin and gravity shifted from under my feet.

I fell to the side, and my right elbow hit the hard-packed dirt with a *craaaack*. Sand billowed up as something snapped under my skin.

Pain rushed my arm like shards of glass as my control on

my magic splintered and broke.

The pain casting rushed out of me uncalled. It slammed into Lynn and sent her back-first into a nearby palm. Lynn slumped to the ground with a hard thud as my magic dissipated, the casting complete.

"Blast it, Ryiah!" Master Byron swore. His aristocratic face was beet red, a common expression around me. "If you can't control your magic, you're never going to be allowed anywhere near a battlefield!"

I scrambled to my feet, my face aflame. "I'm sorry, sir. I didn't mean—"

"The Black Mage made a mistake." The man puffed his chest. "You shouldn't be here. I don't know what Marius was thinking, granting you an apprenticeship. You may have gotten away with that trickery in your trials, but it will not fly here."

"Yes, sir." My elbow was on fire, and I was too busy looking to Lynn across the way. She had pulled herself up, and her expression was full of pity. She was far too patient— this wasn't the first time my magic had accidentally knocked her into a tree.

It wasn't as if I'd intentionally cast; it just happened. Other apprentices lost control too—but in the two months since my apprenticeship had started, the training master only seemed to criticize me.

"What good is a girl in Combat if she is always embracing her gender's weak-minded ways? Learn to deal with your pain, Ryiah, or go back to a convent."

That's it—

Ella's fingers clamped over my left wrist before I could

retort. I bit down on my cheek until I tasted blood. If I angered the master enough, I'd find myself at the end of more than just his insults, and I had four years left.

A throaty chuckle broke the tension nearby. "If the girls are the only ones who feel pain, then I'm living a lie."

"Your sarcasm, Apprentice Ian, is not appreciated." The master glowered at the tall boy from earlier. "I was simply making a point to Ryiah that she would be better suited elsewhere—"

"For accidentally using her magic?" The boy kept on. "Sir, we've all done that. In my second year alone, I—"

"Perhaps she is not the only one who shouldn't be here!" The master bristled as he turned on me. "Ryiah, see to that arm. You will have to make up the rest of the exercise later."

I couldn't see how with a broken arm, but I didn't bother to reply.

All twenty apprentices stepped to the side to allow me to pass, although none of them met my eyes as I did. Most of them hated Master Byron as much as me; the difference was they had learned to avoid his wrath.

Holding my head high, I began the short trek to the infirmary. At least there would be one bright spot to this day. Alex would be with the rest of the Restoration mages— which meant I would get to see him when I checked into their base.

I'd barely seen my brother since the start of the apprenticeship—our factions kept us busy training in opposite ends of Ishir Outpost. Any excuse to see Alex was welcome at this point.

"Hey, Ryiah, wait up!"

I turned and found Ian jogging to catch up with me. His hair was windblown, and his eyes crinkled as they locked on my own. Even out of breath, the third-year was handsome—not like the prince, but then again, no one ever was.

Ian was just Ian. When the apprentices had arrived at the Academy to pick up their newest recruits, most of the older students had been wary of me. I was the sixteen-year-old girl who destroyed the school's armory during the first-year trials. I was also the sixth apprentice to join our faction's year—a rarity since the Council of Magic only ever selected five students to apprentice per faction.

Ian hadn't cared. The moment the third-year had spotted me, he'd let out a loud whoop and set about to collecting his winnings from the rest of his friends. Apparently there'd been a wager going for which of us first-years would make it; since I'd been considered a long shot during the mid-winter duels, Ian had been the only one to bet on me for an apprenticeship.

I was surprised the boy even remembered me from our short time during the solstice ball, but he assured me he'd remembered "everyone that counted."

Since the apprenticeship started, Ian had quickly become one of my closest friends, after Ella. The third-year's sarcasm matched my own, and he knew firsthand how horrible Byron could be. After all, until I arrived, Ian had been the master's least favorite apprentice.

"What are you doing?" I scolded the third-year. "You should be mentoring Darren."

Ian chuckled. "That self-important prodigy? He'll be fine without me..." The boy gave me a disarming smile. "You, warrior girl, are the one who needs help." He hooked my good arm with his own. "That prince has the training master worshipping the very ground he walks on. Darren could be *us* and Byron would still insist he was the next Black Mage."

"Byron's going to stick you with latrine duty." I grinned despite myself.

Ian's green eyes danced wickedly. "He can *try*—but I'll just tell him it interferes with my mentoring, and we know how the master feels about his precious prince."

I laughed loudly. "You are trouble."

"Anything for Byron's least favorite apprentice. It's the least I can do since you took over my torch."

"I wouldn't be so—argh!" I ducked under a low palm's hanging branches and skimmed my bad arm against the side of its trunk.

"You okay?"

"I'm fine." I gritted my teeth. "I just want this pain to end."

"We're almost there." Ian pointed to a set of wooden doors protruding from the base of a large cliff, a quarter of a mile away.

Like most of the city's housing, the infirmary was built into the rocky face of desert crags, a seemingly endless elevation that separated the Red Desert from the northern plains of the capital city, Devon, and the rest of Jerar. I'd always heard tales of a desert city carved into mountains, but I had still been speechless the first day we arrived.

Author's Note

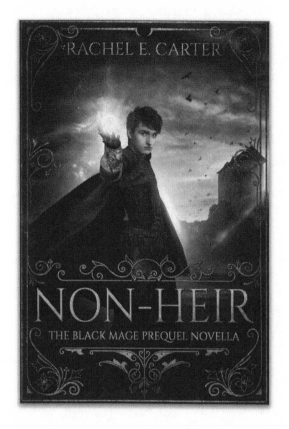

Want to read Prince Darren's backstory before he met Ryiah at the Academy of Magic?

Sign up for Rachel's newsletter on her website so you can receive the exclusive e-novella and be notified of new releases, special updates, freebies, & giveaways!

www.RachelECarter.com

ACKNOWLEDGEMENTS

Publishing a book is like raising a child; it takes a village. Here are the people who helped me raise what I fondly refer to as "the preciousssss."

First of all, MY READERS. Seriously all of the fan art, messages, reviews, and every single status update (yes, y'all know I read more than my fair share on Goodreads) make me proud to be an author. The bookish reader-reviewer company helped launch my books, and y'all are the reason I can now write full-time (SQUEEEE).

COURTNEY MORALES. Because the second I told you I wrote a book, you asked for it. And you read it the very next day (in all it's yucky, terrible first draft form). And you kept cheering me on every step of the way.

BOTH FAMILIES (new and old). For all of your support and the usual family stuff. Special shout-out to my adorable niece, STEFANIE, who let me present at her school, and my mother-in-law, SUSIE, for cheering me on and not calling me crazy. Oh, and I suppose I should add the HUSBAND, who literally has put up with me through *everything* for years and never once told me to go back to a regular job or stop talking his ear off about my characters.

ROTNA SIMMONS. I know Jan said you were the evil one and I was the angel, but we both know it's the other way around. When I didn't know what to do with my life, you held my hand and told me to follow my dreams. Even though those dreams were crazy. Even though those dreams were mad. Thank you for being my rock and sounding board and listening to me complain all these years.

All of my LOVELY AUTHOR FRIENDS, thank you for your support. I have the best coworkers, hands down.

EDITORS (Hot Tree Editing) and my amazing COVER ARTIST (Milo) who dealt with all my nit-picky details.

Lastly, *huge* thank you to my PROOFERS of this new edition for taking time out of their busy lives to spot all the typos and whatnot I missed: NIKKI ALLEGRETTI, TIFFANY KIMBRELL, ERICA STOKES, COURTNEY HOOVER, SARAH KATHRINA SONG, and ALEXANDRA MEYERS. All of your lovely messages and meticulous notes helped make this edition what it now is, and I *so* appreciate your selfless act to help me!

About the Author

RACHEL E. CARTER is a young adult and new adult author who hoards coffee and books. She has a weakness for villains and Mr. Darcy love interests. Her first series is the bestselling YA fantasy, *The Black Mage*, and she has plenty more books to come.

Official Site:

www.RachelECarter.com

Facebook Fan Group:

facebook.com/groups/RachelsYAReaders

Twitter: @RECarterAuthor

Email:

RachelCarterAuthor@gmail.com

ALSO BY RACHEL E. CARTER

The Black Mage Series

Non-Heir (e-novella only)

First Year

Apprentice

Candidate

Last Stand

61500763R00192

Made in the USA
Lexington, KY
12 March 2017